The Changeling

The Changeling

Just for a moment, believe with me.

K. D. Lathar

P

TARRAGON PUBLISHING

First published in Great Britain in 2005 by Tarragon Publishing
41 Anstruther Road, Edgbaston,
Birmingham B15 3NW, England.

www.TarragonPublishing.com

A CIP catalogue record for this book is available from the British Library.

ISBN 0-9548333-2-5

Typeset in Great Britain by Mousemat Design Limited
www.mousematdesign.com

Printed and bound by
Rakesh Press, India

1 2 3 4 5 6 7 8 9 10

For Ian, for his unstinting hard work and advice,
and for Nina, who helped me more than
I could imagine.

Chapter 1

IT WAS COMING

It was coming. It was coming with frightening speed. And, it was invisible.

He was running blind in the darkness, dragging the body of the man, and all the twists and turns he made to avoid his stalker seemed to lead to a narrower and narrower place, until finally there was nowhere else to go but back. He could feel himself changing as he turned around – tough, coarse hair sprouting all over him, the hands becoming thick and padded, the nails elongating into points, and his jaw becoming wider and more powerful – and then his vision altered. He was breathing hard, he was sweating, and fear was making his hair bristle. There was nothing he could do but turn and face it.

Hovering over the bleeding man, hunched on all fours, he waited.

He could see it gliding forward on thousands of legs. The jaws snapping, the staring blind eyes, the wild movements of its large head, it lurched forward and came closer. The predator was hungry, its body covered in boils, its back scraped raw and haemorrhaging. He could see the long, hairy tentacles whipping around. It was searching, hunting, but not for food – for life. The man hadn't moved and he was going to die. He could not save him.

The creature dived at them, opening its jaws and revealing its vicious fangs. He could see them in the dark.

There was no way out…

'Peter, what're you doing?' his mother shouted from the stairs. 'Hurry up!'

Peter was doing exactly what he didn't want to be doing: lingering on his dreams and scrambling around his room looking for the Book – *his* Book.

'I'll be right there, Mum!' he called down.

He surveyed his room, his little place: the only place his nasty uncles and aunt would never enter. In his opinion it was the most organized mess that anyone could have, and he was the only person in the world who could ever find anything in there.

Desperately, he tried to get a glimpse of where it could be. Sometimes his Book just simply wasn't there. Sometimes it moved when no one else was around… Where it was now was anybody's guess. As long as it was in his room, Peter didn't worry.

His grandfather had given him the Book exactly five years ago, on the day his father, Allan Badger, had disappeared without trace, leaving no message, no note, no trail. There was no sign of him anywhere.

Peter glanced at the picture of his father on the bedside table; the wavy hair, dark eyes and casual clothes gave him the appearance of a man who had all the time in the world. He missed his father a lot, and at first he had cried himself to sleep every night.

Then the dreams started.

Then the nightmares came.

The tears dried up, but not his hope that his father would return. The police had searched for months, and the months turned into years. And all the time his uncles and aunt tried to destroy his belief, telling him to 'grow up'.

His mother, Jenny, they really abused, shouting and screaming at her, always trying to get the house, always trying to take what was not theirs. He was terrified of them, and there was nothing he could do. Every day his feelings of helplessness grew. Every day he felt a little bit more worthless for not being able to help in some way.

'Peter! Come down!' his mother shouted again.

Cursing mentally, Peter was about to give up the search when he spotted it. Propping up the door, waiting expectantly for him, was his accursed Book! A beautiful old leather-bound volume with a clasp to keep all the secrets within it hidden – until, of course, they were ready to be read. On the cover, a strange curly figure three was emblazoned in gold, with extraordinary symbols to the side of it, and it was surrounded by six hexagonal indentations. There was no author's name, not even on the spine, which Peter found strange.

Although he had read it hundreds of times, Peter could not remember what was in the Book. In fact, he couldn't remember getting past the first page. Or even what was *on* the first page. He knew – no he *felt* – that it was always different and was always changing. He picked up the reassuringly solid Book, the leather soft and warm to the touch, and tucked it under his arm.

He glanced quickly in the mirror. A twelve-year-old with dark, mysterious eyes stared back. Spiky black hair with an animal sheen framed an animated face.

'Are you ready?' he asked the image in the mirror.

The reflection shimmered momentarily as if Peter had finally caught it out. It shrugged its shoulders.

'Are you?' it replied.

A shiver ran down his spine. Images in mirrors did not move by themselves. He must have imagined it.

They turned almost together and left the room. Peter thumped down the stairs, dashed into the kitchen – and stopped.

His mother stood there, waiting, intense brown eyes boring into him. She was dressed neatly in a plain blouse and a pleated grey skirt that had known better days. With her old worn shoes, she tapped the floor impatiently, which was a dead give-away that she was really annoyed. The strain of the last five years was beginning to tell on her face.

Knowing he was in trouble, Peter tried the flattery trick – 'Hey, Mum: you look lovely!' – but Jenny Badger wasn't about to be distracted so easily. Her left eyebrow rose, yet at the last moment, a smile touched her lips.

'Have you washed your hands?'

Putting the Book on the table, her son raced to the bathroom, yelling over his shoulder, 'Be right back!'

A sudden violent banging on the front door stopped him in his tracks.

No one else knocked in that imperious manner. No one else would try to break down their door. No one else was that rude.

He peered through the spy-hole where he could clearly see the outline of man dressed in black. The profile of the man

was as unmistakable as the two shadows that accompanied him.

'Oh, no…'

Uncle Ramsey!

Anxiously, Peter opened the door, dreading the moment, detesting the man. The door was barely off the lock when Uncle Lorenzo, who must have been waiting to the side, slammed it fully open. He glared down at Peter, his gaunt face thin and drawn, his nervous twitch under control. His treatment must be working.

'Mum –'

'Shut up, boy!' Lorenzo snapped, his ugly face pushing past, uncomfortably close to Peter's, making him flinch. The boils and pits on his cheeks were clearly visible.

His breathing already fast, Peter backed away nervously into the hall until a wall stopped his retreat. He couldn't go any further.

Uncle Ramsey stood in the outside light, perfectly poised. His handsome features and sculpted face were framed for maximum effect by an immaculate black designer pin-stripe suit, a white monogrammed shirt and a contrasting blood-red tie. The scar on the left side of his face stood out, but it seemed to enhance Ramsey's appearance rather than detract from it.

Holding red roses in one gloved hand and a black leather briefcase in the other, he examined the house critically before entering it royally, not even hinting at Peter's presence. Peter wanted to keep it that way.

Despite his uncle's obvious attractiveness, Peter's skin crawled every time Ramsey came. There was something evil about the man.

In the background, Aunt Petra preened herself, waiting for Ramsey to finish his examination. Draped in a wholly inappropriate black and white fur coat and high-heeled shoes, she tottered forward unsteadily, threatening to fall at any instant and break her neck. Her black hair was scrapped back and tied together in an elegant bun, her eyeliner sufficient to draw attention to her angular face which somehow always managed to look cool and detached.

Her perfume preceded her like a skunk; having been applied with a heavy hand and very little reserve, it wafted in noxiously, making it hard for Peter to breathe. She made a blatant attempt at showing off

her new acquisition by smoothing down the fur while trying to negotiate the steps into the house.

'Don't you think it's to die for?' she commented, walking past.

Peter wanted to follow the three harbingers of doom at a safe distance but got waylaid by Uncle Lorenzo, who seemed to appear out of nowhere, his breath rancid and horrible.

'Get me a drink, boy!' he ordered.

Peter practically jumped out of his skin and ran ahead to the kitchen, filled a glass with a scotch and hurriedly placed it on the table, spilling some of the liquid in his urgency. He backed away to a dimly lit corner and tried to make himself invisible, fighting the rising panic. He didn't know what Ramsey wanted, but he knew his uncle would be up to no good.

Lorenzo had already got to the kitchen and proceeded to glare at his mother. Uncle Ramsey, having taken his time, sauntered in, smoothly drew up a chair and sat down, absent-mindedly crossing one leg over the other.

'*Enchanté*, my dear,' Ramsey began, eyeing Jenny up and down. 'Ravishing as ever.'

Petra sniffed in the background as Lorenzo hurriedly pulled out a chair for her. She draped her fur coat over the side, before attempting to sit down in her skin-tight white dress. She struggled halfway to the seat before failing.

Her dress was too tight.

Jenny met Ramsey's gaze with contempt as he continued, 'I have come to give my deepest condolences. It has been five years to the day since Allan –'

'That is not till tomorrow, and who knows what can happen between now and then?' Jenny corrected him without a hint of her true feelings.

'A mere formality,' Ramsey said dismissively. 'Speaking of which, I have brought you these.'

He offered her five red roses.

'Be careful of the thorns,' Petra hissed.

Lorenzo crawled forward, accepting the roses from Ramsey's proffered hand and taking them over to Jenny, who did not move.

'I almost forgot,' Ramsey said, removing his fine black leather gloves, and drawing out some papers from his expensive briefcase. 'You are, as always, in the forefront of my mind. I cannot imagine the hardship you and my nephew endure.' He did not bother glancing in Peter's direction. 'Sign these, tonight. They'll ensure you are not evicted when you are bankrupt tomorrow.'

Jenny simply crossed her arms. '*You're* the big corporate lawyer who's trying to make us bankrupt? And don't you worry about us being evicted tomorrow – that's not going to happen!'

'You always have my protection.'

'*Protection?*'

'I am the king of my castle and will treat you like a queen.'

Petra, still fighting to sit down, froze midway at Ramsey's words.

'I wouldn't want Allan turning in his grave thinking that his brother had done nothing for you,' Ramsey replied, setting the papers on her table.

'It will *never* be yours. Nothing that was his will ever be yours. Now get out!' Jenny ordered, her emotions at breaking point.

Petra snorted. 'You're so ungrateful.'

'Allan was always out trying to save the world. Ironic. He's losing his house and family. Shouldn't he be *here*, saving you?

'Get out of my house!'

'It's hardly as if I'm billing you for the work,' Ramsey feigned hurt.

'The sooner you come to your senses, the better,' Lorenzo hissed.

'OUT!' Jenny shouted, picking up a knife and pointing it threateningly at him.

Peter, who had been paralyzed with fear, dashed forward shouting, 'Mum! Don't –!'

In his haste he forgot Ramsey's outstretched leg and tripped, falling hard on the stone floor, his head banging into the sink. The noise and his cry immediately brought Jenny to her knees.

The three obnoxious relatives hovered over Jenny and Peter like ghouls. Ramsey glared at Peter with contempt. 'He's just a clumsy kid. What do you believe *he* can do for you, Jenny?'

'Your brat's bleeding,' Lorenzo said with a sneer.

'Just leave,' Jenny said dismissively, all her attention turning to her son. 'Peter and I will manage.'

The ghastly three filed out, looking like shadows, not completely human, with Ramsey in the lead. There was an oily nastiness about the man that always made Peter's skin crawl.

'I should have known this was going to happen. I'll get a plaster for that grazed knee. I swear you get more bruises than anyone I know – oh, Peter!' Jenny exclaimed, grabbing his head, the bruising on his leg completely forgotten.

Blood was pouring from a cut in his forehead.

'Here – hold this,' Jenny ordered, pushing the nearest kitchen towel into his face. 'Keep it there.'

She ferreted round and quickly came back to the huddled boy, his face covered, his other hand grabbing his knee. Jenny cleaned up the head wound and put a plaster on it and another one on the grazed leg.

'You'll be fine now. I'll light the candles. We're already late...'

'Thanks, Mum.'

In the background, Peter heard the fuse-box trip as the lights went out. He had been half-expecting the blackout. He was not afraid of the dark and he knew the lights always went just before they prayed every year for his father.

He took one of the lit candles from his mother as she continued to light others around the kitchen. The light provided a warm, glowing rescue from the dark. The small flames flickered and the smell of the incense and wax blew away the lingering odours of the three unwelcome and unexpected guests.

His mother sat down at one end of the kitchen table with three empty chairs positioned expectantly around it. She gave him a weak smile, not daring to break her concentration and letting her fears pour out.

A single candle burned in the centre of the table, its holder shaped like a medieval tower with a badger curled around its base. Wax clung to the walls in globs, like moulded white warts, each fresh drip corrupting and eroding the original shape.

Peter knew that underneath the table-top his mother's hands

were clasped hard, as if in a prayer. The candles cast shadows on her face, making her look strained and old beyond her years. Still, she had regained some of her composure.

'How're you feeling? Do you think we should start?' she asked, breaking the silence.

'Not yet,' Peter answered, feeling the time was not quite right. His head pounded and the graze on his leg pulsed with a stabbing pain. Drawing up his chair, he added, 'Mum, I've being thinking…'

'Mmm. A dangerous thing in your condition.'

It was an old joke and he ignored it.

'Mum, are we *really* bankrupt?'

'That is complete nonsense!' Jenny snapped. She was furious. 'Ramsey's simply trying to take advantage of an unfortunate situation.'

'But he's got the papers –'

'This house is *ours*. There is no way they're getting their nasty hands on it, despite all their scheming. They're not touching anything of your father's – not while we're here to defend it. They've always wanted what was his. Their greed's out of control.'

She took the papers and threw them in the bin. The fierceness in her eyes told Peter that it was best to let the matter drop. He wished he could do more. He wished he *was* more. Ramsey's words came back to him: *Just a clumsy kid.*

It was close to midnight. He looked through the window into the darkness outside. The wind immediately sensed a change in mood and a gale began to bang on the door, seeping through the gaps and making the candles flicker harder, threatening to blow them out. His mother always believed that the weather would get better on the anniversary, but so far, it had only got worse.

'Peter,' his mother asked, 'can you just make sure that the back door is properly closed? The wind is particularly strong tonight.'

As he approached the farmhouse door, there was the softest knock on the old wood – a knock that he could not miss.

Chapter 2

WITHOUT WARNING

Without warning, the back door flew open. Outside in the darkness stood an old gentleman wearing a white hat and dark sunglasses.

'Grandfather?' Peter asked hesitantly.

The old man was dressed in 'proper attire': a gentleman from a different age. He wore a blazer, a white shirt open at the collar with a gold silk cravat underneath, dark trousers, brown shoes and a walking stick, the handle of which was carved in the shape of a dragon whose body wound its way down the shaft.

Peter had not seen his grandfather in five years, but he always felt that he was around. Elated, he launched himself at the old man and hugged him tightly.

The wind whipped up against them, causing the old gentleman to hold on to his hat. Grandfather briefly returned his embrace with warmth, and somewhere around them an ancient whisper in an eternal voice spoke inside Peter's mind.

He is close to breaking. In death they will gain the key. Your beliefs will count for nothing and we will all be lost.

The old man released Peter and dragged the boy into the shelter of the kitchen. As Peter followed, he shouted, 'Mum, Grandad's here!' as the distinguished gentleman slowly removed his hat and placed it carefully on the arm of the chair.

Despite the walking stick's lethal steel tip, Grandfather never made any noise, not even while walking on the stone kitchen floor. He crowded out the room somehow, filling it with spirit, with *life*.

His face was ageless. Fine lines covered his leathered cheek, making it look smooth. Catching the candlelight, his silver hair glistened and his neatly cropped eyebrows stood out straight over the rim of his sunglasses.

Peter found the dark sunglasses a bit weird, but he remembered his grandfather always wore them, even at night.

Was he blind? Peter wondered. He had never dared to ask.

Jenny Badger burst into tears as she got up to hug the old man, finally seeing someone she could rely on. Peter knew how much his mother hated showing any weakness in front of others and he wasn't surprised when she said, 'Excuse me for a moment.'

Feeling light-headed, Peter sat down facing the old gentleman. He was beginning to find it hard to breathe, but that always happened whenever his grandfather was around.

His mother returned, more in control of her emotions, and placed a full bowl of water and a towel on the table.

'You'll want to clean your hands, Father.'

Grandfather rose, cupped his hands and dipped them into the bowl, savouring the moment. The water swirled around his palms in eddies. He smiled and passed them over the elaborate candle in middle of the table. The flame flared abruptly and engulfed them.

Peter was struck by how much the elderly gentleman's appearance reminded him of his Book: comfortable, sort of lived-in. He was a bit strange but Peter didn't mind. He was just glad to see him.

In the background, the clock started to strike twelve.

Jenny Badger seemed not to notice, fidgeting nervously with her skirt. Softly, she began to speak in a whisper.

'Allan, I hope you can hear us. Wherever you are, our spirit is with you. I –' she paused, her voice breaking. 'I do not for a moment believe you are *dead*. When you can, please come home…'

Peter, his stomach in knots and his fingers absent-mindedly tracing the curly figure on the Book, looked at the empty chair. His attention was drawn to the heat beneath his fingers. The cover of the Book glowed a dull red, and light was leaking out from between the pages.

Grandfather, however, ignored it. Instead, he was looking intently at his daughter-in-law. As he did so, she began to change visibly; her features relaxed, the frown and worry lines disappeared. She continued talking calmly to the air, convinced that her husband could hear her.

'It's been hard these last five years while you've been gone. Most people have been kind, but it's not the same. I'm working now. It keeps me busy. And as for Peter – what can I say? He's a darling.'

'Mum!' Peter cringed. She shouldn't say that in front of his grandfather. He was *twelve* now!

The clock was still chiming in the background. Peter, his irritation forgotten, was confused. Hadn't it struck twelve times already?

'He's growing up; a little like you – well, actually, *a lot* like you. Determined as hell. He has your wanderlust and your unshakable faith. I've lost mine, I'm afraid.' She paused. 'We've lit this candle to remind us of you. I know how much you like…'

Her eyes fell on the moulded wax badger at the base of the tower. Jenny began to sob silently and couldn't go on.

Peter, feeling helpless, felt compelled to say something. 'Uncle Ramsey and Uncle Lorenzo came today with Aunt Petra. They tried to throw us out of the house, saying it was theirs, that we're bankrupt, but Mum gave them what for. She's not scared of them. *They* should have disappeared instead of you…'

He stopped, knowing he would only upset his mother further if he continued. He changed the subject. 'We think of you all the time, and in my dreams I visit you.' His thoughts returned to the nightmare from the previous night. In it he had been chased by something.

'But they're not very nice, either.' He tried hard not to remember the dream – a prayer shouldn't be about bad things.

'It's OK,' his mother reassured him. 'I understand.'

'No, you don't!' Peter replied, upset. 'It's like nothing you can imagine! It's got a life of its own, Mum, and it's coming after me!'

'What is?'

'Last night, I had one of *those* dreams, but in it I had a fight with a man, and the man released this – this *thing* and I couldn't get out.' Peter could still see the fangs coming after him. 'It was…'

He looked down. A bruise had started to emerge on his left arm. Wasn't that where he had been scratched in his dream the night before?

As Jenny's eyes followed his gaze she let out a horrified gasp.

'Peter! Where did you get that from?'

Grandfather was listening, his being focussed on his grandson. Peter could feel it in his soul.

'I had a bad dream. It hurt me in my dream, Mum.' Peter glanced at his mother, then at his grandfather, hoping they understood.

An awesome whisper filled his mind.

There is no more time. They have begun to hurt you. You are my hope, and the dreams have prepared you. They are close to finding the key and they will cross over.

The old man made as if to reach for his sunglasses, and time seemed suspended. Peter's heart raced, his pain forgotten at the thought of seeing his grandfather's eyes for the first time. He was going to remove the glasses!

You must go, and I have to believe that you are ready, for I cannot enter there.

The sunglasses were coming off; the light leaking from behind them began to spill over. The table was suddenly black on the outside, its edges crumbling and decaying away. The sight was horrible – ugly and unclean. Hideous black things crept towards the candle and the light.

Peter's body jerked with revulsion and he kicked out, trying to get away from it, his knee colliding heavily with the table-top and knocking the bowl over. Water spread quickly, steaming where it touched the eroding table. All the dreams from all the years were flooding back as fragmented memories – a fight here, a juicy morsel there, the warm earth, the freezing cold…

From the side of his grandfather's chair, the walking stick began to rise, splitting as it stood and turning into monsters with frightening fanged heads that rose behind his grandfather like a multicoloured fan. Peter had no more time. The dark sunglasses finally came off, and the overspill became a flood, bleaching everything in ultra-white light.

The dreams were flowing into his waking world! Either that or he'd lost his mind!

His heart pounding, Peter knew he had to get away from the nightmare that surrounded him.

Go. I will protect your mother.

'But – Grandfather…?'

The time is now.

There was only one place to go.

He was about to dash away when he saw the creeping darkness approaching his Book. He couldn't risk losing that! He snatched it from the table, his knuckles white. He had to hide the Book. He had to get it away to the only place it would be safe.

If he lost it, he would lose his link to his father.

As his mind filled with thoughts he couldn't control – going to different places where he met different people and did different things – he knew he had to get to the bridge, where the Book would be safe!

Peter ran from the kitchen, burst open the back door, and threw himself recklessly into the howling winds outside. He ran oblivious to everything but his Book, clutching it protectively to his chest. He ran to a place that had always been a haven to him: a bridge surrounded by water, a place where he spent his happiest moments these days. The echoes of an awesome benediction followed in his wake.

Bless you, my son.

He ran down the road, cutting through the grounds of St. Martin's Parish Church, past the grave of Sir Winston, and headed towards the churchyard gates, the poster on the notice board briefly catching his eye:

'Be of good cheer. The hour of your deliverance will come.
The soul of freedom is deathless.
It cannot and will not perish.'

Winston Churchill, broadcast 11th September …

The year had been torn off.

He didn't linger as usual but hurtled past, panicked, the gale doggedly following his footsteps. He crossed the road in a haze, not remembering how he got over the wall separating the ordinary from the extraordinary, dashing across several small bridges.

He covered the vast grounds in a blur until at last he stood

beside the stone bridge that spanned the two lakes of a great estate. He stepped onto the bridge, not even noticing the lack of echoes, and immediately his panic subsided.

The Book was his key, and he would fight to keep it. Sweating heavily, he placed it carefully on the walkway, and hung over the side of the bridge to rest, failing to notice his reflection in the river.

Silence.

There was only the merest whisper of a breeze, as if something moved. Afraid, he glanced around into the darkness; everything seemed quiet. There was no hint of the earlier gale, no swaying branches – nothing.

Yet for some reason, the hair on the back of his neck prickled.

The lights were still out in Bladon village – *his* village – which meant that Grandfather was still around; otherwise the darkness would have lifted by now. His normally dark eyes were gleaming more like those of a nocturnal animal than a boy's, and a spirit stirred deep inside him.

Peter went to move the Book, but it was perched precariously on the side of the bridge, next to him, about to tip into the water below. It hadn't done that before! It never moved while a person was nearby. Reaching forward carefully, he grabbed it, hugging it to him before it toppled over.

He recalled the night his grandfather had given it to him – the night his father had disappeared. After the police had gone and his mother had thrown out his horrid uncles and aunt, Grandfather had glided into the room and presented him with a valuable gift: an old, leather-bound volume, covered then in what looked like rags. It could easily have come to him straight from an ancient land. He remembered that the rags had practically turned into ashes at his touch and then disappeared into the air like hundreds of lights.

The Book felt hot next to his chest. It was demanding to be released. Compelled, he slid into a sitting position, his back leaning against the side of the bridge, undid the heavy clasp and turned to the first page for the thousandth time. The little glow of white light leaking out from under the cover became a torrent as the Book was opened.

Peter never remembered what he saw on its ancient pages, but he knew that things moved in there and that those things changed. His eyes felt heavy and his head began to drop. It was warm and inviting; the colours of the rainbow danced around him, but this time there was also something else. He wanted to wake up a little to see it clearly, but he couldn't. He did not see anything as he fell forward, fast asleep.

When he awoke, a light cool breeze was blowing over him, making his fur tingle. He was curled up in a ball, eyes tightly closed yet enjoying the feel of the grass underneath him, the smell of the fresh earth gently warmed by his body heat.

He became aware of something buzzing at his flanks, disturbing his peace. He flicked at it with his stubby tail, his sharp senses allowing him to pinpoint the source of annoyance with great accuracy. He smiled, his whiskers scraping the ground on one side and tickling his fur on the other. He was exactly who and where he was meant to be: a badger, just coming out of his afternoon nap.

Another fly buzzed over him, and again he flicked at it with his tail, this time making contact with the insect and batting it away. It felt good. He was enjoying the sensation of waking up in this world – *his* world – secure in his fur.

Peter had had this particular dream many times during the past five years, but this time it was subtly different. In the distance he could hear all sorts of other noises; some even sounded like people. He was not going to be disturbed, though – not yet. This was *his* dream, and right now all he wanted was to curl up and enjoy it.

He snuggled into a tighter ball to get rid of the noises, covering his snout further with his thick furry tail. He could smell the musk mingled with the earth and it felt real.

A bit *too* real!

He opened his eyes and immediately wished he hadn't. The world pitched as he did so, leaving his head spinning and his stomach queasy. Disoriented and nauseous, he waited for the earth to stop moving, keeping his eyes tightly closed. He thought the feeling would never end, but eventually it began to fade.

Tentatively, he opened first one eye, then the other, aware of the breeze against him – this time, on his bare skin.

Peter was lying face down. He turned over slowly and looked up. He was lying in the middle of a green field, looking at the sky. He sat up carefully, in case the queasiness returned. The breeze, at least, felt refreshing.

This was not good – not good at all. He could hear his own heartbeat. He hadn't felt like this in any of his dreams before. Could you think you were dreaming and still be asleep?

He realized he was halfway up a low hill. At the top was a wood, and at the base he could see people, mostly men, hurriedly packing up their implements after a day's work in the fields. In the distance, he saw part of a village. All of this gave him little comfort.

He was definitely losing it.

It was too real. Everything was so clear and so detailed. Normally he was detached in the dreams – not quite part of them. He had never experienced a spinning head and queasy stomach before.

Noises below drew his attention. One of the men had spotted him and now others were pointing and gesturing frantically. Turning towards them determinedly, he started down the hill.

I can handle this. It's only a dream, he told himself, desperately wanting to believe it.

As they came closer, he realized that they were calling to him. It wasn't in any language he knew, but to his surprise, he found he could understand them. How was this possible? There was no time to think about it now. The shouting was becoming more and more frantic.

'You! Child on the hill! Come down! Come down quickly!'

Behind him in the woods there was a growing movement. Peter's stomach tightened and he spun around instinctively, ready to face whatever the danger was – but he couldn't see anything. The mid-afternoon sun was just beginning to disappear behind the trees. Inside the shadows, something rustled and moved.

'Come down, child! Come down quickly!'

The shouting was more urgent than ever now.

His heart beating wildly, his mouth dry, Peter turned and

started to run towards the men below. His stomach begged to be violently ill, but he dared not stop. He had definitely felt this way before: always when dreaming of being in grave danger.

Behind him, he could sense something pursuing him. Something that moved with terrifying speed.

Something not normal.

Something not human.

Something was coming and it was coming for him!

Chapter 3

'DON'T LOOK BACK!'

'Don't look back! *Run!'* someone screamed.

Peter ran as hard as he could downhill towards the men, who by now were gesturing wildly at him. His heart pounding wildly, the cries from the men urging him on, his own nature blazing into life and screaming at him to run faster, Peter had no doubt that in this dream he was running for his life. He had no idea whether or not the people were friendly, but he was more frightened of what was behind him. The men continued shouting and running towards him.

'Run, child! Run!'

'Quick! Hurry!'

Peter glanced back. He could see nothing tangible, but his vision seemed to be playing tricks on him, one moment creating an outline of something horrible gliding over the grass, obliterating it the next. His sense of panic increased as his primeval instincts shouted in alarm. He could see that a stream at the bottom of the hill separated him from the men, and behind him, he could hear a rushing sound that was gathering strength.

He could feel its malevolence.

One of the men had almost reached the other side of the stream. 'Hurry!' he cried. 'Jump! I'll catch you!'

There was nothing else he could do. Putting on a final burst of speed, Peter launched himself into the air with all his might. With a jolt, he collided with the man, knocking the breath out of him and sending them both sprawling to the ground. Behind them, something large abruptly changed direction, leaving behind a foul, acrid stench. Looking backwards, Peter could only see the trees. The sun was disappearing behind the woods, sending its shadows all the way to the stream.

The man was breathing hard, his black ponytail bunched up underneath him. Peter found himself being scrutinized by intense blue eyes. The brows knotted hard in the middle, making two lines stand out on the man's forehead. Satisfied that Peter was not hurt, he nodded.

'You are fine,' he stated in his strange language, relieved, the lines between his brows fading.

Peter didn't react, stunned to find that he somehow understood what was being said.

Unexpectedly, the man rounded on Peter. 'What were you doing there, young master?' he demanded through clenched teeth, his weathered features taut.

The photograph of Allan Badger flashed in Peter's mind. 'I–' he started to speak but his voice caught in his throat. The rising panic in his stomach him made his palms sweat. He looked up at the man, who was obviously still expecting an answer. 'I don't know,' he said, amazed at being able to answer the man perfectly in the same foreign language.

Concern flickered over the man's face; he struggled to bring his emotions under control.

'I am Ebo, young master. You have been very lucky today,' he said, looking up towards the darkening trees which rustled together as if signalling to each other. 'Those are the Whispering Woods. Where are your guar–' He was about to say something, but changed his mind at the last moment. 'Where are your parents?'

By now, some of the other men had reached them. They were all bare from the waist up, apart from Ebo, who had a white bead necklace that looked as if it were made from tiny bones. They all wore leather trousers and were covered in hay and grass seeds from working in the fields. Each man was wary and alert, surveying everything and often glancing nervously across the stream.

'What's the matter with you, boy?' one of them shouted.

He was furious, leaning forward aggressively and towering over the fallen boy, who was only just getting up. Peter was beginning to bristle at the tone.

'Easy, Arva,' came Ebo's commanding voice. 'Young master here seems to be a bit lost.'

Something in his words struck a chord with his men, forcing them to calm down.

'We have to go,' Ebo said. 'You will come with us.'

From his tone, Peter could tell that Ebo didn't expect to be disobeyed. Without a backward glance, the leader started off towards the rest of the workers. Not knowing what else to do, Peter followed, aware that the rest of the men had formed a protective circle around him, those at the front occasionally glancing back over their shoulders.

His palms were continuing to sweat and felt wet and clammy, his body shivering with cold despite it being warm. Even the presence of his dreaded Uncle Ramsey had not made him afraid like this.

If this was a dream, should he be feeling like this?

Peter had frequently fallen asleep on his Book. Often his dreams had been strange; occasionally they had been violent. Most of the time they had been of being an animal, but this dream was completely different.

How could he understand their language? He wanted to ask questions, but one look at the stiff backs and the stern faces convinced him that now was not the time. His escorts walked in silence until they got to the fields, where people were hurriedly packing up tools and finishing off some stacks of grain. One of the women strode confidently towards them. She had an angular, sculpted face with arched eyebrows, long black hair and brown eyes. Without thinking, Peter ran straight into her arms.

'Mum!'

Although surprised, the lady returned his hug. Then Peter looked up into her face. He was wrong! This woman wasn't his mother. She had the same face, the same eyes but longer hair. She knelt down so that they were face to face. Peter was too stunned to move.

Idiot!

Her eyes were alive and searching with an intensity that only his mother ever used, especially if he had done something wrong. In that odd-sounding language of theirs, speaking slowly, she asked, 'What is your name?' Her eyes never left his face.

Peter's throat was dry with embarrassment. Imagine making such a mistake! He should know his own mother!

'Peter,' he replied lamely.

'*Pe-ter,*' she said, her voice sharp, her enunciation perfect. Getting straight to her feet while still holding onto his shoulders, she looked down and said, 'I am Jasmine.'

She was a harder image of his mother and her manner was frosty. Jasmine glanced at Ebo, who shook his head slightly, concern creeping into his face.

The wind began to pick up and the leaves appeared to whip each other in the trees. He was well aware of Jasmine's grip on his shoulder.

'Everyone! Pack up quickly! We have delayed long enough!' Ebo commanded, his voice galvanizing them into action. The sun was going down fast and noises rose from the direction of the woods.

Tinny howls rose in the distance, the sounds mixed with screeching and the snapping of branches. There was a rumble and the ground shook ominously.

Peter noticed there were guards running in to join them from all around, loaded with torches and wearing daggers in wide belts around their waists. They looked alert and waited on the edge of the group. He also became aware that the rest of the women had all stopped work and were staring at him. Some were looking stunned and others had their mouths open in surprise.

Realizing the reaction Peter's presence was causing, Jasmine ordered quietly, 'You will come with me. We will go back to the village before we decide what to do with you.'

Panic gripped him. What if he wasn't able to get back home? Before he realized what he was doing, Peter pulled away, and yelled, 'No!' His backward jerk surprised Jasmine with its strength and made her lose her grip on him. She stumbled to the ground.

His urgency and hysteria were almost out of control. 'Please! I have to get back to my mother. She'll be worried…' his voice trailed off, uncertain.

Alarm showed on Jasmine's face as she quickly picked herself up. 'You cannot stay here!' she declared, her voice unsympathetic.

Peter's head snapped up. A screeching and wailing rose in the deepest part of the woods; it sounded frighteningly close. A breaking of branches and crashing through foliage quickly followed. A howling started, only to be cut off abruptly, as if it had been swallowed up by something larger.

Why were the noises in the distance so clear?

'We have to move now!' Ebo yelled, his voice urgent. 'Someone grab him.'

'You have to come with us,' Jasmine commanded, looking around nervously.

One of the men moved closer and was about to nudge Peter in the right direction. Energy surged from deep within him and a spirit not quite his own reacted instinctively to the stranger. Sensing the hand about to be put on his shoulder, Peter's world shimmered and he lashed out, catching the man in the face, sending him sprawling to the ground. Shock showed in the man's eyes, a trickle of blood ran from the corner of his mouth, but his attention was glued on Peter. A single word escaped the man's strained lips.

'*Changeling!*'

That was it.

Peter, in his shocked state, felt the animal spirit in him tear free, growling and snarling at its captivity. It didn't like being manhandled and it was ready to attack again. Peter was wrestling with it and finally, having lost the battle, all he could think to do was run.

He saw the opening and dashed through it. Heedless of the danger, several of the men tried to jump on him, yet they were slow and clumsy and Peter avoided them easily. Ebo's attempt was wilier. He tumbled and rolled in front of him, trying to bring him down. Peter leapt over and was soon past him. In the background, a woman's familiar voice was yelling 'Leave him alone!'

Peter headed away from the woods and away from the people. He was running hard, quickly putting distance between himself and the men who had just tried to capture him.

Ebo was shouting for him to come back, and then he was simply yelling at his people to run. Looking back, Peter saw that they were all rushing after him. Behind them, underneath the

trees, shadows moved and things were shifting. The occasional howl broke through the noise of the wind. The sun was going down and the howling was like nothing he had ever heard before.

By this time, the whole group was charging towards him, and Peter, spurred on by fear and fright, found himself heading down the valley. Even at this distance, his ultra-sensitive nose picked up the smell of their fear. The people were running for their lives.

*They're not after me! Something's after **them**!*

The sparse valley quickly gave way to lush foliage, and coming round a small wood, Peter turned to the side and carried on racing, his lungs ready to burst.

The villagers were still moving fast, but strange noises were rising in the distance. Peter looked back in the fading light but couldn't make out exactly what he was seeing. The shadows all seemed to move and his vision was again playing tricks on him. It flickered in the dying twilight, superimposing a brilliant image, allowing him to see it one moment, making it invisible the next.

Strange creatures began to move out of the woods. What he saw made his fear vanish, replacing it with an hysterical panic completely out of his control. The creatures were all chasing after the villagers. He looked towards the scattering of trees he was closest to, and in the centre, away from any light, more things moved inside. In front of him, the light was almost gone.

He looked around frantically, trying to decide where to go next. The creatures were moving closer to the edges as the light faded and the running group of workers headed out of Peter's sight. The animal spirit tried to hold steady, but Peter's terror was out of its cage and it was running blind. Suddenly light flared from the direction of the village as if something had been set alight, and all around him screams of agony erupted.

Peter stopped listening. All he wanted to do was hide, and he forced his tired legs into motion and ran away. The odd, vibrating vision he'd experienced at the stream was happening again, slowing down his escape. This time he could see another image of the world around him made entirely of sound. Superimposed ghost images

extended through everything, but they faded in and out and made his head spin. Sounds turned into images, becoming clear for an instant before disappearing again. Every time the image stayed with him longer.

He had to get out of the open. He could see that the darkness in the woods was now alive with moving shadows.

They had woken up.

He knew he was still visible.

Despite his tiredness, the thought that he was now utterly alone terrified him. He needed to find shelter fast, otherwise he wasn't going to last the night. Edging further into the open, he could make out the river. It continued further down the valley where the creatures had now moved out of the woods. They milled around the edges, leaving the spaces near the water free.

Peter had to find safety quickly. The howling and screeching rose from the scattered woods around him. Often the noises tore apart and became screams instead before being abruptly silenced. A shiver crawled down Peter's spine. It dawned on him that this time there was no one to call for help. No one would hear him if he screamed. The further he went from the village, the further he went from anything familiar. He turned around to retrace his steps and froze. His newfound vision kicked in, allowing him to see perfectly in the dark.

For a moment, he couldn't move, frozen with fear. One of the smaller creatures near him was sniffing. Suddenly it let out a shriek and the other beasts around it responded by freezing and then also sniffing the air. Peter stood very still. The small creature seemed to be blind and was shambling towards him haphazardly, probing ahead with its extended snout. Peter turned his head slowly to look towards the river, and instantly noises rose behind him.

They had spotted him!

He ran for his life, knowing the creatures were close. The baying behind him rose to fever pitch, a cacophony of madness. He was running blind, unable to handle his fear, his mind on the brink of insanity until at last instinct took over and he ran without thinking on all fours. The spirit inside him lacked the ability to feel fear in the same way, and forced into Peter a strength of old, making him pound the ground with every ounce of strength he had left.

He headed for the river and dived in, the cool water refreshing, bringing him back from the fear-induced insanity. He hoped, rather than believed, that the monsters would not follow.

Frantically he swam, the waves throwing him about, his fur heavy but his mind clear and fresh for the first time. Looking back, he could see that the creatures had stopped chasing him well short of the water. The current rapidly carried him downstream.

Peter fought the river while trying to find a safe place to haul himself out. Eventually he gave in to the tiredness and swam ashore, ready to jump in at any moment, fully expecting the creatures to respond and to chase him again. They continued to linger away from the water's edge and none of them came close.

Dripping wet, he looked around in the darkness, accidentally catching sight of his reflection in the water. Intrigued, he went closer to the edge and peered down. A large, black shape stared back. He struggled to see himself clearly, getting closer and closer to the water in order to get a better look, the ripples in the river making it hard to see.

The spirit inside was calmer, but the boy was confused.

A scream erupted in the woods, reminding him that he was still in danger.

Peter shook himself vigorously to get the water out of his fur. If he stood there any longer, they could come after him and he would not survive.

There was only one thing he could do.

Dig!

His senses alert, he followed his animal nature and started to burrow. Going deep, he purposely twisted the tunnel in places, his senses reaching up to the surface and showing him where all the creatures were, the vibration-sound image completely clear. Tired and exhausted, he collapsed.

The sound of sniffing suddenly broke through his doze. It was close. Something was tickling his paw. Peter came awake just as a long-nosed animal tried to take a bite. He lashed out, making

contact with the snout, hearing something paper-thin snap and crumble. It had no substance.

The creatures were packed into the mouth of the burrow – things were shuffling in, one after the other. Peter could see them with his special sight. His breathing rapid, in sheer panic and fright, he turned and started to dig desperately once more, going deeper and filling the tunnel in behind him. More creatures followed.

He put as much earth between him and them as he could, cutting off his own entrance. He could hear them at the seal. They were sniffing and beating against the earth. He could see them, their bodies squeezed tightly in the passage, one after the other, with nowhere to go but back.

The creatures could not break through. Their thumping grew weaker as Peter waited. Breathing hard, feeling suddenly very small, he curled up into a tight ball, failing to notice that the burrow around him had suddenly become huge.

He felt alone. He felt tired and hungry but much worse than that, he felt scared. A tear fell from his eye. He was salivating. His paw felt wet and there was a sharp, pulsing pain in it. Another tear fell. He started to cry. Bleeding and in pain, his body convulsing with sobs, he cried and he cried.

It was dark outside.

Chapter 4

WRIGGLY WORMS FILLED HIS HEAD

Wriggly worms filled his head. Peter woke up tired and hungry and the only thing he could think about was biting into a fat, juicy, wriggly worm. He could feel himself salivating at the thought of biting through the soft, succulent morsel; the idea of the cool liquid and rubbery flesh slipping down his throat was overpowering.

He couldn't believe he had just thought such a thing.

Yuck! Gross!

Trying to distance himself from the disgusting image, he squirmed, instantly becoming aware of the closeness of the walls and then the complete lack of movement. In the pitch black of the warm burrow, his paw stinging, Peter was calmer. He reached upwards with all his senses but could not detect any movement.

Cautiously he dug back through the seal he had made the night before, alert for any signs of life.

Nothing.

Pawing through first the dirt, then the soft ash, he broke through and gagged on the smell of charcoal. Staggering out of the tunnel, he gasped for fresh air, the smell of burnt flesh singeing his nostrils. There were no predators from the night before. Only their ashes remained.

He peered around, twitching at every sound, ready to dash back at any moment. Eventually he spied the flowing river and the badger realized just how thirsty he felt. He edged to the water, still wary, leaned over and took a quick lick. After that, there was no stopping him. The licking became a wild frenzy.

Finally, he drew back from the water having satisfied his thirst. Something wasn't right; someone else was here. Then he saw it: something staring right back at him from the water.

The face was familiar, as if he had known it all of his life, but

it wasn't one he recognized. He leaned forward again and the creature brought its snout closer to the surface, its face striped in black and white. The eyes held the fierce clarity he had seen before. The creature did not look away. It watched him with the same fascination as he was watching it. He tried a smile, and then scrambled back to the bank. The animal's bared fangs were large and too close for comfort.

Peter was ready to flee, expecting the creature to emerge and give chase.

It didn't.

Warily, his stomach doing somersaults, Peter crept forward again, his belly scraping the ground. He could feel the wet bank underneath him. He waited a moment for his heart to stop thumping and his breathing to steady. Those fangs were chisel-sharp, and he did not want to be somebody's next meal.

Again he crept to the water's edge. It was still there, its snout practically underneath Peter's nose. The creature mimicked his movements, and slowly, a realization dawned on him. The nagging sensation at the back of his mind became crystal clear. Peter was repeating something he had done many times before: a game he played in front of the mirror, jumping quickly in front of it and trying to get there before the image, trying to discover if it was somehow different from his own. He always felt excited at the thought. The scary sensation would make the hair at the back of his neck rise.

Peter had got his wish. Now he wanted to take it back.

At first, his mouth dry, Peter rejected the image that he had just seen – the familiar eyes, the mimicked movements. Then he wanted to wake up from his nightmare. He tried to stop thinking, but in his mind the eyes wouldn't go away; they kept looking at him.

His thoughts darted around, trying to gather his courage. He looked once more in the water. The fluttering in his stomach got worse. Finally, the queasy feeling become too strong for him to control and he retched, his empty stomach convulsing with spasms, the pain making him double over. He lay there heaving and panting – lost.

The world shimmered and he was Peter Badger again, hungry, aching and alone. He was not going to survive out there. The prospect of another night in the open was already scaring the daylights out of

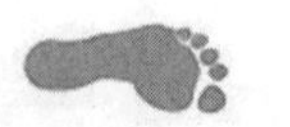

him. Another night with those things and he would be a shish kebab.

Feeling the bitter wind bite into his skin, he instinctively covered most of his body with fur. Looking down at himself, he discovered that he was half human, half furred badger.

This was what the dreams and nightmares had been preparing him for!

The pain in his foot demanded attention, and when he examined it, two long gashes showed him how close he had been to becoming a meal. No Mum and no plasters this time. The scrape pulsed with pain, the skin standing up in bits, blood coming through in tiny red droplets. Still, the gashes were just superficial, and Peter decided the pain was bearable, given the alternative. He had to ignore it.

Only the villagers resembled something familiar. They weren't going to be much help, given the way he had run off, but he decided that he needed to be closer to the village. Perhaps he could burrow underneath their walls. Their light and torches would at least give him some protection. Any hope he had that he would wake up from this nightmare, as he had done many times in the last five years, was gone. It wasn't going to happen.

Anything was better than being in the open. Even the village.

He trekked back along the river for most of the day, but due to his complete exhaustion, he'd slept late and the afternoon was fast disappearing. He was tiring; he hadn't eaten in over a day, and his stomach rumbled – alarmingly loud to his sensitive hearing. It made him glance towards the murderous woods each time it happened.

Peter's strength faded with the daylight. The river had forked several times and he followed the course he thought he had come down. His will to continue searching weakened. The village was nowhere in sight and the life-giving sun was going down. He couldn't think properly, and his body was shivering from weariness and lack of food. He had tried to stay close to the river for safety, but several times he had missed his footing on the steep banks and had fallen in. Filthy, muddy and long past caring, he sat on the bank of the sparkling river, watching his dangling paw despondently. He was going to have to dig soon. He lay back, too tired to worry or even to struggle. If he didn't start to burrow now, this particular night would be his last and he would die – a meal for one of those ugly creatures. He didn't care.

'Hey.'

Peter was sure he was hallucinating. His soundscape was playing tricks on him.

'Changeling – where are you?'

He tried to lift his head, but it was too heavy. He blacked out.

Peter woke the next morning. He couldn't help but feel disappointed. The warmth in the bed was welcoming, but the blanket was light and coarse. This wasn't his duvet. His eyes snapped open, already aware of the person standing in the doorway.

'Interesting night?' Jasmine asked, her manner cold.

He simply nodded. She turned and walked away. 'Come on,' she said without looking back.

Peter dragged his aching and tired body to the other room where fruit and bread were laid on a table.

'Help yourself,' she said, yanking out a stool and sitting directly in front of him.

'I'm sorry,' Peter admitted, ravenously tucking into the food.

'About what? Hurting our man, or running away?'

'Is that man alright? I didn't mean to attack him,' Peter asked. He was genuinely concerned.

'Yes, he is, and Ebo was furious that he let you get away,' Jasmine answered with vehemence.

Peter quickly glanced towards the door: his only way out.

'Do not worry. It was to prevent you from having to spend the night out there.'

Her words didn't reassure him. He heard her voice catch in places as she decided not to say certain things. Peter could hear the apprehension in her words. He had to remain on his guard.

'I didn't think I'd make it,' he admitted nervously, trying not to think about it.

'Neither did we. They only come at night, the worst ones come just before dawn, at the darkest hour. That is why we burn the torches. You, out there, no light, alone… No, we did not think you would make it,' she said matter-of-factly.

Peter nodded. 'What are they?' he asked.

'The creation of a power-crazed man called Blackheart.'

Her tone was hard. Peter had touched a raw nerve.

'Our self-declared king,' she continued, 'Romulus Blackheart. For such a beautiful man, he truly has a black heart. He respects nothing and takes everything – even our children.' Jasmine sounded bitter. 'He is an outlander from a race called the Rumanni. They are a harsh people and he is harsher than the rest, surrounded by his stone walls – a castle he built in a single night. Here, take this.'

Jasmine shoved a hot metal mug into his hand.

Peter didn't understand. 'No man can build a castle in a night.'

'Exactly.'

The drink gave off an odd aroma and distracted him. Hesitantly, he sniffed it.

'It will not hurt you.'

He tried a small sip – it was delicious! 'This is lovely. I'd have killed for this last night - how do I get home?' Peter asked, trying not to gulp down the sizzling liquid.

Jasmine stared at him. For a moment, her iciness melted and she could have been his mother. 'I do not know what we are going to do with you. Ebo is talking to our village elders, so that he can decide.'

Peter's apprehension increased. 'You could just take me back to where you found me,' he suggested, although knowing already that wasn't really an option.

'That is not going to work. We have seen this before.'

The tension in Peter was increasing.

At that instant, Ebo walked through the door. He glared at the boy for a moment and shook his head disapprovingly.

'Well, at least he is not dead – yet.' He looked tired as he slumped into a chair. 'The Shaman could not find him, and so we had to send out the runners. I must admit I am a little surprised. He should not have run away like that.' Ebo was talking to Jasmine only, ignoring Peter as if he weren't even there.

'He knows that now.'

'I have discussed it with the Elders and the Shaman. We have to take him to the castle. It is where he needs to be.'

'I'm sorry, but isn't that the same place as Jasmine was just telling me about?' Peter asked hesitantly.

'All our children reside there for their safety,' Ebo said.

'But – I'm not your child! And didn't you say that this Blackheart guy is half-crazy? I don't want to go near him,' Peter stated, not wanting to anger the man.

'*Enough!* You will do as you are told, otherwise I will throw you out of the village myself. I have spoken to the Shaman – there is no alternative. It is a choice; we can take you to Castle Craven or we can leave you out there in the dark. The Shaman will not risk the lives of all our children for you.'

'But why would I be risking the lives of your children? What's that got to do with –'

'ENOUGH!'

This time, there was silence.

'We will take you to the Castle. And that is final.' Ebo stormed out of the room, leaving Peter to wonder if coming to the village was such a good idea after all.

Surely the people in the castle, the Rumanni, couldn't be any worse than these villagers.

Throughout the day, Peter listened with his ultra-sensitive hearing to the babble of rumours flying around the village. One story swore that Changelings had suddenly appeared in different villages; another that a Shaman was coming to take them away, warning of terrible things if they did not obey the Law of Romulus.

Ebo and Jasmine had argued throughout the night – mostly about him. All voices ceased when he, Jasmine and Ebo stepped outside the house.

What were these people so afraid of?

Peter could only wonder at this point, but he had to find some answers and he expected them to be in the castle.

There was nowhere else to go.

No one approached them as they made their way out of the village, but worried stares followed his every move.

He shouldn't have come here.

Chapter 5

CLOUDS STARTED TO FORM

Clouds started to form. They travelled a path overlooking woods and fields. Just visible in the distance were the creamy spires of a perfect miniature version of a monstrously large castle.

Castle Craven.

It looked as if it had been etched into the mountainside, its soaring towers standing out harshly against the darker mountain rock, its lofty escarpment clearly joining hefty watch-towers.

'We will reach the Guarded Cave before dusk,' Ebo said, looking towards the sun.

'But I thought you were taking me to the castle?' Peter burst out.

'That is too far,' Ebo said, irritated, and pointed into the distance. 'We would never make it before the night falls. Have you forgotten so soon what happens then?'

Peter didn't say anything. He hadn't forgotten. He wasn't ready for another night like the last one but he felt a stab of anger at Ebo for not having told him earlier about the cave.

Before long the light started to turn golden.

'There!' Ebo said pointing.

In front of them, halfway up the side of a hill, was the mouth of a cave, where two men stood waving at them. Ebo picked up the pace and they were soon there, being greeted by several others. The men stared openly at Peter with undisguised interest and unspoken questions. Their scent told him that they were not aggressive, just curious.

The Guarded Cave had torches at its mouth and a trench had been cut into a wide channel at the entrance where a plank lay across the water, allowing them access. Inside, it was large, clean and warm. Torches and lamps provided the light. In addition, there was

a cooking fire in the middle of the cavern, which produced the most heavenly of smells. The fire spat and crackled; smoke circled and rose to the roof. The heavy aromas gave the huge space a warm, cozy feel. In his present hungry state, Peter thought he would probably find anything delicious.

All the men were armed, and more spears, bows and arrows were stacked up against the circular wall of the cave. They looked ready for an attack. Jasmine and Peter were led to the boiling pot, while Ebo went to one side to talk to some of the men. Now that he had stopped walking, Peter discovered that he was quite tired and flopped down to the ground in front of the fire. Its flames danced and flickered close to his face, warmth flooding from them.

'It's all that fresh air,' Peter commented, more to himself than anyone else. 'It's well-overrated.'

A man, overhearing Peter's remark, burst out laughing and even Jasmine gave a tiny smirk before handing him a plate full of food. 'It is better than the smells in the Castle.'

With a full belly, Peter gave a long yawn. Jasmine showed him where his bed was laid. Given the taut faces and short conversations, Peter was happy to crawl straight into the pile of furs. He yawned broadly, somehow wanting to throw his head right back with the gesture. Even the hard floor was more inviting than staying in the sombre company. A warm, drowsy sensation spread rapidly outward from his stomach, and soon it filled his body, making him feel as if he were drifting. His hearing, however, was giving him problems, roaming uncontrollably over the Cave.

'There are others,' he heard someone say.

'How many?' a familiar voice asked in a whisper.

'A boy.'

'A girl.'

'The Shaman will…'

Peter found it hard to keep his eyes open, and tuning into the conversations was becoming difficult. The whole cave was pulsing with sound – one moment alive, and the next, dead silent. He was too tired to resist the dragging warmth and fell asleep.

★

He awoke with a start. It was pitch-black. The fire in the centre of the cave had gone out and even the torches weren't burning. His senses began reaching out automatically. There was a strange, tense, exciting feeling spreading outward from his heart and he felt the earlier animal spirit within him stir. Once his senses adjusted to the vibration, Peter could make out Ebo and three of the other men near the mouth of the cave. They were huddled to the side, ready to attack, the smell of their adrenaline sharp. A beast was moving towards them from the outside, its outline horrifically large, especially when compared with the tiny men crouching to the side. Barely visible against the early morning sky, a man lay face down, unconscious, across the water at the cave entrance. To Peter's vision, the trickling blood from the the man's mouth blazed into unnatural colours as it cooled rapidly.

Peter's heart now raced with fear and he crouched automatically. Jasmine was awake and put out her hand to him, motioning for him not to make a sound. With her other hand, she reached for something on the ground, moving as quietly as she could. In the darkness, Peter's sense of hearing and smell reached out to all corners of the cave. The noise from the men's breathing, the movement of the creature's fur, the whispering of the voices, and even the men tensing their muscles while waiting for their opening, all helped define the surroundings for him. The echoes formed patterns, allowing him to see in the dark – a badger's night-light.

Suddenly, the beast attacked. With a swift movement, it swiped at one of the men and smashed him across the shoulders, flinging him across to the other side of the cave. With a roar, the others launched themselves at the creature, but they were attacking blind and it was far too quick for them. It lashed out with its hind leg, hitting another man, and as Peter watched, the man's image turned a strange colour: his temperature dropped as the blow knocked him unconscious. He flew backwards, colliding into the advancing Ebo, and trapping him. The beast was already advancing on the pinned leader and it was apparent that Ebo was not going to get clear before the creature struck.

All sense of fear forgotten, with a piercing scream, Peter attacked, the world vibrated and buzzed for a split second before settling down. His giddiness passed in an instant, and Peter didn't take the time to fully appreciate the incredible power pulsing through him. He was focussed on saving Ebo. Powerful jaws, serrated claws and great size all came together in one fluid movement. On all fours, leaving behind his humanity, Peter covered the distance between him and the beast with unbelievable speed, launching straight into an attack at the animal's throat.

Sensing something far more dangerous than the men in front of it, the creature rounded on Peter with primeval reflexes, knocking him to one side with its shoulder. Peter tucked and tumbled into a natural athletic roll, landing on all fours. Instinctively, he turned and launched into another attack before the creature could react.

It sensed Peter's movement and turned blisteringly fast, but it was too late. Peter's powerful jaws were already closing on something furry and soft but foul-tasting. A bone snapped. With his newfound hearing, it sounded like a thunderclap and a scream of agony erupted from the beast as part of its shoulder was torn from it. Peter jumped clear, whirled round, ready to attack again, but he did not need to. He watched the beast charge out of the cave, howling in agony, its neck and shoulder ripped open. Using his rough tongue, he cleaned his front paws, scraping the skin and bones off them and spat out the foul-tasting warm blood.

Peter felt quite calm as he turned to face the people in the cave, shaking his mane and snout as he retracted his claws. A new confidence awoke inside him as power surged round his body. He could tell from the smell of the men that they were anxious, but still not afraid. It brought a smile to his face, his whiskers twitching at the corners of his jaws, his laughter coming out as a deep, satisfying growl.

Suddenly, the men were backing away, scared. For a moment, Peter wondered why – he was alert to any new danger and ready for another attack. Then he understood.

A man-sized badger in front of them was growling!

It was the sound of his laughter that had made them feel anxious. He calmed down and backed off slowly, smelling their adrenaline fade away along with their fears.

Two of the men helped Ebo out from underneath the unconscious man. The sense of danger receded and Peter got up on his hind legs, changing back into a boy at the same time, again feeling the strange sensation of the world vibrating, shimmering for a moment and then settling down. He felt quite calm and in control. He was not even breathing hard!

The torchlight cast eerie shadows over the mess in the cave: blood was splattered everywhere and a large piece of the animal lay on the ground. The men were all staring at it. Their eyes finally came to rest on Peter, who was steeling himself for their condemnation but determined to face it. He looked straight back at them, apprehensive about what they might be thinking. If they thought he was something unnatural, what would they do – throw him out or kill him?

One of the men slowly started to nod and then broke into a smile. 'Are we glad you were with us, young master!'

There was general laughter suddenly from the others.

'Are we ever glad!'

Peter couldn't believe it.

Relief flooded through him. He was conscious of how casually the men were accepting him. The transformation had felt completely natural, he was convinced he had done it hundreds of times before, even if only in his dreams, but the sensation of power he had not experienced. More importantly, whatever he was expecting from someone who had witnessed the transformation, it wasn't casual acceptance. He realized he had been holding his breath and now, slowly, he let it out, still waiting for them to change their minds and condemn him.

Images flashed through his head, all the dreams and the fights he had had previously – including the one he had just been in. He couldn't tell the memories apart. Peter felt emotionally drained. What exactly had he just done? He had become – changed into – an animal; not like before, but fully, where he was always conscious of it.

A badger.

His namesake.

At first, he wanted to reject the thought but he couldn't; he had transformed into the animal and he could not deny it. It wasn't just his body but his spirit, too. How was it even possible? Maybe this was still a dream after all. Peter felt confused by all the unanswered questions in his mind. Emotionally fragile, his feelings confused, he was suddenly acutely aware of the cold. His body started to tremble violently.

It was then he really noticed the cave. The torchlight cast eerie shadows that danced with the movement of the men; on the blood-splattered floor and walls, the red seemed even darker in the flickering light, turning into black ugly stains.

Could *he* have done this?

He looked around again, wanting some reassurance that the world hadn't turned crazy. In the strange setting, he couldn't be certain that the mess wouldn't become something else.

How was it possible that he caused this mayhem? He even shied away from most of the fights at school. His mother had taught him to turn the other cheek, and he had always felt like asking why. Especially when something was wrong.

His attention kept returning to the large chunk of the creature lying there. The dark stain around it had stopped growing and the blood glistened unnaturally brightly. He needed a reason for all this destruction and his gaze fell on Ebo.

The men were helping him up. He remembered then the certainty with which he had known that the creature would kill him. He had known that none of the men could help him in time. It had to be Peter. Ebo would be dead now if he hadn't done what he did.

He remembered all the bullying his uncles and aunt had done over the years, pushing his mother around. An anger and regret rose in him at the thought. He wished he had shown the same courage as he had shown tonight and defended his mother against them. If he got back, a part of him was determined never to be weak again, and his uncles and aunt would be getting back some of their own treatment.

'Thank you!' Jasmine said her voice shaking, bringing his thoughts back to the cave.

'What just happened?' Peter asked sharply, his mind suddenly snapping into focus, looking directly at her. '*What am I?*'

'You are the Changeling,' Jasmine whispered under her breath.

Ebo was on his feet again. Peter turned slowly to face him, his anger rising, his dark animal eyes glistening dangerously, locking onto the leader.

'Am I some kind of freak?' Peter asked.

'No.' Ebo paused. 'You are our hope.'

The man squatted, looking lost, searching the ground for answers. Taking a deep breath, he reached a decision, and finally started to explain. 'You are not alone. There have been others – people who came from your place. Who had powers similar to yours.'

'Others?' Peter exclaimed. *He was not alone!*

'We have a Shaman, a wise leader, in one of the other villages, who is bringing them here tomorrow. We will be going on to Castle Craven together…' Ebo's voice trailed off.

Peter, his head buzzing with questions, drifted towards the fire to get warm. Shaking with cold and fear, vaguely aware of the powerful spirit in his soul, he couldn't help but think that this dream had turned dangerous.

But then again, so had he.

Chapter 6

HAUNTED BY MEMORIES AND HUNTED BY CREATURES

Haunted by memories and hunted by creatures, Peter had a dreadful night. He tossed and turned, unable to get the images out of his mind: creatures scurrying into the protective darkness, the rivers running red, the sun rising on horrors. He awoke with all the pains of someone who had slept on the ground.

He had got up especially early and stood watching the creatures, just like in the dream. Then the sun had come up and transformed the whole landscape.

The others didn't arrive in the morning. He could hardly contain his frustration, and his thoughts and feelings kept drifting to other things. Disappointed and bored, he moved away, sensing the people around the cave. Sometimes he was able to look straight through the walls with this new ability to 'see' sound. His control faded in and out, but when it was there, the walls themselves disappeared.

Ebo had said something about starting out as soon as the Changelings arrived, but having decided where they were headed, Peter wasn't eager to begin.

What had happened to his dad?

What was happening to him?

How was he going to get back?

The morning wore on, and the afternoon came. All of Peter's anticipation faded and he lost interest in keeping watch. He wondered off to an isolated part of the cave and sat there thinking about all that had happened to him. It was hard to concentrate on any specific event; only the impressions seemed to remain. Part of him was still trying hard to reject the changes, and the power.

At the thought of power, Peter raised his right hand to examine it. It looked a perfectly good human hand. With just a feeling and a thought, he felt a change flow into his arm and his fingernail transformed into a claw. Peter was fascinated.

He lifted his hand, turning it this way and that, examining the long, protruding claw with the serrated edge from every angle. A smile played on his face, his nostrils flared with every breath and his heartbeat increased. He was still undecided about whether he liked it or not, but more importantly, he hadn't decided if it was a good thing. Looking down at all the extra bruising on his body, he decided that there wouldn't be enough plasters in the house. His mother was going to kill him!

Another thought, another surge and his will changed a part of him into an animal. He covered it with fur and changed its textures. The hair tickled his skin. Peter hadn't noticed that when he had been too busy running for his life, but now…

There was no one around and he transformed his feet to padded paws; he retracted the claws and padded his hands instead. He extended the claws one more time for good measure. He had decided.

They were evil and he liked it!

A normal set of claws would have been great, but these – these were something else. He couldn't even imagine an adult-size badger having these claws. They were huge, serrated like a crab's, and hard. But the most surprising thing about them was their sharpness. Their ridges were edged finely with tiny razors, each facing a different direction. A subtle, dull yellow-grey colour belied the true nature of the weapons, their strength derived from a belief and their size from a lack of imagined limitations. Peter, the boy, thought he could do anything, and in this world, the badger was about to find out what he could really do.

He snapped out all of his claws. The five razor edges appeared as if from nowhere.

'It's not *that* impressive.'

The cool female voice caught him off guard. Surprised, he felt sheepish as he looked up.

A frosty cold blue-eyed stare met his gaze. It was the look of a predator eyeing up its prey, the jury still out as to whether he was a meal or something else.

'Hi. I'm Michelle. And you must be Peter. I expected you to be taller.'

The girl staring down at him with the piercing look had long, straight blond hair down to her waist, high cheekbones and the olive complexion of someone who spends most of her time outdoors. The worrying thing for Peter was the flame of the life force he could sense inhabiting her skin – a predator with a variable disposition bordering on intolerance, and an insatiable appetite.

She snapped open a wing briefly, just to demonstrate, raised her left eyebrow and said, 'I hear you wanted to meet us.'

'Us?'

'Hello. I'm Paul.'

The brown-eyed weasel-like boy, coming out of the shadow of the blond girl, was dark-haired, freckled and hesitant. His demeanour concealed the strength of life flowing through him, but it was easily apparent in the soundscape image Peter could see. He seemed to glide rather than walk, his rhythm always ready to change, every noise a distraction.

Paul smiled and paused, as if deciding what was the right thing to do. He quickly darted a look towards Michelle, who ignored him.

'I didn't hear you come.'

'Why should you? Only real predators are that alert,' Michelle stated, her assurance overpowering in its conviction.

'I'm a bit of an animal myself,' Paul beamed, extending his leg and transforming it into a black, fur-covered otter's leg.

'I can do that,' Peter said, joining in, his leg already black and silver-furred.

'But can you do this?' Paul challenged, his face transforming into half otter on one side and half human on the other.

'No problem.' Peter concentrated and his face turned instantly into a half-badger.

'Mild improvement, boys,' Michelle yawned, 'although a bag over both your heads would be better. As I was saying, only real

predators are alert!' She snapped open her wings and obliterated the otter from Peter's view.

Paul sneaked around her, spitting out a feather. 'But I can also do this,' he said, transforming just his ears into points and covering them with oily fur.

Michelle's face changed as she turned to face the otter. A large beak transformed her nature from the cool to definitely predatory. Paul squeaked and jumped out of her way as she took a nip.

'They are waiting for you.' Jasmine's voice broke into their conversation. 'We have to get going soon if we are to catch the boat.'

Ebo and the tribesmen had been joined by a one-eyed man with black dreadlocks, who was wearing an old heavy brown cloak, and a woman with reddish hair tied in a neat bun, wearing a colourful orange and yellow dress. The woman looked up immediately at the children's return; her blue-green eyes gazed critically at Peter before going to Michelle. Michelle nodded slightly and went to join her.

'What's with them?' Peter asked Paul in a hushed whisper.

'Don't know,' Paul answered, puffing out one of his cheeks and making a blowing noise.

The severe-looking one-eyed man was having a heated argument with Ebo. His other eye was permanently closed, as if the eyelids had been glued together. It gave him an air of danger – someone you didn't tangle with unless you had no other choice.

'That's their Shaman,' Paul stated, 'a man of few words, mostly rude ones. I don't think he can say any sentences without swearing.'

The man Paul had called a Shaman towered over Ebo and was practically yelling at him.

'Boom-Basa, Ebo, they go to the castle! Damn it – that is final! It is the bloody Law!'

'I know the Law, but why can you not see our opportunity? This could be our last chance to rescue them!' Ebo was sounding loud and frustrated.

The wise man, abruptly becoming aware of the children, relented. He threw a venomous look towards the three of them before stomping off in a sulk.

Turning towards them, Ebo took a deep breath. 'As I told Peter –' he seemed to have trouble pronouncing *Peter* properly – 'our children live in the Castle, but what I did not say at the time was that they are – *prisoners* there.'

He was fidgeting, his hands in constant motion, and he sounded awkward. 'We have made many attempts to free them, all of them unsuccessful. We have to hand you over to the castle folk, the Rumanni. We have no other choice.'

'*What?*' It was Paul who shouted at him.

'No you're not!' Michelle stated crossing her arms.

'You *lied*,' Peter growled at Ebo. 'You said it was for their safety.'

Ebo looked towards Jasmine and then at the three of them. 'The king has the Sight. It allows Romulus Blackheart to spy on anyone. He can look anywhere in this land, wherever he likes. And, he can do it all sitting comfortably in Castle Craven!'

'You lied to us,' Peter growled again.

'Listen to me. Romulus can see almost everything. Even though I am convinced he cannot see *you*. Your gifts somehow hide you from the Sight, but I cannot be certain. Sooner or later he would find out something was wrong if we were hiding you, and then he would punish us by doing nasty things to our children,' Ebo explained, the worry lines between his brows deepening. 'The Sight is the main reason why all our attempts to rescue our children have failed. The Rumanni were waiting for us. They know what we are going to do before we do it.'

'Then don't hide us. Let us go,' Peter added, looking round to see how far he would get.

The Shaman was instantly on his feet, his one-eyed gaze fixed intensely on Peter, his hands already moving in strange rhythms.

'When we first fought the Rumanni,' Ebo continued, 'Changelings were with us. We could not be seen, and the castle-folk could not second-guess where we were.'

'Boom-Basa – for a while we were even *winning*,' the Shaman chimed in with resentment. Almost an afterthought he added, 'With the help of the Boom-ba Changelings.'

Ebo flashed an angry look towards the Shaman. 'We found out

that if one or more of the Changelings were with us, the Rumanni armies would always be confused as to our exact location. Even our own people with the Sight could not find us. They could only reach us directly, by the stones,' Ebo explained.

The hair on the back of Peter's neck rose. 'These Changelings, who were they?' he asked softly. He was not sure he wanted to know the answer. He felt the Sight was suddenly trivial.

'Mar-ray, Al-leone,' Ebo said with his heavy, aspirated accent, as if it were an explanation in itself. He seemed to have trouble pronouncing the names. 'We thought that you came to help us, like them.' He turned to Paul. 'Mar-ray and Dah-vid Ot-tar,' he emphasized slowly. Turning to Michelle, 'Jo-sephine Haw-uk,' he swallowed. 'Al-leone Bad-dar…'

A frightening sensation crept over Peter, making his breathing faster. Blood rushed to his face, the redness accentuated by the fires that burnt day and night.

'Allan? Allan Badger? My dad?' Peter said leaning forward. 'He was *here*?'

A stunned silence fell over all of them, the immensity of the cave accentuating their isolation and stillness.

The thought kept going round and round Peter's head. He couldn't believe it. His imagination ran riot, until finally it came to rest on Ebo. Peter stood there, his eyes boring into the leader, who was having difficulty meeting his stare.

Michelle's was almost fighting herself, her voice rising, sounded shrill. 'Where's my mum: Josephine Hawk?'

'And *my* parents – Mary and David?' Paul demanded in an angry screech.

Ebo looked up and met his gaze.

'They died.'

For a stunned, silent moment, Peter didn't even understand. His mind reeled from Ebo's words. *They died.*

There it was! This was always what he needed answering but it was not what he wanted to hear.

Peter had waited all this time. At the back of his mind, he had always hoped that his dad would come strolling back into his life

with his quirky smile, that brightness around him. He didn't even remember his father's voice properly and he was finding it harder still to remember the face. The more he tried, the more he saw Ebo's.

'He – *died*?' Peter asked, his question mistakenly taken for a statement. He was numb, a million emotions clambering to get out. 'How?'

Ebo took a deep breath and licked his lips nervously. Glancing quickly at Michelle and Paul, the same questions on their faces, he started to explain. 'In our final battle, your parents somehow got separated from us and we were unable to protect them with our magic. All your parents are dead,' he said quietly, knowing he could not hide it from them.

Peter heard the truth in the man's voice. With Ebo's last words, Peter sagged to his knees, utterly alone. Struggling to understand, desperate to come to terms with it, Peter latched on to an image. He had never felt such a surge of violence and it was all directed at the Clan leader.

Ebo had let his father down. Now he was going to betray the three of them as well.

'None of our captured people were ever seen again. Their spirits were never reclaimed and so they wander the earth. They should have returned to the Well of Souls.'

Peter's eyes were stilled glued to the leader's, a hatred rising through the centre of his entire universe.

'Romulus first imprisoned them, and then he killed them.' Ebo sounded desolate.

A slight parting of Peter's lips showed his teeth, and anger and hatred flowed into his hands. Ebo backed away. Peter stared down at his paws and from the grey, white and black fur of his forearms protruded a set of even larger serrated weapons. He slowly flexed them to see how they felt. Peter's eyes came back to meet Ebo's and he left the leader in no doubt of his feelings. The animal inside was struggling to be free. Its emotions were far simpler and it wanted to lash out, but Peter calmed it down.

When Peter took a deep breath, he retracted his claws and Ebo's sharp intake of breath gave away his relief. The Shaman had

stopped weaving his hands and stood in the background, transfixed.

'I am sorry,' Ebo said sadly. 'Al-leone was my greatest friend.' He sounded bereft.

Without another thought, Peter ran. He ran into the heart of the cave. He ran to a place he knew: to the darkness where he was comfortable. His tears, flowing freely, gave his feelings full rein. His love for his father, whom he had known all too briefly, was absolute. He ran, his mind screaming, not tripping once, not caring, but seeking the comfort of the darkness. Wanting to be alone – utterly alone.

It was a very long time before his tears stopped, and even longer before his body stopped trembling.

Peter's eyes were shining very bright. An internal fire had been lit and it was coming alive with a fierce hatred. A hatred that had a name.

Romulus Blackheart!

In his mind's eye, Peter, in his agitated state, his abilities flaring to their full potential, flew across the land to see the king tossing and turning in a four-poster bed with the sun just starting to stream through the window. He descended into the king's dream, where Romulus was riding fully armoured on his black horse, progressing through the streets, his sword glinting in the sunlight and a blood-red crystal blazing in the centre of a black armoured breastplate. Crowds were waving and cheering as he passed. They bowed: a sea of humble servants.

He smiled at them in a cruel way, almost a sneer, and waved, the scar on the left side of his face and his pointed aristocratic nose stood out prominently in the sunlight. He looked back over his shoulder and his crooked smile froze.

Over the mountains the dark clouds gathered and the rain began to fall on his parade. Out of the darkness came something he recognized, a black and silver fiend with vicious claws and teeth, carried on huge wings, flying through the parting clouds, the red furnaces of its eyes lit like a volcano, erupting with vengeful fires.

'It can't be!'

In that moment Romulus knew there was no escaping this one and he awoke screaming as the fires caught him.

Peter's mind came back from his righteous fancy. He was drained of all emotions. He stayed still, feeling washed out, not wanting to do anything. Finally, he picked himself up and his feet started to move back towards the entrance of the cave where he knew the others were waiting. They were all gathered around the fire and the torches had been lit. Night had fallen, and the howling and screaming had begun again outside.

'I'm going to the castle,' Peter stated to the sombre gathering.

Ebo looked up and then looked to Jasmine. The Shaman was shaking his dreadlocks in disbelief.

'It is all right,' Jasmine said, nodding to the lady with reddish hair who was standing close to Michelle. 'Charm and I have decided to hide you.' Her manner was different; something had changed.

Peter looked to Michelle and Paul, who were nodding at him. A slight, imperceptible smile started to appear on Michelle's determined face. Paul was nodding and the colour was coming back into his face, too.

Romulus Blackheart now had an old enemy. He already knew them. They were the Changelings.

Inside, an animal gave a deep, satisfied growl.

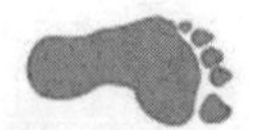

Chapter 7

HIS DAD WAS DEAD

His dad was dead. Peter had thought that finding out the fate of his father was all he wanted, but for him, it was just the beginning.

Having slept the sleep of the dead, every bit of him hurt, but the physical pain was nothing compared to the emptiness he felt inside. He kept his eyes tightly closed, staying in the warmth of the blanket a bit longer before facing the bite of the day. His emotions were raw from the revelations of the previous night, but they were no longer intense. Instead, he felt a little jaded, and slow.

The memory of a screaming Romulus Blackheart came unbidden into his mind, his arrogant face changing from a sneer to sheer terror when the razor-sharp serrated claws descended. Peter's feelings were in turmoil, and his hatred was threatening to choke him, making it hard for him to breathe. He was enjoying the violence bubbling up inside him, feeling guilty as he tried hard to suppress it.

He had agreed to help the villagers initially out of a sense of revenge, but now that he'd had time to think, he had no idea how he was going to do that. He needed to be by himself to figure it out. Silently he walked off into the comforting darkness of the Guarded Cave.

He went a lot further than he intended. The darkness was pitch-black, but with his soundscape vision, it didn't matter. He could see perfectly.

Peter walked aimlessly, going deeper with every step, his mind numb. The air was damp and clammy, the walls became wet and eddies appeared, swirling in the corners. He was about to turn back, when a light unlike anything he had ever seen before caught his eye. It was leaking out from around a corner. Curious, he went forward.

A low, mournful wailing rose, getting louder the closer he went towards the corner. The edges of the wall were dripping wet and covered in slimy algae. He stood a moment, his senses alert, his heart pounding. Warning bells in his head shouted at him to get away, and the animal inside him was whimpering in terror.

Something was pulling at him. It was not physical; instead it was pulling at his spirit, tugging just underneath the skin. He felt a cold, wet touch slip between him and the world, an iciness burrowing into his spirit. And it spread. His feet were rooted to the spot, his breathing became shallow, and he could feel the temperature drop. He was being separated from his body. His senses screamed for him to run before it was too late. Sheer panic gripped him. He was terrified, but a horrible fascination compelled him, almost like the Book, to look around the corner.

Just once…

Frozen to the spot, he desperately needed to see what it was and he tried to force his feet forward. Apart from his eyes, he couldn't move. Taking that last small step was impossible. How long Peter stood there, he had no idea. Then a greyish wisp of mist came slithering around the wall. It moved over his feet. He could feel its soft touch through the cold as it stopped and lingered: deciding.

'*PETER!*'

Paul and Michelle's shouts startled him out of the spell.

Petrified, Peter turned in the direction of their voices and fled, screaming: 'Run!'

Paul and Michelle were immediately alert and drew their claws and talons, but on hearing the sheer terror in Peter's voice, they, too, turned and fled.

Peter should never have gone that deep into the cave. It was, as he later found out, forbidden.

On the way back, he didn't say a word. He was reluctant even to remember what he had felt. The slippery, oily feeling of the wisp's touch still lingered and made him feel unclean. He wanted to scratch it off, remove every trace of it. This place had more evil in it than he had uncles and aunts.

Paul and Michelle looked back over their shoulders frequently,

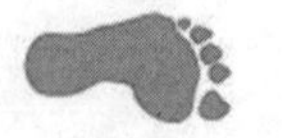

and when they were far enough away, Michelle stopped Peter by grabbing his arm. She stood facing him, those piercing, angry eyes burrowing into his.

'What do you think you're doing! Next time you want to go off like that, we'll be coming with you. You're not alone in this,' she shouted at him.

'They were our parents, too,' Paul added. 'We're just as upset and angry. '

Peter nodded. 'I know. I'm sorry,' he said sympathizing with Paul and feeling the icy veneer melt from the predatory blond girl. He was determined never to go there again anyway.

'If anyone's gonna do any killing, it'll be me!' Michelle stated, turning on her heels and walking away

Paul stared at her retreating back and whispered, 'I don't think she's kidding.'

Ebo and his wise man, the Shaman, were sitting silently around the fire when they returned. The dreadlocked Shaman threw Peter a vitriolic look and said, 'Boom-Basa, boy, don't you know anything? It's not wise to go into the bloody depths of this wretched cave without protection.'

Ebo flashed an angry glance at the Shaman. 'What happened?'

'Nothing,' Peter replied for the three of them. 'Just had to be alone for a while.'

'You are walking close to the edge. Be careful,' the Shaman advised him.

'We're going to the castle. You've tried rescuing your kids from the outside; I thought we'd do better from the inside.'

Ebo frowned but he let the comment drop. He gathered them round and admitted that their children were being used to mine tunnels underneath Castle Craven. The children's lives were used to blackmail the Clan into behaving. No Clan adult had ever been allowed near the mines. The stones they were being forced to mine were holy.

Even after hearing Ebo's confession, Peter was undeterred. He was going to make sure his dad had died for something.

Time was short and Ebo could not finish his explanation. They would journey through woods and then by water. He ordered them to stick to the path where the light penetrated the branches.

They started off immediately, walking in single file on the narrow rough path. In the gloom, shafts of sunlight pierced the thick canopy of leaves. What little light there was burnt the sparse foliage white and dazzled their eyes with its brilliance.

Peter could hear rustling in the darker areas and his memory of that morning was sharp. His thoughts kept straying to the terror of the cave, even though he tried to keep them elsewhere. It had felt unreal: the touch of smoke unclean. He shuddered just thinking about it.

'Peter, stay on the path,' Jasmine ordered. Seeing his ashen face, she asked, 'Are you alright? You were gone a long time this morning.'

'What's in that cave?'

Jasmine hesitated. 'Peter, how deep did you go?' Her voice reverberated with fear.

'To a place I didn't like.'

Jasmine swallowed loudly. 'Don't go there again! It is a closely guarded secret of our Clan. There is an entrance to another life – one that the Maker left behind. We call it *The Well*. It is where our dead go to wait for their next lives.'

Abruptly, the woods ended. In front of Peter was a sight that took his mind off morbid thoughts and left him speechless.

He was standing on the bank of the widest river he had ever seen, yet it wasn't that which had caught his attention. On the far side, giant trees of the forest loomed threateningly, their branches interlaced and thick, the canopy so dense that inside it looked black and evil, even in broad daylight. It brooded, like a great meandering black snake, slumbering and resting before its next feed. The expanse of the river was simply dwarfed by the size of trees that rose straight into the sky for hundreds of feet, casting a huge shadow over the water. Large exotic fruits hung from branches where no one would dare climb, and Peter's sensitive nose picked up a subtle but pungent smell of the twin destroyers: death and decay.

'That is the Foul Forest,' Jasmine spat out the words with loathing, 'once our greatest forest.'

The sickly sweet smell was overpowering Peter's senses and it clung to the roof of his mouth. 'Yuck! It's like Aunt Petra's perfume – deadly at close range,' he said, gagging.

'It is. Never venture there. *Never!* Do not touch the fruits of those rancid trees.' Jasmine spoke vehemently, her expression serious. There was dread in her voice, fear in her warning, and disgust in her words. 'They are deadly. And, if they do not get you, the creatures in there will.'

Just then a dark shape flickered in the branches and latched on to one of the giant fruits, its weight dragging it down into the light. Instantly it burst into flames, leaving behind a black residue on the bobbing fruit.

'That is not all you have to be careful of,' Ebo reminded them, pointing at the water.

Wherever the sunlight fell, the river sparkled, danced and flowed free. However, in the shade of the homicidal trees, where the thick, bloodthirsty shadows lay, the river was enticingly still. The surface took on an unusual sheen, lay quiet like a thick film of oil: inviting to the eye but hiding the corruption underneath.

'This is The Great River Sindu,' Ebo said with pride, 'even now it holds true. We travel on this side; never must we stray to the other, or we, too, will fall like all the poisoned fruits and seeds.'

'That's a funny river. Shouldn't the waters mix?' Paul asked.

Jasmine was uncertain. 'We think the clean water is moving too fast for the evil to catch it.'

Their attention was drawn abruptly by a large, portly man who came out of the clearing trying to hail them at the same time as hauling up his trousers. His black, shaggy hair and beard, along with his general appearance, gave him a shambling look of a well-dressed tramp.

'Greetings, Ebo!'

'Greetings, Griphand! Are you prepared?'

Griphand strode forward and clasped Ebo's forearm. His eyes roamed over to the children and lingered longest on Paul, who had

grabbed a branch and was leaning over the water. 'The boat is ready whenever you are,' he said heading off, his booming voice carrying easily over to them.

Rounding the bend, Peter was just in time to see Griphand stomp across a plank to a moored boat. It bobbed gently, its light beech-coloured wood shone in the sunlight and its single sail in the middle of the deck was folded neatly on its mast. On the outside it looked sleek and tanned, covered in carvings as if warding off evil. Smooth lines were carved into its sides and ran along its length before disappearing into the water. An engraved three-headed serpent stood guard at the front, staring out at the river and the forest. The waves bashing into the sides caused a constant knocking sound.

Michelle jumped aboard and Peter could hear her talking. 'How come you have a boat? Did you steal it?'

He tuned in.

'We are not the Rumanni. The river is the most effective way to transport the things we grow,' Ebo answered curtly.

Peter was disappointed. The Rumanni had stripped them of everything but the basics.

Obviously having overheard Ebo, Paul asked as he, too, climbed abroad, 'Do these – Rumanni – *do* anything at all?'

Jasmine saved Ebo the effort of answering. 'Yes. They build and trade with others like themselves. Metal, power, things. I say let them get on with it, but unfortunately they are dragging us into the same mess they are in.'

'But isn't trading a good thing?'

'No. Not for us. We used to take only what we needed. We kept the natural order. The Rumanni, they do not care.' She sat and snatched at one of the many knotted ropes that ran the length of the boat, tying it round her waist.

'Hold tight, everyone. Griphand is on board,' the Shaman commanded, quickly getting into place, his nervousness showing. Peter hadn't thought the Shaman would have been afraid of anything.

No one was manning the sails on the large boat and Paul pointed out that there were no oars, either. He leaned forward and

whispered to Peter and Michelle, 'How's he going to move this ruddy great thing? There's no wind!'

Peter shrugged just as Jasmine jerked their grips and adjusted the ropes attached to their waists. Her manner had somehow softened towards the three of them. 'Hold tight. The man is a lunatic with speed,' she whispered.

Peter couldn't help but look backwards at Griphand as he bent over and released the securing rope. His copious backside cheekily peeked out over his trousers, and an almost imperceptible trumpeting sound escaped from his rear. He straightened and, noticing Peter's gaze, smiled good-naturedly as he hauled up his trousers at the back. He placed his feet apart and grabbed hold of the tiller. The sail in the middle of the boat unfurled itself and the runners chased themselves to the end of the poles. They watched in amazement as the boat came alive and set sail – by itself.

The exuberant man at the tiller let out an unrestrainedly joyous yell. 'Griphand on board! I've got wind,' his voiced boomed, echoing off the shore.

Griphand's loud laughter vibrated in the very timbers of the boat. He raised his hands and, out of nowhere, a wind sprang up. The single large sail caught it and the boat lurched forward. Peter was only just recovering his seat as the first spray came over the bow and hit him in the face. The boat bounced several times before it picked up speed, and the spray became a fine mist on their faces.

'He is not called Griphand Windmaker for nothing!' Ebo hollered over the sound of the rushing air.

'How's he doing this?' Paul shouted back.

'His name is his power – at least he still has it!' Jasmine yelled.

Paul's expression said he didn't understand, but he let it drop because he was too busy holding on to his seat. They picked up speed gradually and Paul's attention remained fixed over the side, fascinated by the water. He let his hand skim the surface.

'It's really weird,' he said. 'Ever since I've got here, I've had this craving for fish.' His concentration focussed over the side of the boat, then his hand suddenly shot into the water and came out grasping a wriggling fish. He contemplated it for a moment before

throwing it back in. Peter had been convinced Paul was going to take a bite.

The fish flew convulsing through the air and landed in the water just where the shadow of the trees lay. Touching it briefly, it stiffened suddenly and dropped like a stone into the evil, still liquid. It didn't even make a splash.

Paul bolted upright. 'What happened to it?'

Jasmine watched the fish in a detached manner. 'It will not be able to move until the shadow does.'

Paul grimaced. 'And I was hoping to go for swim in it.' He sounded disappointed and repulsed.

'I don't think so,' Peter said.

They travelled north, hugging the shore and keeping to the clear water. The sound of the boat moving crisply over the clean water was in stark contrast to the deathly stillness of the other side, which seemed to be hoping for them to make the tiniest of mistakes. The waves left in the boat's wake stoped abruptly as soon as they hit the shadows, their energy swallowed up by the brooding, oily blackness.

The three children watched with morbid fascination as the darkness chased the sun, moving with the shade of the trees. Wherever it fell, the water changed suddenly, and the fish in it froze until the shadow moved on. Peter's eyes kept being drawn to the huge trees on the far side, where shadows moved in the darkness, and eyes glinted briefly as they caught the light. They would wink out quickly when Peter spotted them.

Great shadowy bird-like things jumped out of the trees into the air, high above the branches. Some burst into flames, while others fell back again, consumed by the immense forest. Sparks flew from them as they fell, their agonized screams cutting off abruptly.

'What type of birds are those?' Michelle asked, shouting to be heard over the noise of the wind.

Charm briefly glanced in the direction of the forest. 'They are not birds,' she answered and did not elaborate.

'I thought so,' Michelle said in a satisfied way as she continued to gaze at the grisly scenes.

Peter had been only partly listening, his thoughts dwelling on what they would do once they were inside Castle Craven. It was this thought that scared him; the constant smell of death was now just a forgotten irritation.

The river had begun to narrow and the shadows reached across further to their side. The closer the boat edged to the darkness, the headier the smells became. Peter's head spun, his stomach lurched almost out of control, and it was only by a whisker that he held on to consciousness. He became delirious with the heady aromas, his lungs filled with the disgusting smell, which contaminated and corrupted them. He tried to get away from the smell by moving to the other side of the boat.

'Peter, sit down!' Jasmine shouted, but it was too late. A low-hanging branch smacked Peter in the mouth and took him over the side.

Chapter 8

HE HIT THE WATER HARD

He hit the water hard, his cheek stinging from the whip across the face. The rope suddenly became taut and yanked hard on his wrists and waist. The speed of the boat carried him forward through the spray and bounced him like a rag-doll close to the deadly black surface. Ever time he touched it, an electric shock went through his body, jolting him and making his arms jerk erratically. Desperately Peter tried to regain his bearings, but the boat was dragging him along too fast, skimming him on the surface. Frequently he went underwater. In the grimy depths of the river, eyes came up to him frighteningly fast and jaws snapped at him.

Swallowing water and choking, Peter was only vaguely aware of someone diving off the boat, changing into a black creature as he hit the river surface and grabbing him. The boat swerved, yanking the rope on his waist, and they both hit the oily, still surface.

It was like hitting a brick wall. The force slammed every feeling out of them, their spirits and bodies froze instantly. Charged bolts of lightning shot through them. Peter lay suspended, unable to move, unable to breathe, unable to fight. He sank deeper into the dark liquid, thinking death must be better than this. The dim light of the surface blacked out completely and he couldn't even feel enough to be afraid.

Then, suddenly, his spirit and vision shifted, and he felt the presence of Michelle – was looking through *her* eyes. In his mind, he hovered above the boat, heard the sound of wings flapping and watched the boat and the two floating shapes in the water; the black one was still struggling against the impossible deadness while the other lay inert. Ebo and Griphand were doing their best to haul the boy and the otter back onto the boat.

Suddenly, they were in the clear water again. Excruciating pain quickly blazed through their bodies. Peter and Paul found themselves thrashing in the arms of an extremely strong man as they convulsed with pain.

Hands grabbed them and pulled them abroad.

'What did I tell you about taking trips by yourself?' Michelle yelled, landing on the deck, but Peter couldn't hear anything. He was too busy coughing up the water, along with the otter and the Clan leader.

'If Paul hadn't jumped in after you...' Michelle was furious.

Peter glanced at the coughing otter, 'You saved my life.'

'That hurt, you owe me one.'

Peter did not answer; he remembered well the creatures with the large eyes that had come when he had been underwater, their icy stares and their hunger for life... The swelling in his cheek was forgotten.

The boat sailed on so fast that everything became a blur. The woods on their side started to thin, eventually ending altogether to be replaced by a rolling landscape framed by gigantic mountains in the background. Coming in and out of view was an enormous castle cut into the mountainside, its creamy blocks of stone glowed brightly in the sunlight, its towers drew the eye like a magnet, its terrifying size a deception.

Peter wasn't interested. Fully recovered now, his attention only came back to the boat when it slowed. The sound of rushing air gradually became a breeze as they approached a docking area. Peter glanced back towards Griphand. The big man on the tiller looked strained, his face glistened as the sweat poured off him. His trousers had slipped down again and part of his ample tummy had popped out. Hauling his trousers up with one hand, he gave Peter a thumbs-up sign with the other.

As they went round the corner from the unmanned dock, any queasiness was immediately forgotten.

Cut into the mountainside, Castle Craven blazed its triumphant glory: man's craft against nature. It was of monstrous proportions, swallowing up the countryside with its size. Peter guessed that the

drawbridge alone could take six horses side by side. At one time, the mountain must have been completely covered in trees, but now most of the woodland had been cut away. On the lower slopes, a deep semicircular moat had been constructed around the main gate.

His stomach lurched at the enormity of what he had promised. *I'm going to help their children escape from **that**?* Peter thought, blanching at the prospect. After all the years of being a coward in front of uncles, not defending his mother as he should have…

Jasmine was prepared for his reaction and whispered in his ear. 'Peter, if you change your mind, we can still hide you,' she said in her most persuasive voice.

Paul and Michelle stopped and looked back at him. He felt like saying yes, but forced down the thought.

His father had died in that place.

A renewed fierce emotion battled its way to the surface: all the suffering his mother had endured, all his lost years. He looked straight at Jasmine and said, 'No. I'm going to wipe that crooked smile off Romulus's face.' He said it with such force and determination that she took a step back.

'How did you know he has a crooked smile?' Jasmine asked.

'I saw him in a dream,' Peter said, without thinking. 'He reminded me of my uncle who wants to live in Blenheim Palace.'

Michelle had overheard their conversation. 'I saw him, too. What's Blenheim Palace?'

Had Michelle been in his vision? 'It's kind of like that,' he replied, pointing at Castle Craven, 'only beautiful.'

Michelle winked at him. 'Perhaps he can fall off that black horse of his and break his neck instead,' she said cheerfully.

'We wouldn't be that lucky.'

Michelle nodded thoughtfully. 'You're right. We're going to have to do it ourselves.'

'It's a pity he's not some sort of reptile,' Paul said, recovering his composure from the ordeal. 'We could have a lot of fun with *that*!'

Ebo and the Shaman seemed to be arguing again.

'Now do you believe that they can hide us from the Sight?' Ebo was saying.

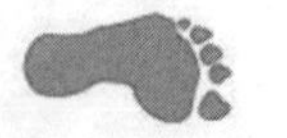

The Shaman looked at them and nodded his head. 'Boom-Basa,' he admitted reluctantly, 'it must be so, Ebo! I will go and prepare, damn it.' He shook his head as he looked towards Peter. 'Your coming – damn it. We have not had hope for a long time; feels like forever.'

With a sour glance towards Ebo, he took his leave and headed away from the castle.

'We are going the other way,' Ebo said. 'You can change your mind –'

'We've already had that discussion,' Peter said, glancing at Jasmine.

'Of course.' Ebo stared at them seriously. 'Just as stubborn as their parents. So be it!'

'Don't worry: you can thank us later,' Paul said lightly.

Again, Peter was struck by how much Ebo looked like his father. He found it frustrating that he remembered only pictures and not his father's real face. It pained him to think that he might have forgotten his father's real face altogether. He closed his eyes and rested in a dark place where he controlled his breathing, and reined in his emotions. His insecurity was rampant. Could he do what he said he would? Only his anger kept him focussed. When he opened his eyes, Jasmine was staring at him.

'Shall we go?'

He tried to smile but failed. 'Yes.'

'Charm needs to see her son and will be coming with us. Not that we could persuade her to stay behind,' Jasmine said, glancing towards Michelle. 'Normally when we bring our children here, the Rumanni are always waiting, but as you see, you three are invisible. After the gates, there is no turning back.'

The castle loomed quite close, surrounded by small trees and bushes. However, its size turned out to be even bigger than Peter had imagined from a distance. The small trees were in fact tall trees, the bushes turned out to be smaller trees and the walls and the drawbridge were simply huge. The immense blocks of creamy limestone were precisely cut and the towers looked brilliant in the light, pointing loftily and defying the heavens, threatening to reach the stars themselves.

'How did the Rumanni snatch children?' Michelle asked.

Before Jasmine could answer, they saw a guard approaching from the direction of the castle. He swaggered along and seemed to be in no hurry. Watching him, Peter realized that he, Paul and Michelle were closer in appearance and clothing to the guard than they were to the people they were going to help.

The guard was dressed almost all in leather, his jerkin over a grey cotton undershirt, trousers, a wide leather belt with a scabbard and pointed metal helmet. He smelled as if he had not bathed in weeks, and he was chewing something pungent, spitting frequently as he walked and leaving a dark stain on the ground. A worn red crest was on his left breast.

Peter could smell his insecurity and anxiety despite his cavalier attitude. Mixed in with his body odour was the acrid smell of a person expecting trouble.

'Halt!'

It was an order.

Chapter 9

THE GUARD HATED THEM

The guard hated them. From the moment he laid eyes on the group, Peter could feel the Rumanni's hatred. His loathing was apparent, his apprehension barely concealed, and his odour was foul. He swaggered arrogantly towards them. The undercurrent of aggression exuding from him was ready to explode.

'*I said HALT!*'

They stopped at his command. The guard was alert for any trouble, yet despite his belligerent manner, his hand rested casually on the hilt of his sword.

Peter bristled at being ordered; normally, he wouldn't have felt that way.

'State your business with these children,' he croaked rudely. 'Why are they outside the castle?' he demanded.

'We are bringing them *back* to the castle,' Ebo said in a measured voice.

'The House Master is going to pay particular attention to you trouble-makers,' he said leaning towards Paul with an unpleasant smile, his saliva dribbling down the side of chin.

Michelle stepped protectively in front of Paul. 'Don't worry about him,' she said. 'He hasn't been house-broken yet.'

The guard grunted in agreement. He turned to the Clan leader. 'Good job you brought them back. The House Master will be expecting the runaways. Don't be tarrying – the sun will be down by the time you reach the Craven,' he said stepping to one side to let them pass. The obnoxious man waited for Paul to come alongside before he screamed, '*Filth!*' loudly in his ear.

Startled, Paul reacted instinctively and faster than the clumsy overweight soldier. His hand whipped out, turning into a padded

paw and smacked the guard in the face, knocking him to the ground. The semi-conscious guard flailed and screamed incoherently, his head lolling about.

'Change – Changeling!' he shouted as he tried to grab his sword.

Peter heard what sounded like the huffing and puffing of a great beast, well before he saw it out of the corner of his eye. Griphand hurtled towards them at an alarming rate, his body wobbling with every step, and before Ebo could react or the guard recover, Griphand had flown through the air, and landed like a beached whale on the semi-recumbent Rumanni.

A solitary squeak escaped from the man before he went limp under Griphand's great mass.

Wiping the sweat from his forehead, Griphand gasped. 'Good smack, Paul,' he complimented the otter, clapping him on the back. 'Followed you. Thought you might need some help.'

The Clan leader's taut face filled with conflicting worries. He pursed his lips. 'Sit on him until I decide what to do with him. We must be extra-careful now.' It was an unhappy Ebo who turned and walked towards Castle Craven, shaking his head.

The might of the castle in front of them was overwhelming. The mountain rose majestically in the background but looked shattered and humbled in comparison. It insisted on their attention but it was Castle Craven that grabbed it.

They gawked in unashamed wonder at the murderous towers soaring upwards and the lethal spires that poked out of the impregnable white blocks, ready to spike any enemies. Inky rectangular arrow-slits cut into the walls watched their every movement - the guards seemed superfluous. Someone must have had a bad day to make Craven so perfect; why else would they make everything in its shadow so unworthy? Such flawless precision was simply inhuman.

All the dusty cobbled roads led towards the main gates, where they finally merged. The three Changelings found themselves unable to resist, and strained their necks to get better look, but their attention soon returned to the increasing number of offensive people on the road with them. The small group was forced to join

the other Rumanni heading for the protection of Castle Craven from the night.

It seemed that every Rumanni had a duty to be revolting towards all other races – at least that was the impression Peter got. The hatred was somehow reserved particularly for the three of them. At first, it was rude stares, but these quickly changed and became offensive spitting on the road in front of them. Ebo ignored their gestures and appeared to be a man out for a stroll.

Peter found the Rumanni scent odd, and eventually it dawned on him that it was not just hatred they gave off, but fear. The presence of the guards at the gate only spurred on their spite. The hatred from the Rumanni children was especially strong, as they didn't bother to hide their feelings. The small tribal group had no choice but to endure it.

'They hate us. What have you done to these people?' Peter asked in a whispered.

'Quiet!' Ebo ordered as Charm drew closer to the group, forming a protective circle around them.

The walk up to the main drawbridge had taken longer than Peter expected because the size of the castle deceived them, its proportions warped any perspective and made it seem nearer than it really was. By the time they finally reached the portcullis, the castle's creamy walls had turned a treacherously comforting warm, golden colour.

'Can you smell the people?' Paul asked quietly, wrinkling his nose.

'Even I can smell them,' Michelle answered, unimpressed.

'I don't think we should do anything that shows them who we are. Things are bad enough already,' Peter whispered.

The two guards, one on either side of the drawbridge, stopped and searched those entering the castle, their gestures exaggerated and their manner abrupt. Both seemed preoccupied in their duties, but Peter knew better: they were deliberately waiting until the last moment.

'Stop!'

The young guard raised his hand, his other gripped his spear. 'Why are those children not in the castle?'

Ebo's reply was curt; he didn't like these people anymore than they liked him. 'We are taking them there.' All that was missing was the word 'moron'.

Before anyone could react, the guard had stepped forward and smacked Ebo across the face. 'You will be more respectful,' he demanded, his spear angled at Ebo's nose. The Rumanni soldier wanted to show his full authority, and he was not about to back down to a mere farmer. Peter could see Ebo's back stiffen, his head stayed perfectly still as he looked down on the young guard.

Under the fierce stare, the young man took an involuntary step back, 'I mean to say, we had not been informed,' he blurted out, gripping his spear hard, regretting the mood he had set.

The smell of danger coming from Ebo was like a physical presence. Even the other people gave the small party a wide berth.

'I am sure that you will be,' Ebo lied.

The older guard interrupted, but Peter got the impression he already knew the Clan leader. 'It must be an oversight. Do you know the Eastern Quarter?' When Ebo didn't reply, the older Rumanni nodded, 'Good. Good. Be on your way then.'

Ebo stepped forward, and although the young guard tried hard to hold his ground, he failed and took another step back.

Once through the portcullis, the stink really hit them. Along with the human odours were the mixed smells of animals and the reeking aromas of cesspools and drains. The foulness of the town was matched only by the vileness of its people. The Rumanni's aggression and bigotry amplified; the shouts became louder, and the reek from the inhabitants became worse. The cowards threw their abuse from a distance and kept well away from the shadow-like man hurrying through their narrow streets.

In the Eastern Quarter, they rounded a corner and Paul got hit in the face by a rotting tomato. There were cheers from the Rumanni children. The adults took this as their signal to hurl more of the decaying vegetables at them from the windows, shouting, 'Animals!' as they passed, not worrying about the presence of any guards.

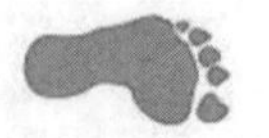

'Well I guess it's an improvement,' Michelle said, looking at Paul, who caught a boiled egg that was about to hit her. 'Thanks,' she added, 'but I *had* seen it.'

Ebo picked up the pace while protecting them with his body and acting as a human shield in front of them.

Peter became aware of a din over a high wall, well before they reached the entrance gates. It was only then that Ebo's aggression began to ebb.

They had arrived.

Livid, Peter scraped bits of rubbish off his body. His senses jumped at every sound. He was not certain that he knew what he had got himself into, but it felt unclean, and he was surprised to find he was not about to put up with it.

At their approach, a smirking guard opened the gates. Squashed vegetables still clung to their bodies and clothes, and made them look like something that the cat had dragged in.

'You know the drill,' the guard barked at Ebo, who nodded, 'and *you*,' he said looking at one of the other guards, 'make sure they go straight there.'

As soon as they had all passed, he went into an animated conversation with another guard, their whispers rose as soon as they thought they were out of earshot.

'Where the hell did they come from?'

'We don't know. We weren't informed, sir.'

Trapped by the high walls, surrounded by hostile people, Peter's thoughts dwelled on his escape. The urge to transform and run grew with every step; unable to control his fears, the hair on his hand grew and his claws started to emerge. His doubts ate away at his feelings and he looked enviously towards Michelle.

'At least those aren't a problem to you,' he whispered gesturing wistfully towards the high stone walls.

'Don't worry. I can throw you over, if you like.'

'Me first, please,' Paul whispered anxiously.

Ebo led them to a place that was as desolate as a morgue, with an unlit fireplace, a single bench and a stone staircase. A heavy chill

hung in the air, a musty dampness gnawed at them. It was obvious that no one ever came here willingly. The emptiness echoed the unhappy memories of the stolen years of those who entered. Ironically enough, it was called the Grand Hall.

'Why haven't the guards followed us in?' Paul asked.

'They don't need to,' Jasmine answered.

'Why not? That means we can escape any time we want to…'

'Our children can't; if one escapes, the others suffer. None of our children would do that to the others.'

'Our families and friends come here to see their children,' Ebo explained, his eyes darting about like a caged animal, the bruise on his face coming up an angry red in the torchlight. 'We stay here, when it gets too late to return to the villages. Just one night together in any fourteen days is all we are allowed –'

He was about to continue when a boy burst through the door yelling 'Mother!' at the top of his voice. He located Charm in an instant and flung himself on her in a bear-hug.

'Storm!'

The boy released his mother, already aware of the three strangers among them but he still took time to greet Ebo and Jasmine formally, putting his hands together and bowing to them in turn.

'So, they have returned?' he asked, turning to them.

'Only younger,' his mother said quietly.

Gaunt and lean, with a close-shaved head, Storm looked tough, with a slim muscular frame, yet scars underneath his shirt hinted at the life he led. He did not look the type to take any prisoners.

Storm obviously worshipped Ebo, and although deferential towards him, he asked, 'Ebo, are you sure about the Sight? Otherwise they will be interrogated tomorrow and it will all be over.'

'Do not worry. They will protect you.'

Paul's natural curiosity got the better of him. 'How long have you been here?'

'About five cycles of the seasons, straight after the Great Weakness,' Storm answered in a neutral tone.

'Same time my dad disappeared,' Peter stated.

'Storm, you have to follow Peter's lead,' Ebo commanded.

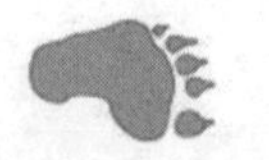

Immediately, the young man's hackles rose but he didn't say a word.

'What's that smell?' Paul asked curious.

'It's Jasmine.'

Startled, Jasmine looked at them. A quizzical expression appeared on her faces before she rushed off. 'Wait here.'

Ebo was on his feet. Charm went after her. They returned with steaming mugs of the most gorgeous-smelling liquid and something altogether different.

Peter, Paul and Michelle took theirs and tried a small sip. It was delicious. The hot liquid tasted like having a feast. Soon they could not help but gulp it down.

'I'm recovering my healing gifts. How could this happen?' Jasmine sat down, her eyes wide with speculation.

'It must be *them*,' Ebo said, staring at the Changelings.

Suddenly Jasmine recovered herself and yelled, 'No – wait! Don't drink that too fast!'

It was too late. The healing potion spread through them like wildfire, picking up all their tiredness, all their hurts. Their relief was so overwhelming that the Changelings dropped to the ground, fast asleep, the rest of the healing liquid spilling on the hard, lifeless floor.

Dreams came that night. Peter was trapped. He was smashing walls, shattering the ground to get out. At first small cracks appeared, the grooves deepened and a strange green light escaped from the opening. From inside the light, he heard an animal crying in pain. Its inhuman sound was filled with aggression and anger. The crack spilt open, the green light flooded out and blinded him, and in his blindness Peter staggered around engulfed in sound, this time filled with hope and joy.

It was singing to the night.

Both Peter and Paul woke with a start and bolted upright. They were in bed, and the others were all asleep.

'Did you hear it?' Paul whispered anxiously.

'It was only a dream, right?' Peter suggested, uncertain.

'Being trapped, trying to claw your way out?' Paul started.

'Cracks, green light,' Peter finished. 'How did you have *my* dream?'

Peter's body shivered and his palms were sweaty. There was a primeval quality to the voice in his dream, a plea to be released. An echo of it remained and he could feel the vibration around the darkened room. It made him feel light-headed. In his dazed mental state, his mind's eye wandered and he saw a far-away kitchen, one that he knew and loved. As he fell into the vision, he saw a lit candle with the badger at the base of a burning tower. Peter, his stomach in knots, thought he was hallucinating.

At least Grandfather was there because the lights were out.

A cooler voice joined them. 'Your kitchen?' she whispered.

'You can see that?' Peter asked Michelle, wanting to believe.

'I can,' Michelle said, in her usual clipped manner. 'We have the same candle in our house.' She turned over and fell asleep.

Peter's apprehensions and worries from the night did not have time to materialize. The morning was a noisy, hectic, frantic affair where everything proceeded with mechanical precision. There were no good-byes and Peter forgot to ask how he was going to get in touch with Ebo.

The large hall, with guards only on the main doors, was filled with the sound of hundreds of children all gulping down their food and talking in whispers, the chatter deafening in the high-ceilinged building. Silently, Storm took them to collect their clothing and food for later. The food was basic.

The other children were all in various groups and wore coloured bands, head wraps, gloves, and padding on their knees and elbows. An excited flame-haired girl came rushing in to find Storm, her eager face flushed.

'Did you see them? Did you? Why were they here?' she demanded, poking her eager face next to his.

'Yes, Ginger. They sent lots of love,' Storm said, trying to be brief. His slight head movement caught Ginger's eye and she noticed the newcomers.

'Who are you?' she asked brusquely.

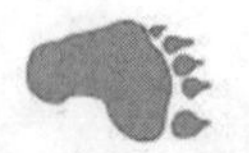

Before anyone could answer, a whistle sounded sharply and a guard appeared at the door, calling out the groups by colour. One by one, the bands got up and walked out of the hall. As the hall emptied, the echoes become more and more pronounced.

Storm was in charge of several groups and he immediately started to hand out green armbands to them. Ginger glanced at them briefly. 'I'll find you in the mines,' she said, hurrying away.

'Charming,' Paul whispered sarcastically after her.

Storm sniffed, got up and quietly led them between the buildings, through an arched gateway and into the open ground on the other side. The vast walled-off area was in fact the site of the mines – it looked like something had hit the ground with cataclysmic impact. Their footsteps made loud crunching noises as they walked on the igneous ground that glistened blue-black in the early morning light.

The crater was hundreds of feet across, and crude wooden platforms lowered the groups of children into the gloom below. The Changelings, lost in their own thoughts, followed Storm mutely onto one of the wooden lifts, where railings on each side stopped them from falling out. One of the guards shouted to stand clear. They were hoisted up and swung away from the edge, before descending into the darkness.

Looking down, Peter felt queasy; it was a vertical drop into nothing, the platform being held by what, to Peter, looked like thin ropes. A bit *too* thin.

By the time they were only a third of the way down, the daylight had gone, replaced by a slight greenish haze. The moisture in the air was cool, and bits of green starlight sparkled around them. The intensity of the glow increased with the depth.

The walls were riddled with hundreds of different-sized holes and in the green light, the blue of the earth now looked black. A slight mist settled on platform in droplets and stopped it from creaking.

They could no longer tell if they were being lowered. The experience lulled Peter into a semi-doze and he was abruptly jolted awake when the platform changed over to a second pulley to take them down further. The lift continued to descend, the only indica-

tion that they were still going down came from the large stones on either side of the platform that went hurtling upwards, close enough for them to feel the rush of air.

It seemed like ages before they eventually reached the bottom, and any idle banter had died.

Peter expected the air to get stuffy, but instead it was the opposite: quite clean and fresh.

'There's more life down here than there ever will be up in the castle,' Storm said unemotionally. 'Welcome to Plateau Periculum!'

The place felt a lot nicer than the surface. This might not be as bad as he had thought.

'What are those straight lines on the tunnels?' Paul asked pointing to the many holes.

'They are the ones we have already explored. They are all dead. Two strikes and we move onto the next one. There are thousands of them yet to go,' Storm said sounding wary.

'What're you mining?' Michelle asked.

A guard had come up quietly from behind them. He pointed a tiny glowing red rock rudely into her face.

'You're looking for these, stupid!'

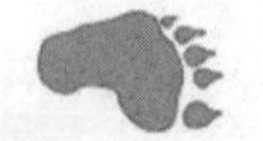

Chapter 10

THE GRUMPY GUARD WAS IN DANGER

The grumpy guard was in danger. Michelle's contemptuous stare was locked on him and he did not even see the problem. Walking towards her and about to poke his fist in her face was not the best thing he could do to a predatory bird.

Storm stepped in front of the guard before he reached Michelle. 'I am sorry, sir, she is new and will learn her manners,' he apologized, trying quickly to appease the aggressive Rumanni.

'See that she does. Make sure they all do, or I'll have you whipped tonight!' the guard barked.

Peter slid in between Storm and Michelle and tried to catch her attention. She was still glaring; her claws out and ready to rip. Noticing Peter, she immediately withdrew her talons.

'Any more, little girl, and I will personally supervise your beating,' the guard promised, spitting out the words with venom. The smell – the hatred, mingled with his unwashed body odour – was overpowering. He glowered at Storm and bawled, 'See that she goes all the way down into each tunnel!'

'I will, sir,' Storm responded and although his voice sounded sincere and subservient, the lie was in his tone.

Another soldier hailed the guard, and he sauntered off, grumbling about 'the filthy lazy savages'.

Storm let out a sigh of relief and then turned viciously on Michelle. 'We cannot afford that!' he hissed.

Michelle's stare challenged back for only an instant before she apologized grudgingly. 'Well, what do we have to do to stay out of trouble?' she asked, her nature back under control.

'Follow me. That glowing thing he had in his hand is a *Lal Shankar*.'

'That red stone?' Paul asked quietly.

'The Shaman had one just like it around – ' Peter started to say but was quickly cut short.

Storm put a finger up to his mouth and looked around quickly to see if Peter's comment had been overheard. 'Yes, but the ones we are mining are Lal. I will show you when we find one. Now stay quiet.'

They went round the lift, and any thoughts Peter had that the situation was normal disappeared. The sight of children tied to the wall, all wearing purple armbands, greeted them. Their hands were bound together with rope, and the bindings fastened over their heads. The rope cut into their wrists and forced them to stand. Some of them had fainted from exhaustion; others just looked on helplessly. Most of the children had looked slim, but down here they appeared even thinner, as if they hadn't eaten for days. Storm looked at his feet as he hurried past them in stony silence.

Peter, however, was too shocked to do anything other than to gawk at them. They had been beaten, their faces bruised black and blue.

'What have they done?' he asked.

'They did not meet their quota,' Storm replied. 'Try not to look at them or we will get beaten, too.'

Peter had to get out of there and he was now more determined than ever to make sure that he took all the children with him. This was wrong; the kids who were tied up were no older than he was. They looked battered, bruised and tired. The Rumanni obviously had no human feelings and they were about to meet a badger with a whole set of them.

'Get working!' yelled a guard.

With Storm in the lead, they set off across the vast plateau looking like insects, dwarfed by the huge area, surrounded in a green glow that seeped out of everything. He led them to a tunnel, next to one with two lines struck across the entrance. It

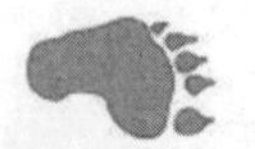

was small and they had to stoop to enter. The ceiling dropped further before opening into a small, circular cave with many exits.

Other children were already gathering in there. They placed their meagre rations in a communal pile, busily paired off and disappeared in different directions. The only evidence of their presence was a single chalk line against the entrance of the tunnel.

'Right, you three stay with me. When we find something, I will show you what to do.'

'Has anyone ever got stuck down here?' Paul asked, looking around with concern.

'Yes, for days. He fell through and we could not find him,' Storm answered pragmatically.

'Fell through? Did he die?' Paul was really worried.

'No. But he was different when he came back. He must have seen something. He doesn't speak now, so we never found –' The noise of a guard outside interrupted him. 'Quick: follow me!' Storm said, marking their tunnel with a cross and entering.

'Where do these end?' Michelle asked, scrambling after Storm's retreating rear.

'We don't know,' Storm yelled back, his answer brief.

The tunnels were roughly circular and forked deceptively in other directions. The green glow was everywhere. Peter found to his surprise that not only could he see perfectly, he could move easily in the confined spaces.

His soundscape vision even allowed him to anticipate directions, and there was a strange, subtle smell that lingered in the air. It was very familiar, and it had been growing as they'd descended into the crater. It was only in the tunnels that Peter had become fully aware of it. He looked back and could smell the direction from which he had just come.

It was him! He was laying down a scent trail almost like a bright, luminous path for his senses to show him the way back!

They had gone a long way in, twisting and turning, having to crawl on their hands and knees as the tunnel narrowed, when suddenly Storm exclaimed, 'Yes! Found one!'

He moved past, and there, in the wall, with just the barest hint

of a tip showing, was a red glow coming from within the rock. It looked sickly and was shot through with dark veins. It reminded Peter of his Uncle Lorenzo's hands: the veins purple and thick, sticking up all inflated and large.

Storm wriggled round in the tight space so that he could face them. 'This is perfect. What I have to do now is get a *Herya Shankar* from the guards, one that is bigger in size than that,' he said pointing at the red glow. 'I think that one is going to be about this big,' Storm said, indicating with his hands. 'There is something else!'

Their attention perked up at Storm's ominous words.

'The Rumanni are not aware of this but every time we grab one of the Herya Shankar, we use its ancient power – depending on its size, of course.'

'For what?' Peter asked remembering the hidden green stone around the Shaman's neck.

'To call our parents. We speak to each other through the stones. I will explain later.'

Storm was gone awhile and looked a lot happier when he returned, carrying a large green Shankar. He looked at them and said, 'Can you all see? It is slightly tight in here…'

Michelle twisted her head back unnaturally and suggested to the others, 'I think we'll manage!' knowing that they would understand.

Peter's world shimmered and he transformed into his alter-ego, all fur and claws. He wanted and needed to be smaller if they were all going to fit – to his surface, he found himself shrinking. The desire alone triggered it.

A big wing smacked him in the snout.

'Sorry,' Michelle squawked.

The three of them all looked at each other, Peter with his distinctive white stripes on either side of his face; Paul, his oily fur glistening black in the green light; Michelle, with her vicious beak, her brown and white head glowing strangely.

Storm stared at them wide-eyed and open-mouthed. He tried hard not to stare, but it was beyond him. 'Can you understand me?' he asked tentatively.

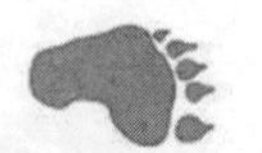

'Only when you make sense!' Michelle squawked back.

'Look: this is what you do,' he continued, amazed, changing the subject and trying to ignore Michelle's vicious beak. He held up the stone until it touched the glowing red surface. 'If the Herya Shankar starts to ooze, you must move it away quickly, and go back and get a bigger one,' he explained, gingerly pushing the green stone in his hand into contact with the red.

Their animal eyes were fixed on the green Shankar. Its glow increased as it came into contact with the wall, and the red glow grew brighter in response, as if battling the other stone, spitting hot sparks. The walls became warm, and it seemed that at the point where the stones met, the red one was melting. Eventually it grew fainter, as it were overwhelmed, and its edges began to soften and ooze out of the wall.

Storm pulled the green stone away, put his fingers into the hole and prised out the last bit of the red stone, letting it drop from his slippery hands. It glowed a virulent, ugly crimson. Storm picked up the solid bit of the red rock and touched it to the gaping hole. The red liquid flowed out and around it, reforming again into a solid red translucent rock.

'It takes a little while, but it will be a whole Shankar again,' Storm said, trying to explain. He didn't need to; they could all see the magic working.

'Let's get back. This is one of the biggest we have ever found. They are getting bigger,' Storm said muttering to himself.

As they all turned, Peter did not move. He hadn't come here to mine. He had come to help them escape.

'What's wrong?' Storm asked.

'You can go back. I need to find a way out. The sooner we get out of here, the better,' Peter stated, his mind filled with horrible images.

'You are going to save us where Ebo failed? Right!' Storm exclaimed sceptically.

'He hasn't got you out of here yet,' Michelle challenged.

Storm stared back, his cheeks flushed, and then his expression changed. 'I'm surprised you would want to go exploring alone. I was scared silly when I first came down here,' he admitted.

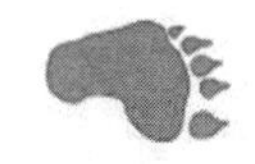

'Go if you want to, but you can easily get lost in these tunnels.'

The insincerity in his voice was clear. He expected Peter to fail – expected him to get lost. Peter looked at his tail. 'No, I can't. It's part of my nature,' he answered.

'Don't! I can smell it already,' Paul said, quickly closing his nostril flaps.

Peter could not understand what the fuss was about. It was just a mild smell – wasn't it?

'I'll go back,' Michelle interrupted. 'I really don't like enclosed spaces. Be careful,' she squawked scrambling past Paul. 'Hmm, Otters don't smell bad, either.' She licked her lips.

Peter looked towards the threatened Paul. 'Coming?'

'I'm with you,' Paul remarked in a shrill voice.

Michelle shouted back, 'Good hunting!'

'We can move faster in this form,' Peter suggested, looking down at his furred body.

'Mind if I lead?' Peter asked looking backwards.

'I think you'd be better,' Paul trilled. 'Can you keep a little distance, though?'

Peter dismissed the wicked thought of laying a thick trail – he couldn't do that to Paul. Suffocating the otter was not high on his agenda.

They headed upwards at an incredible pace. Behind him he heard Paul squealing, 'This feels grreeaaaaaaat!'

'You're not kidding,' Peter shouted back, sifting rapidly through the changing images, using the echoes to find his way up.

He could sense and feel the tunnels ahead of him, and in his badger form, his human apprehensions faded. He felt as if he had been doing this all of his life. He knew which way was up, and as they raced on, he instinctively laid a trail with his musk. Occasionally, he had to double back whenever he came to a dead end, and then he headed up again in the next tunnel. His ultra-sensitive hearing gave him the clues he needed to judge the direction and the length of each tunnel.

Peter found he could adjust his body size when the tunnels

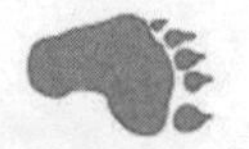

narrowed, and subconsciously he kept the same distance between his body and the walls. As soon as he relaxed, however, he reverted to his original size.

On the way up, they passed several red, glowing sections, but there was only one thing on Peter's mind: to escape and take the children with him. If he got caught, he knew what fate awaited him; the memory of the tortured children was fresh and the badger gave an angry growl at the thought.

Exhilarated by his changes, feeling the sheer strength and power in this body, Peter felt invincible. At the back of his mind, a little voice warned him not to get used to it.

After climbing upwards for a time, they found themselves in a wet, slippery tunnel that was gloomier and darker than those they had just left. Peter slowed his pace.

Quite abruptly, the tunnel opened up and they found themselves in a small cavern with a pool. Water dripped into it from cracks in the walls. Peter stopped, but Paul continued to hurtle past. With a squeal, he launched himself into the air, did a double-flip, and belly-flopped in the water, spraying everything.

Paul flew out of the water, in the same instant transforming himself back into a boy, and landed in front of Peter.

'Wow! I just had to do that!' he enthused as he looked around. 'That's the first time I've felt whole.'

Peter shook his head his head in disbelief – otters were scatty. He was now human apart from his midriff down, where he was still covered in a thick black coat of glistening fur.

He looked down at the thick grey fur that covered his legs, and Peter finally began to accept his true nature. 'If my dad could see me now…'

'Where are we?' Paul asked, not interested in bringing up painful memories.

Peter stretched his senses to the far side of the cavern as he walked across. A smell of unwashed people emanated from it.

'Nice! What a pleasant smell you've discovered,' Paul commented, wrinkling his snout, closing the small flaps over his

nostrils and making his whiskers twitch. He tiptoed carefully over to Peter.

They had found the sewer. It joined a small stream heading downwards, the water in it completely discoloured. 'That stream must lead to the outside of the castle,' Peter said.

'You've gotta be kidding! It's through the *sewer*? We'll end up smelling worse than the enemy!'

'Guess my tang isn't so bad now.'

'It's the difference between choking and dying.'

'Come on, weasel: show some grit!' Peter shouted back to him as he set off once again. The sewer ran for a considerable distance and the glow from the walls had faded altogether by the time they found themselves facing a small algae-covered opening cut into a wall. Peter already knew the surface was close. They had found a way out. The stench, however, was horrible.

They cleaned up in the pool before returning. The small cave was deserted but there was a commotion outside. Peter and Paul crept forward and quietly joined the group of children who were all gathered in a circle. Peter peered over the shoulders of the others to see what all the fuss was about.

A man in black armour and cloak was standing with his back to them, staring down at a fat, bulbous guard. The Rumanni was shaking with terror, his eyes darting about, looking for an escape that wasn't there.

'It's King Romulus Blackheart,' someone whispered back to them. 'Keep quiet!'

Romulus turned around, his cloak flaring behind him, and for the first time Peter saw his face.

His heart stopped.

He had seen the flawless features before. The man's perfectly sculpted face was in stark contrast to the squashed features of the other Rumanni, the symmetry tainted only by the scar on the left side of his face, somehow making him look harder and more regal.

Peter ducked quickly. Paul followed suit, a nervous, confused expression on his face, but he stayed quiet.

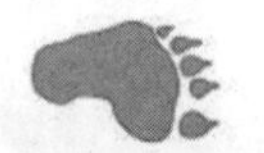

'Children, children!' Romulus's melodious voice carried easily. 'One has been receiving some terribly alarming news. This *man*,' he said emphasizing the last word and pointing to the shaking blubber in front of him, 'has been beating you for not making his quotas. Outrageous. One feels your pain. As he has not met Our quota, One feels, it's only fair, that *he* shares in *your* pain.'

He smiled unpleasantly.

Romulus signalled to one of the guards, who turned and signalled towards the walls. There was a heavy creaking noise as several guards pushed forward a cage on wheels with a matt-black cover, and a wooden ladder on the side that disappeared on top. It rattled loudly as it moved. Something large snarled and slammed against its sides.

Another guard stepped forward to offer the quivering man a short sword.

'Splendid. Go in there and if you come out, you keep your job – and get some benefits,' Romulus ordered, not bothering to look at the guard.

'But, sire: I will not come out of there alive!'

'Stop snivelling. You might get lucky.'

The trembling man knew he could not disobey the king's orders. Reluctantly, he climbed the stairs to the platform. His face hardened and his eyes took on a fatal gleam. He turned to the king, saluted, and jumped in with a cry. A frenzy of screaming and shouting erupted from the dark cage, which shook manically, followed by a sudden deathly silence.

No one emerged.

'Shame,' King Romulus sighed, placing a hand on his chest. 'Good help is so hard to find.'

Twirling his cloak around his shoulders and looking at the ugly muscle-bound guard next to him, he added, 'Congratulations, House Master. Try to last longer than your predecessors.'

The guard grunted and grinned mirthlessly, revealing a set of yellow teeth.

'Oh, by the way, wear a mask in future. You don't want to frighten the little ones,' the king commanded as he left.

★

Peter was pale as he headed for the winching lifts to take them to the surface, the sound of whip-cracking followed by a scream. Despite Storm's earlier warning, he could not help but stare at the bound children. Romulus had seized his heart with fear; his resemblance to Uncle Ramsey was uncanny. Peter wasn't ready to feel helpless again. He wanted to fix at least some of the things that were wrong.

The sun was setting by the time they reached the surface, and a red horizon had all but faded. Various children came to pat Storm on the back, and have a quick look at the newcomers. They lined up, collected their two large pieces of bread and a large bowl of steaming broth made from vegetables. At least the bread was fresh.

Peter's mouth salivated at the smell and he took a bite, but he had no stomach for conversation. For all its unsavouriness, the meal was surprisingly filling. The three Changelings ate in complete silence.

They followed Storm mutely to the bedchambers, where rows of beds were laid out in a long hall. The beds were made exactly like the ones in the village: entwined ropes with a hard mat and a blanket on them. Ginger came to join them in their corner. Silently and furtively she eyed them up and down, especially Peter.

He was still hungry; he was used to that. But he wasn't used to being a slave, and he was not about to be beaten by anyone, let alone by a bigoted race of people. And, Romulus terrified him. The badger was still growling and he couldn't keep the anger from his voice.

'I'm going to get us out of here,' he said, his growl just above a whisper.

Chapter 11

THE CASUAL MURDER

The casual murder, the horrible whippings, the smells... He felt trapped. It made him sound harsh as he stated his intentions to the others in the hall: 'I'm going to get us all out.'

'But – you've only found the way to the sewers,' Storm argued. 'They go outside of the castle building, to the castle grounds.'

'And?' Paul couldn't see the point.

'The grounds are still walled off, so that the creatures of the night cannot enter. I guess you could say they are there for our protection.'

'We'll get past the walls,' Paul said with confidence.

'We could go over them,' Michelle suggested. 'I could drop you on the other side. No problem.'

Paul couldn't believe what they were saying. 'Have you *seen* the drop?' he asked, his eyes bulging.

'I can make it higher if you like, weasel. If you need a bigger challenge,' Michelle threatened softly.

Paul realized he'd lost the high ground. 'No, from the wall will be fine.'

'You cannot possibly carry us all in time,' Storm said firmly, thinking it was a silly idea, 'and besides, you are not big enough for that.'

'I might surprise you,' Michelle replied, her raptor-like stare fixed, as if eyeing up a tasty morsel.

Storm shook his head. 'It would take far too long to get everyone across.'

'Then we'll go under it,' Peter said, thinking out loud.

'How?' Storm was still unconvinced.

'Leave that to me,' Peter answered. 'Here's what we're going to do. When you talk to Ebo next, tell him I've found a way out but we'll need his help from the walls.'

'The Clan has not the power to take on the might of the Rumanni,' Storm argued.

'That's why they need to be waiting for us at dusk.'

'At *dusk?* But that's when all of those "nice" things come out!' Paul said, looking round as if they had all gone mad.

'Yes, they do. That's part of the plan. This castle is basically fortified at night. So, any pursuit would be short-lived and they would have to start again in the morning, giving us a head start.'

'But we'll all be out *there* – in the *dark*,' Paul hissed.

Suddenly understanding, Storm nodded. 'We can flee to the River Sindu.'

'We're spending the night on water.' By this time, Michelle had caught on, too.

'So?' Paul said.

'So they never go near water or light – or hadn't you noticed?' Michelle sounded annoyed.

'Griphand can bring a large boat,' Ginger put in. 'He is my uncle, you know,' she said, beaming with pride.

'Now *that* makes me feel better,' Paul piped up sarcastically.

'I'd better get started,' Peter said, more to himself than anyone.

'Ebo thought you would find a way out. I should not have doubted him. He said Al-leone did once.'

'Allan,' Peter corrected, blood rushing to his face. 'My dad? If he escaped from here, then I can, too. I've got to go and dig a hole.'

'I'm coming with you,' Paul said.

Michelle thought about it for a moment. 'I think I'd better come with you, too. Never know what kind of trouble you two might get into without me.'

'You know you'll have to be silent?' Paul quipped.

'You'll be making more noise than me soon,' she warned, daring him to say another word.

The three Changelings made up their beds so that it seemed like someone was sleeping in them. Storm opened the hall door sufficiently for them to slip through.

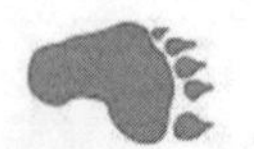

Sticking to the shadows, close to the walls, Peter and Paul raced to the far side of the crater. In the moonlight, with no one around, it looked surreal and haunted – apart from the outline of a bird that should not have been there. Noises from over the walls came in loud and clear: howling, shuffling, and the occasional scream that was invariably cut short. The towers were manned, and most of the guards on patrol were on the walls. The limestone blocks glowed creamy white with the reflected moonlight, but Peter's other sight was all he needed to see clearly. He was hoping they wouldn't be looking for a couple of small animals, but even so, he stuck to the shadows.

The ground changed from the hard blue-black to a more normal earthy brown. Peter could smell the difference as he dashed along. Storm was right – the outer walls were far too high to get over for so many. Peter was searching for another way.

'Too many guards watching. What're we going to do?' Paul asked.

'We need to go further away and more towards those bushes,' Peter pointed with a shake of his snout.

The unused ground he pointed to had grown wild with thick bushes and shrubs. Peter picked a secluded spot, completely hidden by the undergrowth, and started to dig.

'Oh, of course,' Paul whispered. 'Badgers.'

This is what Dad would have done…

'Peter?' Michelle trilled. 'Don't be digging all the way through. The night-creatures are right outside.'

Peter concentrated, turning into a man-sized badger, and with the extra strength and leverage, he enlarged the tunnel he'd started. It was the size of a large child.

He dug down for some distance until he was underneath the foundation of the wall, then he turned and headed upwards, stopping just short of breaking through to the other side. He could sense the thickness of the layer above and he left it so that anyone could punch through it. He restrained his impulse to continue upwards and get out of the stinking place despite the images of the creatures milling around outside the walls, sniffing at the ground and letting out erratic howls.

'Done!' he exclaimed. 'Let's go.'

Overhead, Peter's sharp hearing picked up the release of an arrow and a hawk squawked indignantly, dropping like a stone towards the trees to the side. Several more arrows were released before Michelle managed the safety of the trees.

'What you shooting at, dummy?' someone shouted from the walls.

'There was this big bird, Sergeant.'

'You are a simpleton. There's nothing flying at this time of night. Those things saw to that.'

Peter and Paul froze at the sound of the guards' voices. Peter got the strongest sense of Michelle looking at them from the trees, ready to come to their aid.

Turning into their smallest forms, all three raced back to the shelter of the hall, where Storm was waiting anxiously for them. They briefly described what Peter had done. He was determined to leave the next day.

'Your father and friends were our heroes, Peter. We hear stories about them and they come up in our legends.'

Peter winced at the mention of his father. He gazed at Storm, not really interested. His father was dead; he didn't want to hear any stories about his battles, but Storm mistook his silence and explained further.

'Our legends tell of a time when the Clan would lose their powers; the land would suffer and strangers would come to save it - your parents! Instead of having powers, they *were* the power. It speaks of The Six,' Storm finished.

'They were only four – not six,' Paul yawned.

'As I said, I do not know what it means, but it is said that strangers would find the source, they would make the Land whole again and rid us of the corruption…' Storm's passion ebbed in the face of their tiredness.

'Let's get some sleep,' suggested Peter, who was also yawning. Paul had already dropped into his bed and was snoring gently. *Otters!* Michelle, too, was curled up with a slight smile on her face, seemingly asleep. Peter knew better, though; he could sense her watching him. Peter thought he heard Storm saying something in the background as he crawled into the hard, ropy bed and fell asleep.

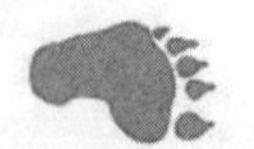

★

Drifting off to sleep, the strange ability to see another place flared into life. He had a vision of his mother arguing with his uncles and aunt. They were shouting at each other. Uncle Ramsey was yelling so hard that the veins in his forehead stood out. Something had happened which made him lose control. His normally handsome face was ugly, twisted and warped with hate, and his scar now made it worse. In front of them was the lit candle: the badger at the base of the burning tower.

Uncle Ramsey looked about to strike his mother when the shadows seemed to shift and blew out all the candles. Somewhere in the ensuing gloom, his uncle screamed and Peter smiled.

The morning's din awoke him. Peter felt tired and longed for more sleep. It was the thought that he was leaving that brought a smile to his face. The children washed and whispered conspiratorially.

They must all know the plan by now, he thought.

He wondered why the tribe's children all implicitly trusted and believed each other while the Rumanni all gave off an air of distrust and fear, even among themselves. Peter finished breakfast in silence, preoccupied with contacting Ebo. His thoughts were interrupted as Paul and Michelle joined him.

They were just getting ready when suddenly one of the guards shouted for them to stop at the top of his voice.

'HOLD!'

The guard screamed came running up, sweating heavily. 'You three will come with me. *Now!*' He was yelling for no apparent reason, his fear and apprehension out of his control.

Storm stepped forward, trying to smooth things over. 'What have they done, sir?'

The guard didn't even bother to reply. His drew back his right hand back and smacked Storm hard across the face. The guard was scared out of his mind. 'Was I talking to you?' he yelled. 'Lord Killjoy wants to see you three – now! The rest of you will wait here until I come back.'

The guard's fear was rampant and Peter stepped forward before any more violence erupted, throwing a warning glance at Storm. A bruise had appeared on Storm's tight-lipped face and a steely glint was in his eye, but he understood.

Seeing Paul and Michelle also step forward, the guard calmed down. He turned and led them through the main gates, expecting them to follow. Peter looked back once towards the fidgeting Storm, who was angry and upset.

Peter, his heart pounding, whispered to Paul and Michelle. '*Be ready.*'

'We are,' they replied together, struggling with their natures.

They went through the gates and turned right towards the high archways leading to the centre of the castle. Walking to the main part of Castle Craven was awe-inspiring: its creamy limestone walls shone, and flying buttresses to the side were topped by gargoyles and towers. The place was built for war and decorated by demons.

The guard did not speak to them again but led them to the side of a tower where someone opened the door at their approach.

'Take them to Lord Killjoy straight away – to the Testing Area.'

The guard sounded relieved to be rid of them.

The other Rumanni wasn't happy to be given the task. 'Follow me!' he said. His voice was cold, not so terrified, but he was still scared.

As Peter stepped across the ominous threshold and into the badly lit corridor, his agitation and worry grew. Inside, the smell of lit torches hung heavily in the air, seeping into the dark passages that led down to the dungeons. He wondered why it was more heavily guarded here than outside. Occasional groans were interrupted by a terrified scream. The voices were human.

Peter's soundscape showed him the various guard rooms, the single cells, and the central chambers. They were in the prison.

He was barely able to control his urge to transform and run. As the screams got louder and more immediate, the children's nerves jangled and danced.

The stocky guard led them deeper, and then he started down a different stairway. The stone was colder and the surface of the walls harder. He was leading them into the castle's very foundations. The

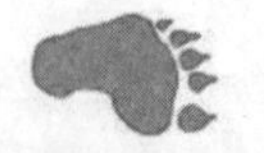

guard continued to descend, past more screaming voices. They spiralled down the large staircase, leaving behind even the merest thought of daylight, it was getting damp and cold. The only light now was coming from the torch the guard carried. Finally, they all stood in front of two enormous doors, heavily engraved and impregnated with metal. The soldier hesitated before knocking quietly.

A velvet voice – more of a whisper – slithered through the door.

'Come in.'

The guard, his breathing heavy, pushed open the door, allowing a red glow to spill out from the chamber. 'My lord – ' he began tentatively, taking great care that his head was bowed and facing the stone floor.

A voice cut curtly through the obsequiousness. 'Bring them in! And you: wait outside until I am through.'

'Yes, my lord,' the guard said, stepping back to let them through. 'Get in!' he ordered through gritted teeth.

Peter stepped past the sweating guard, closely followed by Paul and Michelle. He wasn't looking forward to this encounter, despite a morbid curiosity.

Inside, the room turned out to be a large circular hall, the centre of which was dominated by an irregularly shaped, transparent, glowing red stone. Two-thirds of it was missing, its surface jagged and sharp. The lower part of the stone had been placed in a golden armature, its red light giving a sickly reddish tinge to everything in the hall. Fascinated by the macabre glow, Peter forgot the reason they were there.

'Beautiful, isn't it?' the velvet voice said lovingly from beside Peter's ear. He turned and almost jumped out of his skin.

Lorenzo!

An old, thin man stood next to him, only just taller than himself, strands of brittle white hair poking out from within his hood, his face almost concealed. One critical brown eye examined the three of them; the other was covered by a milky cloudiness, the pupil hardly visible, giving the man a disturbed, unholy look – not unlike Peter's ghoulish Uncle Lorenzo. Peter swallowed and held his breath. The man's aura was cold, and a thick smell of death and

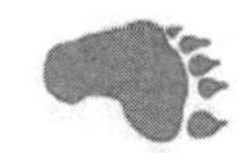

decay hung around him. The malevolence seeping from him made Peter's skin crawl.

'I,' he said, his big hand curled upwards at his chest, revealing long, curled yellow nails, 'am Lord Lucas Killjoy.'

Peter could not be sure, but he thought the man was trying to smile. His thin lips became even thinner. It was an ugly sight. His voice, however, was lovely, almost caressing. Lord Killjoy asked casually, 'Which village did you come from?' He appeared distracted by something on the table. His flowing robe gave him an androgynous look.

Peter could feel the voice urging him to speak. Urging him to tell the man everything. He tried to resist. 'Ebo Shalimar's,' Peter answered, despite the voice in his head screaming for him to stay silent. Lord Killjoy's voice compelled him to answer, and as an afterthought Peter added, 'Sir.'

'Charm Dawn's, sir,' Paul and Michelle answered in unison.

Peter's senses were rattled and the warning bells were going off in alarm. This was no time to transform – not the right time to change! He pushed his abilities down, as deep as he could, desperate to hide even a hint of them. He was hoping Michelle would keep her fierce temper to herself.

'Hmmm.' It was a guttural growl. 'Still keeping children hidden from us,' Lord Killjoy said, stroking his chin. 'Now, why would they do that?' He looked revolting as he smiled again at the thought. He moved over to a table strewn with papers and various-sized glowing red and green Shankars. 'Come over here.'

The power of his voice was persuasive, and Peter found himself moving forward without willing it. He struggled to gain control of his legs; he tried to stay focussed but to no avail. His heart pounded loudly in his ears. His nature screamed to be released – to change and run.

'Let us see what you have, shall we?' Lord Killjoy said in an off-handed manner, as if making casual conversation. 'Hold out your hands. Do not worry: it isn't going to hurt – *too* much.'

There was something very nasty indeed hidden in the undertones of his voice. From the table Lucas Killjoy picked up two small red crystals and closed his hands tightly around them, the whites of

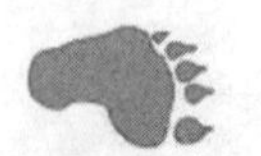

the bone showed through his already pale skin. The gaunt man's hair stood up and his eyes took on a powerful glint as he stepped forward. Looking more wraith-like, his flowing robes darkened as he started to glow from within.

Standing in a row against their will, the children were amazed to find their hands rising upwards, lifted by an unseen force at the sound of Killjoy's voice. Peter tried to control his instincts, and made himself stand there before the ghoul. He was worried about his friends and he darted a quick glance in their direction. Immediately he wished he had not.

'How did you do that?' Lord Killjoy asked, shock written on his face. His eyes bulged and threatened to pop out of their sockets. 'HOW DID YOU DO THAT?' he screeched.

Peter's fright bordered on hysteria, the desire to transform almost out of his control as he looked at the raving spectre before him, its shadowy face thrust next to his. He tried to hide his feelings, frantic to keep the horror from showing on his features, the man's foul breath making him feel sick. 'Do what, sir?' he asked, dread starting to bubble to the surface.

'Look away from me, boy!' Lord Killjoy screeched again, stained yellow teeth showing between his lips. His hands were glowing and he placed his clenched fists into Peter's outstretched palms. Peter flinched as the paper-thin dry skin touched his. Momentarily, a confused look passed over Killjoy's features. He examined his hands and then Peter's face. Nothing. He concentrated harder and Peter started to feel something warm emanating from the withered old hands that quickly became hot and unpleasant.

Peter could not withdraw his hands. The panic that had been rising now gripped him fully. The fear of getting burnt made him struggle harder and he tried to wrench his hands away, but he could not. He called for help and in his mind he was no longer alone. Suddenly he felt Paul and Michelle's spirit there with him, adding their strength to his, looking through his eyes, seeing what he could see, feeling what he could feel.

Lord Killjoy gazed at him and Peter knew that Killjoy could see his hatred. The royal councillor stepped back, preoccupied.

Peter, the sudden heat gone and the relief instant, collapsed to his knees, breathing hard, his eyes closed.

Like a whisper he heard Paul's panicked thoughts. Instantly in his mind he was next to his friend and watching Killjoy approach them through Paul's eyes, feeling Paul's horror rise.

This is no time to transform, Paul. Push it down.

Peter forced his thoughts into Paul, willing him to stop the urge.

Lord Killjoy moved over to the trembling boy and repeated the gesture. Paul flinched involuntarily when the old man's hands touched his. His fright had risen to an alarming level and he was about to change and run.

Paul, stop! We're with you. Look straight ahead! Peter shouted telepathically to his friend. He could feel Michelle's tough spirit standing silently beside him in Paul's mind.

His awareness still with Paul, Peter pushed himself to his feet, remembering to look straight ahead this time, hoping Michelle was doing the same. Lord Killjoy's ugly face still hung disgustingly close to Paul's and Paul could not hide his revulsion. There was a lot more apprehension and fear in Paul than Peter had suspected, and he felt Paul was shaken by his unpleasant experience.

The old man's face began to show confusion by the time he moved to test the defiant-looking girl. Without thinking, Peter's thoughts moved over to Michelle. Now he was looking through her eyes and he could suddenly feel a more serious Paul standing next to them, physically and in spirit.

Michelle was not even scared of Lord Killjoy, nor did she want to run. Instead, she felt as if she were about to smack the man. No revulsion, no panic – no reaction other than pure contempt. If her life was threatened, Lucas Killjoy would die.

Lord Killjoy finished with Michelle faster than he had with Paul. He turned away, distracted and puzzled. 'Pretty girl,' he said as his appearance shrank from the demon-like persona he had taken on while he tested them.

Peter was too drained to worry about what he saw. He watched Lord Killjoy shuffle and limp back to his table having completed whatever it was, but not happy with what he had found.

'So even the Clan's children can be giftless,' he muttered to himself. '*Guard!*'

Killjoy's commanding shriek brought the children quickly to their senses, their energies drained by the weight of ordeal.

The door flew open instantly.

'Take them back. They are *useless*.' Killjoy spat out the words.

Peter noticed that Killjoy's gaze followed Michelle as they were led out. He glanced at Peter again, astonishment appearing briefly, but quickly masked. He, too, looked drained, having got nothing out of the torture.

'Do not eyeball me again, boy,' an angry Lord Killjoy warned, glaring at Peter.

An animal spirit leapt at the challenge. He wanted to lash out and take the look off the ugly man's face but he kept his eyes down. 'I am sorry, sir,' he said, trying to sound humble, desperate to rein in his emotions.

The guard pulled them through the doorway in a hurry. 'My lord,' he said closing it quickly behind them.

He hustled them away from the chamber as fast as he could, practically dragging them up the stairs, and threw them out of the doorway into the sunlight where the other guard still waited. Relief washed over them, and Peter saw that the guards felt the same.

The three friends looked at each other and silently acknowledged that this was not an experience they wanted to repeat.

Storm paced back and forth and stopped only when he saw them come through the gate. Without speaking, they all headed for the mining area and only after they had entered the inner cave did Storm's curiosity overflow. 'What happened? Lord Killjoy is not someone anyone wants to meet, even on good day.'

'He's a nasty old man,' Michelle said disgusted. '*Little girl.* I'll give him "little girl".'

'I'm glad you didn't,' Peter said gratefully. 'I was trying hard to tell you not to.'

'I heard it. You should have been more worried about *him*,' she answered, her temper ready to explode.

'I was,' Peter replied.

'*What?*' Michelle sounded outraged.

Storm held back and waited for them to calm down. 'Where did they take you? How did you get away?'

Paul started to explain at the same time as Peter. 'We didn't.'

'The guard took us to the prison area – nasty place – and then he lead us down further into the dungeons – even nastier place – underneath the main castle,' Peter said, shivering and feeling once again the life-draining cold from the dungeon walls.

Paul simply wanted to forget the whole thing. 'There was this round hall with a broken bloody rock.' He shuddered as he spoke.

'You saw the Lal Shankar they are rebuilding? How far have they got?' Storm asked intently.

'It's a third done. That old man, he tested our hands with those bloody stones you mine. Then he said we were all "useless",' Paul said indignantly.

Peter remembered the brittle feel of the man's skin. 'He didn't find what he was looking for and was really disappointed.'

Storm let out a surprised whistle. 'They cannot detect your powers. You cannot be seen.'

'But what was he looking for?' Paul insisted.

'He was looking to steal your powers, like he has stolen all of ours,' Storm's voice shook with anger. 'We all had them: powers to make flowers grow, powers to call up the wind.'

'Griphand Windmaker!' Paul exclaimed intuitively.

'Exactly,' Storm sounded despondent.

'And you are?' Michelle asked, halting their questions.

'Storm Bringer. It has been a long time since I have felt that.' There was a deep sense of loss in his voice. 'I can hardly make a cloud in a mug now. Funny – over the last few days I have found I can do some tiny things again. Right now, though, we need to make things look normal. And try and find some gems.'

'I've had enough. We're getting out of here today.'

'Have you been Killjoyed recently?' Paul joked nervously. 'I'd rather it had been yesterday.'

'We cannot get everyone to the surface in time today.'

'Fine, we're leaving tomorrow. Tell Ebo. And by the way, I saw lots of those red glows,' Peter said dismissively.

'What? And you did not –' Storm stopped and realized how he had been conditioned. 'Can you find your way back to them?'

Paul butted in and answered for Peter. 'I'll follow his nose,' he said pointing. 'What would you like? One or two?'

'Today? Nothing. For tomorrow, two,' Storm requested.

'Won't they be suspicious?' Paul asked.

'No. They don't see us much during the day and they think there is nowhere to go from down here. Certainly not *out* of here. Not if we give them a gem or two as well. Besides a few of us will stick around to make it appear normal until the last moment, while the rest are making the dash to your tunnel, Peter.' His voice sounded different, somehow.

Peter nodded. 'So, basically, today we make ourselves scarce and don't attract too much attention,' he said, already heading towards one of the tunnels. He could hear the guards moving towards their cave. 'Coming?' he said, looking towards Paul.

Paul was already transforming.

'I'll stay here, weasel,' Michelle teased.

With a nod they were off. Now that they were working to a plan, Peter felt better and wanted to see if he could avoid the sewer. He shuddered at the thought; it had smelt foul, like the Rumanni.

The released badger, exhilarated, started to head upwards but Peter stopped abruptly. 'Paul, ready to find another way other than those sewers?' he suggested.

'Good idea. Don't mark it too strongly; I'm coming up behind you, remember,' Paul said with a sniff, closing his nose flaps.

Peter bared his fangs and smiled, and then he headed downwards instead, negotiating the passages underneath. The tunnels widened rapidly as Peter headed deeper in his quest to find a better escape route. They searched for some time, travelling underneath the main plateau area, all leads coming to dead ends. Peter noticed that the walls were thinning out. They were brittle, and occasionally, when Peter stopped abruptly, he skidded into one, bursting through the tunnel wall to the other side.

He had slowed his pace and was exploring with greater care when the floor of the tunnel suddenly gave way and he crashed through it. The tunnel underneath also collapsed under his weight, and then Peter found himself falling through one floor after another, wildly trying to get hold of something solid. He could hear Paul crashing through above him and, with a final panicked effort he extended his claws fully, burying them into the soft earth as he crashed through the last floor. He found himself dangling from the roof of an immense underground cave. Below him, a long way down was a crystal-clear lake glowing with a blinding bright-green light. Madly he tried to haul himself up as he could hear Paul rolling closer, unable to stop.

Paul came crashing through, failed to grab hold of anything and smashed into Peter with a force that almost knocked the breath out of him. Peter's grip held only for a moment, before they both fell screaming into the water below.

Chapter 12

THE FALL WAS ENDLESS

The fall was endless. Peter twisted and turned uncontrollably. He could hear Paul screaming something above him about it being just a lake, before the impact blew all the breath out of him. He was frantic and struggled to get to the surface because he knew he was in deep water. Suddenly he lost control and changed back to a human. He couldn't hold his breath.

Completely disoriented, and not being able to feel which way was up, he feared he would not make it. Out of nowhere came a graceful, sleek man-size otter that grabbed him. They broke the surface, with Paul whooping and shouting about how great it was. Peter gulped in the fresh air, coughed up the water he had swallowed and was grateful for every breath. Paul did a few more fast loops around him. Peter was staring into the distance trying to spot the hole through which they had fallen.

'Peter, change back, come on!' Paul squealed.

'Badgers only swim when they need to,' Peter yelled irritably.

'This way!' Paul trilled, setting off.

Trusting Paul's senses, Peter swam after the otter. The shore came into sight, a long, curving sandy stretch, and Peter dragged himself onto it and collapsed, irrationally wanting to kiss the sand. He closed his eyes, giddy and disoriented. The fall and fear hit him and all he wanted was to lie there.

Paul was shaking him vigorously. 'Wake up. God, I thought you were dead!'

'Not yet. I'm working on it, though,' Peter answered.

They were on the shores of an underground lake just like a deep bowl, its waters crystal-clear and sparkling. The lake was immense, and scattered around the bottom were various bright lights, the

strongest of which was at its centre. The radiance drew their attention but from where he stood, Peter could not make out what it was. He could, however, feel the power radiating from it.

'You OK? This is fantastic!' Paul exclaimed enthusiastically.

Peter wished he could show more appreciation but he couldn't drum up the energy. 'It's not a way out,' he said. 'Can you feel that?'

Paul nodded. 'I'll go find out what that is,' he offered, leaving without even a splash.

Peter suspected that the otter was finding any excuse to be in the water. Paul was gone a long time, and when he finally broke the surface he was near the centre of the lake, screaming joyfully. Peter shook his head. Paul was enjoying this far too much!

'You're not gonna believe this!' Paul blurted out even before he changed back.

'What?'

'There's this huge green Shankar down there. It's *massive!* You've *got* to see it! *That's* what's giving off the light.'

'How big?'

'The big part is really big,' Paul ranted. 'It's all fractured inside, so maybe it'll just come apart. It's absolutely beautiful down there. You've got to see it.'

'How deep is it?' Peter asked apprehensively.

'Not very,' Paul said coyly, looking eagerly towards him.

'Let's go. And Paul? Thanks for getting me out of there,' Peter shouted after Paul, who had already dived back into the lake.

Now that he'd got his breath back and had transformed, swimming wasn't as bad as Peter thought. They swam almost to the centre, where Paul indicated taking a deep breath before going down.

The lake was shallow and shards of brightly glowing green translucent rock lay scattered everywhere. The buried Shankar was bigger than Peter imagined. Inside he could see thousands of fracture lines running through it. It must have shattered on impact.

He swam back to the surface and took a deeper breath. Swimming underwater wasn't as hard as he thought, and the weight of his fur helped him sink faster. The pulsing power surges became stronger the closer he went to the stone. It drew him like a magnet,

tempting him, daring him. The smooth surface cried out to be touched, its fracture lines flaring with pulses of power that begged to be released.

He touched the stone and a spark flew from it to his paw, gluing it. Light burst in his head, making his mind spin, and suddenly he felt that he was everywhere. There he could see himself in the water; there he could see Storm in the small cave; Grandad and Mum in the dark kitchen talking; Ebo and Jasmine making their way towards the castle; Romulus Blackheart looking down at his bloody hands, his sword buried in a smoking creature. But strongest of all the visions was that of the red glow emanating from the Shankar hall. The vile man, Lord Killjoy, stood with his back to him, hunched over one of the tables.

Peter felt Paul pull him clear and the contact broke. They both got to the surface gasping for air.

'What were you *doing?*' Paul screamed at him, furious. 'You were falling into it. Couldn't you see?'

'Didn't you see all those places?' Peter shouted back in amazement. 'You must have seen them!'

Paul looked at him as if he had gone crazy.

'I was everywhere – bits of me, anyway. It was as if I was actually there. That's what Storm must have meant when he described how to call.' Peter was ranting.

'Storm! We've got to get back, or we'll be left behind!' Paul shouted, looking worriedly at the many tunnels in front of them.

Getting back was slow. There was no trail to follow and the walls were alarmingly brittle in places. Peter concentrated and led them upwards until he accidentally crossed one of his earlier trails. Retracing it was simple – Peter could gauge direction from the strength of the glow and the smell.

They burst into the small cave, surprising Storm and Ginger, but Michelle only gave them a raised eyebrow. They had been unable to find an alternative route to the surface, but all Storm wanted to hear about was the buried green Shankar and its size.

'The Rumanni have not guessed what they really are. They

know that the Lal contains power, but they do not know it is *holy* power – that it is a Shankar. They have no idea about the other stones.'

'So what *is* a Shankar? Can it get us out of here?' Paul asked.

'Ahhh, no. Originally the Maker made six; each contained His holy power. Placed in the heavens, they battled each other, but then something happened and they fell and shattered on the ground. That is what you see today: different Shankars all over the place. The larger piece wins the battle over a smaller one.'

'You mean size matters,' Michelle said, raising an eyebrow.

'Yes, but it's no good. It always go back to its original shape,' Paul said, trying to follow Storm's tale to its logical conclusion.

'Yes. They are eternal; they cannot be destroyed by us. They protected us. We understood that the Land needs to be in balance, but all that changed when the Rumanni discovered the powers from the Lal Shankar…'

'Holy stones in Killjoy's unholy hands,' Peter remarked.

'Careful how you address him. He is *Lord* Killjoy. He can suck out the very life you have. It was he who stole our powers. We were taken one by one to the hall. The Lal Shankar was not so big then,' Storm said, remembering. 'The king laughed manically throughout as the rock grew brighter with every gift.' There was fear and pain in his voice and he rubbed his palms together, nervously. 'The Rumanni are not at all like our Clan. They even have prisons for their own people.'

'What's going on in there?' a guard barked from outside.

They had been careless and loud. Storm quickly asked in a whisper, 'How big a Lal Shankar can you find in a hurry?'

Peter indicated the size of his fist, and Storm dashed out of the cave to enthuse to the guard about their find. He was soon back with a green, glowing stone. As he handed it to Peter, again there was the power surge and Peter was back in lots of places.

Storm quickly jerked the stone away from him. 'What is that?'

'I forgot to tell you. When I touched the green Shankar, I felt like I was in all these different places at once.'

'*You?* A *Caller*?'

They had no time to debate the matter because the guard was

still loitering outside. 'We need a Shankar. Paul, can you carry this?'

Paul hesitated.

'Callers are rare,' Storm said with pride. 'You could not be one as well.'

He passed the gem to an apprehensive Paul before he could protest. Paul jumped back startled, ready to drop it at the first sign of power. He looked at the stone in his hand and replied, 'Yes. Yes, I can.'

They quickly extracted a red stone and brought it back for Storm who hurried off to appease the aggressive guard. When he returned, he indicated with a gesture that the guard was still outside, spying. The Rumanni loitered awhile, finally he got bored and wandered off.

The rest of day was a blur for Peter. His thoughts lingered on being a Caller. It had felt like he had been looking through an eye but something had been there with him – infinitely more powerful, detached and inhuman. A vast energy pulsed in the stone from another time, able to see through anything. He felt confused, agitated, and he bristled at everything. His behaviour did not go unnoticed by Michelle and Paul. They tried in vain to talk to him several times before giving up and leaving him alone. What he wanted, more than anything, was to talk to Storm. He had seen his mother. There had to be a way he could use his power to call her.

'Peter, this is a rare gift even among my kind – one that we keep secret,' Storm said when they were finally in the sleeping quarters. 'When you touched the Shankar, what did you feel?'

Peter could not really describe it. 'Electricity – sort of like lightning bolts. I was everywhere.'

Storm nodded slowly. 'That is just the start. You have to be careful. When you see these people and places, *they* can see *you*.'

Peter heart leapt. 'What? I'm really there?'

'Yes.'

The thought stabbed him with fear as he remembered Lord Killjoy. What if he had turned around?

'You have to think yourself invisible and only then should you touch it, and even then you have to remain focussed on a single object, or an image. The power will take you there.'

'I saw my mum,' Peter said quietly, his stomach in tight knots. 'Does that mean…?' he asked slowly, but he already knew the answer, even before Storm's nodding head confirmed it.

'Sometimes you will not see the object and get a blank, but I think, that is because of the lack of power in the stone you are holding,' Storm explained, but Peter's mind was already back at the lake. He *had* to try again. He needed to reassure his mother that he was fine – that he was alive.

'Sometimes I get the images when I am falling asleep, but I cannot control those,' Storm continued in hushed tone.

'So do I, but I'm not holding a stone then.'

'Stop your chattering!' a guard yelled from outside as he banged on the door.

Peter lay wide-awake on his hard rope-spun bed and stared at the ceiling, his gaze mindlessly tracing the circular patterns embossed in it. He drifted in and out of his strange thoughts until, eventually, he grew tired and his eyes drooped.

Without warning an image forced its way into his mind.

He was in his mother's kitchen and she was making tea. It was late afternoon, judging from the light outside. She turned, surprise transformed her face and she dropped the teapot. The china smashed on the floor, its shards flew off in a million directions and made Peter open his eyes quickly, the reflected sparkling lights on the lake cave roof blended into his vision for an instant and he could not tell them apart. He was suspended between the green light below and the kitchen above. He heard his mother's voice cry out, its echoes followed him.

'I'm alive, Mum.' He didn't know if she heard.

Peter awoke with a start. Light crept underneath the doorway and he remembered they were leaving the dreadful place that day.

All the children were in a sombre mood, their many previous failures weighing heavily on all their minds. Though they tried to act normally, their nervousness increased as the day wore on, and the banter and boisterous chatter sounded hollow. Their feelings were contagious; their eyes darted about and the clamour in the

dining hall was subdued. The guards, however, didn't seem to notice.

Having seen the scars, Peter could well imagine their previous punishments. If they were caught, the three Changelings could still escape, but that was not what Peter had promised. He had to get them out. Otherwise, it would be his failure, and they would pay for it – with their suffering.

The children disappeared into various tunnels, only to double back and gather quietly in a larger hidden cave. Storm picked out several older boys, ordering them to be the last ones to start up. Others he picked to mark the route up. Finally he turned to Peter.

'Get us out of here.'

Peter started off with a gangly dark-haired youth called Chameleon, who looked half-starved. The children outwardly appeared to be orderly and disciplined. Their scent was a different matter; it was rampant and their terrors were close to panic. Their jitters barely contained, they kept bumping into one another in their anxiety to get away.

At the base of the sewer, Chameleon took over and led them straight towards the opening that Storm had described to him. The children reacted in the same way as they waded through the filthy stream and its contents; some vomited and gagged on the stench. Chameleon hurried them through the passage to the opening; he stayed to one side and reminded each one that they needed to hide until dusk.

The train of children emerged quietly out of the sewer exit into bushes, and disappeared into the thickets and the trees. Peter pointed out the tunnel he had burrowed to the dark-haired boy, who nodded. He made sure that Chameleon knew to wait till the last moment before they dug through to the other side.

By the time Peter returned to the cave, only Storm and a few of the older children were left.

'I will go and get a Shankar,' Storm said, taking a deep breath.

'Why? We haven't got time! Let's go!' Peter said.

'We need to talk to Ebo.'

'Would this help?' Paul said, holding up a green Shankar, 'I crept out earlier.'

'Yes. I will be the last one up.' Storm was visibly relieved.

'You're needed on the surface,' Peter argued. 'You're the only one the children really follow.'

'We will stay behind and give an impression that we found something,' one of the elder boys offered, nervous but determined.

'I'll stay and bring them up at the last moment,' Michelle offered, expecting everyone to have understood what was on her mind. 'You do realize as soon as I step out onto that plateau, they will sound the alarm.'

'They will be too heavy,' Storm objected.

'No they won't, but a man-sized hawk even they will notice,' Peter interrupted. 'Let's go,' he said, giving Michelle a quick look.

She simply smiled back, fearless.

'Ebo is on the other side,' Storm informed Peter as they emerged from the sewer exit and ran to cover where the other children were waiting.

Daylight was just beginning to fade when from off in the distance came the sound of an alarm being raised.

They heard yelling and shouting, and the sound of bells ringing.

'They have found out!' Storm said looking back into the vast mining area, terrified.

From the crater a hawk rose, like a phoenix from the green fire, with two boys dangling in her claws.

'Peter!' Storm screamed, but Peter was already in the tunnel, digging through the last part. His head broke through to be confronted by hoards of armed Clansmen, with Ebo and Jasmine in the lead. The reunions were short-lived as the children poured through rapidly ushered into small groups and herded north in the direction of the river.

During the exodus, Peter dashed back to join Paul on the other side. There was a lot of shouting and he could see soldiers running towards the escaping children. They would not all get out before the guards reached them.

Michelle disappeared over the wall before reappearing, having dropped off her load.

Peter looked towards Paul and Michelle. 'They're not going to make it! We've got to slow the guards down!' he shouted.

They were already following his lead. He could hear Michelle's heavy wings behind him as he rushed forward. All of a sudden the powerful flapping stopped, and Peter knew she had gone into a dive, swooping with deadly accuracy at the guards in front. Coming in low and brushing the ground at speed, Michelle scattered the Rumanni. She then glided over the inner wall and disappeared from view.

Confusion and fear spread among the guards. In front of Peter were five soldiers, braver than most, dashing forward with outraged faces, but as Peter grew to a full man-sized badger, their outrage turned to panic. The pandemonium spread quickly to the soldiers behind them. Most stopped and ran the other way; others came on, still swinging their swords. The steel was met by hard ivory as Peter and Paul tore through their metal armour and snapped swords and bones with their claws and teeth.

Peter was in an animal fury, his reflexes inhuman, dodging in and out of the soldiers with ease. Vibration and sound warned him of every swinging blade, and the harder the guards swung, the more warning he got. To Peter, they all seemed to be moving in slow motion. Their fearsome armour wasn't as strong as he had thought, or else he had underestimated the hardness of his own claws. His mind exploded with anger and rage, both of which he was finding difficult to control, lashing out with more force then he intended. He was trying to keep focussed, spreading as much confusion and mayhem as possible to give the Clan and their children time to get away.

Thumping vibrations in the ground alerted Peter to a new threat. while he was momentarily distracted, a soldier's blade got through and sliced the top of his shoulder – the pain was excruciating. The guard had already swung back for the killing blow to Peter's neck when a black shape materialized as if out of nowhere to pound the man to the ground. Paul continued to roll past and flew at yet another one.

Peter didn't even have time to bleed! Guards on horseback approached through the archway and sped towards the fleeing prisoners. They were all in full battle armour and charged towards the badger with their spikes lowered, ready for a kill.

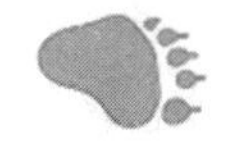

The leader was grabbed by powerful talons and lifted off his horse. He was dragged flailing into the air before Michelle decided to drop him on another mounted guard. Both crashed heavily to the ground. Another soldier behind them had just enough time to swerve out of the way of the falling guards, but he failed to miss Peter's lethal leap and had his chest ripped open by a powerful swipe.

Peter was aware of Paul having his own battle, and much further back he could hear the clashes with the Clansmen. There was more shouting coming from the walls, warning screams, then the heavy flapping stopped and everyone dived for cover as Michelle went into another swoop.

Peter could sense that reinforcements were arriving in increasing numbers. The vibrations were heavier and the foot soldiers started to withdraw, letting the horses behind them charge through.

Peter turned to find Paul, who was close by and shouted, 'Let's go! Hurry!'

They turned and fled for the burrowed escape tunnel. On the far side, more mounted soldiers approached the area. The Clan people were fighting a losing battle at the escape route and urged them to make haste. The mounted soldiers were going to get there first.

The tribesmen shot arrows but with little effect. They were being forced back and there was no way Peter and Paul would reach them in time.

Suddenly, from the direction of the prison tower came a blazing fireball, lighting up the sky and hitting the hawk.

Michelle screamed in pain and started to fall.

The cavalry had already made it to the Clansmen and their escape was cut off. In the sky, Michelle only just avoided another burst of red fire.

'Join the Clan!' Peter yelled at the top of his voice, and tried to wave her away. 'Get away, Michelle!'

Peter looked at the mounted soldiers who were now riding at full gallop towards them. He looked at Paul. They each came to the same conclusion.

'*The sewers!*'

Chapter 13

THEIR RETREAT WAS CUT OFF

Their retreat was cut off. In front of Peter and Paul, the mounted soldiers were going to reach their only remaining escape route – the sewer. Even with their inhuman speed, it was going to be close as to who got to the entrance first.

Faster than any man on horseback, they raced with desperation, fear of being caught driving them on. The pungent smell of the sewers already told the badger how far he'd have to go before reaching safety, and it was not in his nature to come in second. The mounted soldiers put on a final burst of speed and tried to block their way.

'Hurry!' Peter growled over his shoulder.

'What do you think I'm doing?' Paul shrilled, high on adrenaline.

'To the pool!' Peter yelled, flying into the entrance, a spear glancing past his head.

Paul scrambled in after him and collided with his back just as more spears smashed against the walls outside. The badger heard the guards dismount; Peter knew they were coming. He followed the route back to the end of the sewer, where he entered the first of the tunnels leading back down to the plateau.

Peter needed to talk to Ebo desperately – otherwise they would be completely cut off, alone in Castle Craven. They hurtled down to the plateau, their senses warning them of the pursuit.

He could sense a number of guards still on the plateau and there was a commotion up ahead. Peter was about to carry on past Plateau Periculum, when he yelled backwards: 'Paul – can you steal another one of those greens?' He needed to discover if he could use the green Shankar properly.

'Shouldn't be a problem. Be right back.'

'Be careful!' Peter shouted after him.

Paul slithered out into the open, his natural blue-black sheen making him almost invisible against the strange rock. Before long, even Peter couldn't spot him from his hiding place at the mouth of a tunnel. On the far side of the protected wooden crate which bore the precious rocks, a dark shape rose briefly over the edge, a couple of green lights seemed to jump out of it, and the dark shape winked out. Paul was soon back.

'*Voilà!*'

Unsure that he would be able to control the Shankar's power sufficiently, Peter was apprehensive as he remembered Storm's words: ***They*** *can see* ***you***.

He took a deep breath, reached out his paw and transformed it into a hand as he prepared himself mentally.

Think yourself invisible... how do you do that? he wondered, twitching his whiskers. *Lock yourself onto one thing.* He tried not to think of the places he went the first time he touched one of those stones. He concentrated on the person he knew best in the Clan: Jasmine.

Closing his eyes, he held out his hand, a picture of his mother popping naturally into his mind. He felt Paul drop a slimy Shankar into his outstretched palm, his fingers closed instinctively around the cool, slightly sticky surface.

It burst into life in his hand, a miniature sun contained in a blazing furnace, and his mind flew across the distance.

There they were!

Peter hovered over the villagers. In his mind's eye, he watched them as they ran hard over rocky ground. He kept pace – the walls of the castle loomed menacingly close behind them. Darkness had fallen and Ebo was shouting from the back of the group.

'Not far now. Move! Go around!'

There were shouts and screams in the background where the mounted soldiers had just emerged.

The children ran as fast as they could, the adults scattered protectively around them. Jasmine held tightly onto Ginger's hand; she practically hauled her along. Turning the corner, Peter spied the

boat that would have meant his freedom. A thin plank connected it to the shore.

Torches lit up the area as the former slaves started to scramble on board – their last chance for freedom. People armed with bows and arrows mounted the front of the boat, shooting into the air over the heads of the approaching children and adults. Ancient arrowheads burst into the skies, causing it to rain, but relentless armour prevailed. Screams behind the fleeing group filled the darkness as the rest of them clambered across.

Peter saw Griphand at the tiller, already raising his hands as the magic runners began unfurling the sails. Everyone started to shout at a small struggling group which had just come into view. The man in front was carrying a girl who was bleeding; her hand dangled limply and she bobbed with the man's running motion, a shock of blond hair flying around her. The people on the boat started to push out the plank again as he ran towards them with her.

It was Michelle!

Charm rushed forward to relieve the man of the unconscious girl. Blood poured from a deep cut on Michelle's arm. Charm frantically tore up clothing to make a tourniquet to stem the flow.

'Get some water!' she ordered.

The man lowered Michelle to the deck and Jasmine tried to squeeze the gushing wound shut to stem the bleeding.

The boat lurched forward and started to turn away from the cliff. The last of the stragglers quickly jumped on as the plank was withdrawn. The magical rain continued to pour down as the bowmen let off their arrows, while on the towers and the walls, torches sprang up out of the darkness. The Rumanni could not follow.

From the darkness rose a cacophony of deafening screams and growls.

Michelle!

Jasmine's head snapped up sharply. 'Peter?' she enquired cautiously.

Can you hear me?

'Yes. Yes. Peter, where are you?'

Paul's hand dropped onto his shoulder and distracted him. The

contact broke. Peter found himself back in the cave, gripping the Shankar so hard that it cut into his hand.

'They're coming,' Paul whispered, looking backwards.

Behind him was a loud noise – guards were moving in. A man's voice was chanting in the background, and the chant was being amplified by the tunnels. The whole place started to reverberate.

Cautiously, they edged to a point where they could observe the plateau clearly. King Romulus Blackheart was striding towards an elaborately dressed priest, who was laying Lal Shankar stones into a pattern on the ground. Romulus did not have his armour on, but his tunic, jerkin and slacks were all in his characteristic black, with the red embalm on his left side. His cloak swirled behind him like a huge moth. Even when casually dressed, the man looked good, especially compared to the stocky Rumanni. Murderous, but good.

'Your majesty,' the priest stopped his task to kneel before King Blackheart.

'What imbecile allowed One's unpaid helpers to escape?'

A burly guard came forward, his head bowed, his body shaking.

'I– I– I did, my lord.'

'Tear your heart out and grate it for One's salad!' Romulus commanded the house master.

'Yes, sire.'

'No – stop! One is being too hasty,' Romulus rubbed his forehead in frustration. 'Go to Lady Pariah for correction – and tell her to keep you alive so you can repent your mistake.'

'Yes, sire.'

Romulus was still agitated and paced back and forth. Glancing down over the kneeling priest's shoulder, he asked, 'Is it ready?'

'Yes, sire.'

'Gotcha!' A guard screamed from behind Peter, grabbing him by his fur and hauling him out onto the plateau. Startled, for an instant Peter didn't react – the sensation of being lifted by his hair was new to him. With his other hand, the guard managed to grab the otter as well, making Paul squeal.

As the gauntlet bit into Peter, however, his fury at being manhandled exploded. Growing in size, he swiped out at the guard, who dropped them both in sudden terror. A look of horror spread over his face.

'Giant *rats!*'

Peter whirled round to see the king staring at him, recognition in his eyes. 'It can't *be*!' The hatred in Romulus's voice was unmistakable. 'Kill them! Release the spell!'

'But my lord: it's not quite perfect –' The priest's protest was cut short by a slap that knocked him to the ground.

'NOW!'

The priest started to chant again, and the amplified vibrations caused the stones to glow brighter. Lord Killjoy hurried from the lift towards the king and the priest. Instantly, smoke began to rise from the Shankar and blood-red strands emerged from the pattern on the ground.

'*Run!*'

Paul didn't need to be told twice. Gaseous red smoke began to flow into the tunnels after them.

'To the lake – hurry!' Peter croaked backwards, running through the passage faster and faster. Their throats hurt and the air began to choke them. The smoke was catching up, and sheer fright drove them through the tunnels at blinding speed.

Peter instinctively ran downwards, having forgotten the crumbling walls, and without realizing, fell through the roof of the lake again.

Falling and screaming, with the otter close behind, Peter could see bright-red snakes of flashing lights and smoke coming after them. The burning strands were surrounded by thick grey smoke and an orange skin that constantly renewed itself. They did not stray from their course, but came on blisteringly fast.

The fall was as bad as he remembered. Just as Peter thought the snake-strands were going to catch them, the impact of the water, sudden as it was, jarred him to the bone. A sleek black otter came and pulled him under just as fireworks exploded above them where the burning strands met the water.

As suddenly as the danger had begun, it was over.

Peter held his breath until his lungs were about to burst, and Paul took them to the surface. Paul stayed underwater while he watched Peter, ready to pull him under at any moment. It was a long time before Paul poked his head out into the cavern air, by which time Peter had finally stopped gasping.

'That was close,' Paul said, his gaze darting around the cavern. His glistening otter eyes reflected his sentiments, nervous and fidgety. He was ready to jump back into deep water if anything happened.

'Have you still got the stone?'

The large otter opened its mouth, two ivory fangs grinned a wide smile. It stuck out its tongue and on it was a green glowing Shankar. 'But there's lots more down there,' he said, indicating to the glowing green lake. The two began to swim ashore.

'Michelle's injured.'

Peter's words made Paul choke as he changed back and almost swallowed the large stone.

'How? Where?' he coughed, struggling to talk while spitting out the rock.

Peter tried to describe what he had seen.

'How bad?'

'Very. Charm was bandaging up her arm,' Peter said, watching a dejected Paul slump down on the sand, his normal playful demeanour subdued.

'What now?'

Peter knew that the Clan could not make a second rescue attempt; it would be far too dangerous. They sat in the green glow surrounded by a burnt sulphurous smell, lost in their own thoughts. He was grateful that Paul was there with him.

The glow in the cavern flared momentarily and in his mind's eye, Peter saw the red Shankar in the hall flare and dim, and on the plateau, a look of terror froze the face of Lord Killjoy. Suddenly, the priest behind Killjoy screamed and collapsed. Killjoy looked down at his bleeding hands, dropped the red stones, and sagged to his knees on the hard ground. The vision faded.

'I don't think the snakes will be coming back for a while,' Peter said, his eyes still focussed in the distance.

Paul looked up and smiled. 'My aunt would probably disapprove, but I got a lot of pleasure from seeing that look on Killjoy's face.'

Peter looked at Paul and then realized he could feel Paul standing next to him in the vision, very much like what he had felt when Killjoy had tested them.

'I don't know if Mum would disapprove if she knew about my Dad.'

Silently, Peter examined the wound on his shoulder. The slice was not too deep. Instinctively his tongue whipped out and cleaned it.

'Are you OK?' Paul asked.

But Peter merely looked at the ground and said nothing.

Curled up in their furs, they slept. Darkness engulfed Peter and the comfortable dreams of home came more sharply then ever. He floated through his house. There was his room - all tidy.

That had never happened before! It was going to be hell finding anything in there!

Semi-darkness hung over it, the morning light only just crept through a slight parting in the curtains…

Peter.

The voice was a whisper. Peter shot awake. Paul was already up.

'What?'

'I didn't say anything,' Paul said, confused. 'I thought you called me.'

Peter. Paul. Put your hands on a Shankar.

The clear voice was coming from the air. Peter quickly located the stone. Paul joined him in holding it as it erupted into life.

The cave faded and they were standing on the boat with Jasmine, Charm and a cross-legged Shaman who sat on the deck. There was no one else. The Shaman was in a deep trance.

The boat was eerily still and Peter felt suspended – unreal – whereas previously he had felt more. In the background was a

transparent ghost image of their own cavern, and in front of them were a relieved Jasmine and Charm.

You have not been captured, have you? Jasmine asked. Her voice had a tinny quality to it.

'We're OK. We're in an underground cave with a lake. They flooded the tunnels with something,' Peter answered.

'Bright-red serpents!' Paul added.

Maker preserve us! Charm's outburst drew their attention.

Did you call earlier? Jasmine asked, ignoring Charm's comment.

'I tried. You were all running to the boat,' Peter started and then he remembered. 'How's Michelle? How badly is she hurt?'

She is fine. The fire-arrow cut across her skin and it was bleeding a lot, but she is fine. Listen to me: we do not have much time, Jasmine said urgently. *We have to travel away from you to ensure that they cannot follow us. But we will be back to get you. Stay hidden – stay out of the castle. Storm said something about you finding a big Shankar. Use that one to call us. Remember to protect yourself: think invisible. Only then close your hands around the stone. And concentrate only on one person. Peter, stay out of the Dragon's Breath. That's what those snakes were. They are death.'* Jasmine hammered home the message.

'Why are there only three of you on the boat? Why aren't you moving?' Paul asked.

The boat is moving, and we are all here. The Shaman is creating this image so as not to confuse you, Jasmine waved at everything. *One last thing: stay away from Lord Killjoy. He will now be looking for you, but Ebo thinks that they have not understood what happened there tonight. We must go…* she said looking around.

The image faded.

Peter dropped the stone to the ground, its normally bright glow now only a faint glimmer.

'Stay away from Killjoy? Is she serious?' Paul repeated slowly. 'I didn't want to go near him in the first place.'

'Nor me,' Peter agreed, remembering the foul breath, the rotting teeth and the evil eyes.

'What're we going to do?' Paul asked in an uncertain voice. 'They're gone.'

'They're not gone. They just had to get away for a while. Jasmine said they would be back to get us.' Peter tried to sound convincing.

'How, Peter? Killjoy is going to use the Sight and find them.' For once, Paul's words fell like stones. After a guilty silence he added, 'And besides: I'm hungry.'

This time it wasn't Peter who growled, but his stomach. They were starving, trapped and a long way from home. Peter's worst fears were confirmed.

'There's nothing for it,' he said at last. 'We have to look after ourselves and there's no food around here. We're going to have to scrounge in the castle.' Jasmine's warning was still fresh in his mind, but the growing hunger occupied his thoughts. 'How about the prison area?'

'*What?* Are you *nuts*?'

'No, just hungry. Think about it. They're guarding prisoners – they must feed them something. They're not likely to be guarding the food, are they?' Peter said, giving Paul a wink and holding out his hand to pull him up.

As they approached the area of the prison, Peter heard odd bouts of coughing and wheezing. A slight chill came down the tunnels, which meant that dawn was breaking outside. Peter watched as Paul shrank to a smaller form. It was so cool!

They approached cautiously, not wanting to slip in any of the liquid waste that flowed in the centre of the tunnel. They headed into the prison quarters, fear lending an extra sharpness to their senses, making them alert to any danger and particularly aware of the voices and vibrations of people up ahead.

The passage ended in a hole in the wall, and the occasional foul liquid flowed through it while they waited for the men in the toilet chamber to leave. Silently they crept through the washroom area. The open door afforded them a view into the main chamber, where all the guards, apart from one, still seemed to be asleep. Peter was grateful for the overpowering smell of burning wood from the fireplace – it masked their new fragrance.

He looked around carefully, and on the corner table, he

spotted what he wanted: some scraps of meat and bread. Paul had also seen the food and, being the better thief, squeaked that he would go and get it. Peter knew better than to argue with an otter on a mission.

Paul's hunger must have added an extra urgency to his quest and he was soon back with the dried meat and stale bread. They tucked in ravenously, their attention completely on the food.

The door flew open abruptly, making them both jump. One of the guards yelled and drew his sword; he tried to skewer Peter and only just missed. They scrambled out of the way, dropped the remaining food, and searched for a bolt-hole. The heavy-set guard blocked their escape. Peter was reluctant to attack and make the guard think that they were anything other than big rodents – just as the not-too-bright guard on the plateau had thought.

With nowhere else to go, Peter dashed into the main chamber, aware that Paul was right behind him. The door at the top of the stairs was closed and Peter quickly ran down the main corridor that housed the prisoners, using his senses to probe ahead. Spurred on by the commotion behind them, they eventually found themselves at the far end of the corridor. The noise ended abruptly when someone got punched and a guard shouted something obscene about being woken up because of rats.

No one followed them down the corridor. Peter located an empty cell and entered, followed closely by Paul. The darkness inside was complete. Both of them were now relying entirely on their ultra-hearing sense which, to them, made everything as clear as day.

A brief search of the cell revealed that it was covered in fine steel netting on all the walls, floor and ceiling. Peter thought it was the oddest room, and he felt a subtle pressure on his mind. He was uncomfortable in the atmosphere, but they both stayed quiet, not daring to move.

'We'll wait awhile, then let's grab some more food on the way back,' Peter suggested, trying to take his mind off the room.

'This room's a bit funny,' Paul muttered, glancing around.

'I've been thinking the same. Not easy to get out of here, is it?'

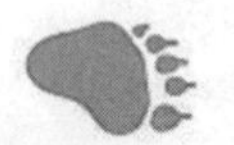

Peter could tell Paul was looking apprehensively around the silent cage. From here, the moans and groans of other prisoners appeared to be even louder.

After what seemed like hours, Peter finally sneaked back to the main chamber, but found the door they had originally come through bolted shut. He looked around. The only other way out was the door at the top of the stairs that had a barred window in the middle, which Peter believed they could squeeze through.

He nudged Paul and indicated the top door. He was relieved to see Paul nod back and start shrinking to an even smaller size. They managed to squeeze through – just – their skins grazing on the rough bars, and jumped down the other side.

The corridor was similar to but not the same as the one that they had gone down to see Lord Killjoy. Steps led off in both directions, spiralling up and down.

Peter's natural instinct was to head downwards towards the protective darkness.

'Down?' he suggested to the tiny otter behind him.

'No!' squeaked Paul. 'What if it only leads to that hall? Let's get out of here!'

He wasn't sure of what else he was going to meet, but being trapped in the middle of Castle Craven in a hall with an evil man wasn't what Peter had planned. The sound of doors opening from below him, however, made up his mind in a flash.

Chapter 14

THEY FLEW UP THE STAIRS

They flew up the stairs. Peter stopped briefly at various corridors that led off the spiral staircase, but decided that too many people occupied them to afford a safe, unnoticed escape.

In their search for safety, they climbed higher, having nowhere else to go but the roof. Peter realized that the tower they had come up was the identical twin of the one in which they had been interrogated by Killjoy, and he had no desire to bump into him a second time.

He squeezed through an arrow-slit and dropped onto the slanted roof leading to a flat gravelled area, but his claws slipped and made too much noise for comfort. At a thought, the paws became feet and hands. The tiles felt hot on the soles of his feet, but at least they didn't slip, removing the possibility of falling to his death in the market square below.

'I think we're safe here, for a while,' Peter said, pointing out the hole used as drainage. 'We can wait here until night falls and go straight back down to the lake.'

Paul looked dubious about being safe anywhere in the castle. They found a heavily shadowed place and crouched in it to rest, their dark fur helping them to blend into the background.

In the market, people were gathered noisily around a raised platform. On it rested a wooden structure for imprisoning people: their head and hands were bound in three circular gaps, trapping them between two wooden slats. Suddenly, from below, cheering erupted as soldiers dragged out a struggling man. He looked like the priest Peter had seen on the plateau, his striking elaborate robes now torn and dirty. The cloth snagged on the wood as the priest was manhandled into the stocks. He groaned when they hit

him, and by the look of him, he had had more of the same treatment earlier.

Peter detected the smell of fear and anger rising from the square. These people were scared, excited and expecting violence, all at the same time. Just as the priest was bound into the wooden structure on the platform, there was a commotion directly below their hiding place. The crowd hushed. Peter crept forward to have a quick peek.

He immediately wished he hadn't.

It was Lord Killjoy.

Surrounded by guards, his hood drawn over his head, he shuffled forward, his left leg trailing slightly. The hushed crowd parted before him and a forbidding silence fell over the onlookers. The crowd watched, fascinated, as the dark-hooded man struggled onto the platform.

He turned, surveyed his audience and stopped, facing the towers. He seemed to be looking directly at the Changelings. Peter and Paul tried to shrink further and pressed themselves into the shadows.

'This man,' Killjoy said in loud voice, the pitch carrying it across the whole square, 'has disobeyed me. He could have captured the Changelings.'

'My lord, it was – ' the cleric started, but was silenced by a swift blow from a guard.

'His incompetence has let you down. He has betrayed you,' Lord Killjoy continued unaffected, ignoring the outburst. His melodiously seductive voice held the crowd spellbound. 'He released the Dragon's Breath, despite my clear instructions, and he has killed them. They should have been taken alive.' There were nasty cries from the crowd. 'As decreed by our king, His Majesty Romulus Blackheart, we will exact punishment from those who fail us. I leave that to you – what punishment should we administer for leaving you in such peril?'

'Tear out his eyeballs!' screeched a hag with a child in her arms.

'Whip him to death!' screamed another.

The horrid crowd bayed for blood, the noise quickly escalating into unintelligible jeering and shouting. A burly muscle-bound

guard stepped heavily onto the platform, his hairy fingers wrapped around a whip. He wore a black hood.

It was the new house master.

'Twenty-five lashes!' ordered Lord Killjoy, to the sound of applause.

Although the people cheered and applauded at Killjoy's order, Peter could smell their fear. He could understand how they would be scared of this man who stood on the platform like a ghoul in broad daylight.

The house master ripped open the robe of the whimpering priest and stepped back. Each snap of the whip was accompanied by a scream, each scream accompanied by a loud cheer, and each cheer by a count for the priest. The voices were shrill, the counting completely wrong.

The smell from below had changed; it was sickly and sucked at the very core of life. The revolting excitement gave way to something worse – it turned into something dead and inhuman. Peter watched, horrified, unable to look away. He strained his neck further to get a better look. By now, the priest merely grunted at each stroke, and soon he passed out altogether. The guards on the platform unbuckled the unconscious man from the contraption and carried him off.

The crowd fell silent and stood rooted to the spot. Not even a baby cried. Peter could see some of their faces; a bluish-grey hue had replaced their normal skin colour. They stood and stared, their expressions vacant. Lord Killjoy, whose gaze still followed his priest, seemed to have grown larger, more filled out, with a hint of creamy tanned flesh underneath the hood. He examined the crowd one last time, his skin aglow, the silence over them absolute.

Casually, he gazed back up towards where Peter and Paul were hiding, his head to one side as if listening to something. With vigour, he took the small number of steps on the raised platform – no trace of the previous limp – and headed back the way he had come. The crowd had to be forcibly parted by the two remaining guards and the house master. They barged their way through the silent lifeless crowd.

Lord Killjoy left behind a deathly silence.

The guards dragged the priest off to the other tower. Peter and Paul couldn't squeeze into the shadows hard enough in their attempt to get as far away as possible from the vileness that had spread below. The cloying smell that threatened to suffocate them faded slowly, but still they did not dare move until they heard murmurs from the crowd, and life returned to the marketplace.

Paul fidgeted. 'Let's get away from here. Killjoy was *feeding* off their suffering.'

'Ugh!' Peter exclaimed, his eyes wide. 'He was stealing their *lives* – not their suffering.'

Fear drove them into the drains to wait for nightfall, as waiting in the open clearly wasn't safe. They stopped only when the passage became slippery.

A voice called from behind him.

Peter.

'What?' he growled back.

'I didn't say anything,' Paul squeaked.

It was then that Peter felt the tingle of a Caller, a slight coolness fell around him and a rhythmic pressure squeezed his mind, as if someone were gently knocking. Paul, who had automatically been designated official Shankar-bearer, spat out his green cargo. Peter rubbed the saliva off it onto his fur before they both placed their paws on it. Suddenly they could see Jasmine, Charm, the Shaman and Michelle, whose arm was extensively bandaged. They were sitting cross-legged on the boat.

Peter? Paul? Jasmine asked.

They looked at each other; a bright-eyed badger stared at a glistening otter. They were still in their animal forms.

'Yes.'

'We cannot transform back here, the drains are too small,' Peter explained. 'How's the arm? I saw you get hit and then –'

I'm fine, but it's going to take time to heal, Michelle said.

Jasmine's interrupted. *The whole Clan is moving into the mountains. With Michelle here with us, and the greater distance, Ebo thinks that Romulus cannot track us.*

'They've just punished the priest,' Paul blurted out in his usual excitable manner.

What? Charm asked, alarmed.

'We saw him in the marketplace. They think we're dead.'

You are in the castle? Jasmine was horrified. *Get out of there!*

'We were hungry – but we're OK,' Peter tried to explain.

With Romulus there, you are not safe! He has other powers, and he will find you. Go down to the underground lake, and stay put for a couple of days. Michelle's going to come and get you.

They both looked at Michelle, who nodded. She started to say, *I'll be OK*, and then screamed: *Look out!*

A sudden rush of water, looking like a tidal wave compared to their small size, bashed into them. Paul had snatched the rock from Peter's grasp at Michelle's warning, before they both tumbled uncontrollably downwards. They were dragged almost to the exit and Peter failed to secure any kind of grip. He could think of nothing else but to increase his size and block the whole passage with his bulk.

Paul, desperately holding onto the Shankar for dear life with one paw, could only make weak attempts to grab with the other one. He crashed hard into the inflated badger. Peter looked down at the sheer drop from the castle wall, the water streaming out from underneath him forming a long waterfall to the river and jagged rocks below.

They had stopped just in time.

Slowly, the water drained sufficiently for them to ease back into the drain. They had tumbled all the way round to the back of the building. Their fur was covered in grime and they both reeked horribly.

'Thanks,' Paul remarked as they reached a relatively dry part.

'Don't mention it,' Peter snorted in disgust.

After the near-fatal experience in the drains, Peter and Paul decided that waiting on the roof was not bad. During the day they would just have to stay well-hidden – especially from any guards on duty on the higher walls. Peter slipped into one of many shadows from

the overhangs to hide and keep watch over the marketplace. He stayed small, his colour blending better into the shadows. After he was certain that there was no one around, he allowed himself a roll on the gravelled roof. The roughness of the stones scraped the larger tangles from his fur and stopped his desire to scratch at the horrid knots.

'I'd kill for a bath,' Paul said, following his example.

'My worst nightmare, but in this case so would I,' Peter admitted, looking down at the hardened clumps on his fur. 'In this case, maybe even a girly bubble-bath.'

Paul examined his reeking fur. 'I'm still hungry.'

Peter, however, was fighting an irresistible urge to lick himself and food was the last thing on his mind.

While they waited, Lord Killjoy appeared several times during the afternoon and early dusk. Each time, his routine was the same: he went to the centre of the square, fidgeted slightly, looked towards the main gates as if expecting something and then walked back thoughtfully – no sign of his earlier limp. They were both grateful to be separated from the evil man by the high wall.

Suddenly, Paul pointed towards the towers. 'Look.'

A man, another prisoner by the look of him and shackled around his hands and feet, was dragged out by several guards from the same tower in which they had been interrogated. He was emaciated and thin; long matted hair and a dirty beard covered his face and grew down to his chest. The heavy guard escort seemed oddly out of place. Occasionally he fought back and resisted them. Despite looking fragile compared to his captors, the guards kept a wary distance from the harmless-looking man.

He was hauled to the centre of the square and hosed down with water. The guards ordered him to scrub the filth off his body. Even at that distance, Peter was able to overhear their commands. Just then, Killjoy made one of his afternoon appearances and barked at the guards.

'What is he doing here? Why is he not washed and back yet?!'

The guard stuttered. 'A-a-apologies, my lord, b-but he was s-still resisting us.'

'Get him back down NOW, you idiot!' Lord Killjoy ordered.

Peter and Paul watched apprehensively as the man was dragged off to the other tower. There was nothing gentle about the way they manhandled him. Peter was conscious of the crowd, their suspicious eyes glued to the prisoner, but no one dared approach him. The badger inside fumed silently at such inhuman treatment.

Near dusk, trumpets sounded and the crowd below was galvanized into action. They were apprehensive and worried. The sound of their nervous laughter rose from the marketplace. They were *afraid*.

'What are they expecting?' Paul asked.

'My guess is, we're about to see the king,' Peter said, anger churning in his stomach. Although he was afraid of being caught, he had to get another look at the man – the resemblance to Uncle Ramsey had been too scary.

At the thought, violent animal passions gripped Peter, wanting to rip into something – anything – but particularly a man with a scar on his face. Peter lost track of time then, the memories of his fights, the biting, the pain and, best of all, the feeling when the enemy ran off – defeated and hurt.

The king had killed his father, and Peter could feel hatred burning inside him. He could feel himself losing his humanity. The badger inside was going to make Romulus pay, and it had nothing to do with justice.

It was *revenge*.

Paul, meanwhile, simply kept his eyes glued to the crowd. He chewed on his lower lip and his mouth frothed at the edges.

The trumpets sounded again, louder and closer, and brought their thoughts back to the square.

A procession entered and continued to the main towers. Initially, only foot soldiers with swords and spikes marched forward, but then some armoured knights on horseback entered, to the sound of genuine loud cheering. Eventually, an even louder cheer went up, and at the far end, two people on black horses entered the area, one horse much larger than the other. On the smaller one rode a raven-haired woman in silver armour,

but all of Peter's attention was focussed on the other rider.

The larger horse was ridden by a majestically arrogant man dressed all in black armour. The armour was exactly as Peter had remembered from his vision: a red crest was emblazoned clearly on left side; his armour interlaced in many places to allow perfect movement. On his head he wore a full plate helmet, and his golden visor, which was moulded into the face of a demon, was down.

King Romulus Blackheart.

It was all Peter could do to sit there, when what he really wanted was to go hurtling towards the man with only violence on his mind. He must have been growing in size, for he found an otter laying a restraining paw on him, reminding him of their situation.

'This probably isn't the best time. We can't take on an army. We need Michelle for that,' Paul said soberly, looking down at Peter's drawn claws.

Peter followed his gaze. 'You're right,' he whispered. The tension broke and the animal lust lifted. He wasn't the only one controlling himself. The smell of aggression rising from Paul was strong, too.

Peter glanced back to the marketplace. Romulus was getting off his horse and Lord Killjoy was on one knee before him. They seemed to be in an animated conversation, and at one point, it looked as if the king were about to strike his advisor. Slowly, however, he lowered his hand and threw his reins at a waiting soldier, who flinched. Romulus stormed off in the direction of the towers, leaving Killjoy on his knees.

Peter couldn't help but watch a bit longer. The raven-haired woman sauntered up to the kneeling man, obviously enjoying her superior position, before following the king. Peter lingered only long enough to see Lord Killjoy get up and start hissing orders at the guards.

The sun was setting, and darkness was fast approaching. The mining area was crawling with men searching the bushes. Peter didn't fancy having to dodge that many guards.

'Well, this is as good a time as any to creep back down through the prison area, ' he said.

Paul simply nodded.

Peter raced down the stairs, feeling an immense frustration. Even if Romulus didn't know it, Peter knew that the king had been talking about them: the Changelings.

They headed down the spiral staircase. At the door to the prison chamber, they waited for an opportunity to dash through the grate. The guards were all laughing and joking about it being a rough day, arguing over who would be on duty for the morning, when the king would come down there. Peter saw no one in the main chamber, but he could hear a guard starting to descend the stairs.

'It's now or never.'

He climbed through, Paul nudging him on. Peter could sense that the washroom was occupied, and raced through the metal bars and into the prisoners' corridor. He quickly went past all the moaning until he had led them into complete darkness.

His senses told him the penultimate cell in the corridor was empty, but an odd smell lingered in it, forcing him to go further. He was sure he glimpsed a body in the cell through the grate as he went past. It was only when they had got to the last cell and Peter was certain it was empty that he dared to go in.

'What was all that about?' Paul whispered.

'Someone was inside, and I didn't want to say anything.'

'I didn't see anyone.'

In the corridor, the voices of the guards rose in excitement.

'That's bad, ' Paul whispered. 'They're catching rats now.'

'I don't think it's rats they're after,' Peter said flatly. 'We'll go when they're asleep.'

'It's not exactly the Ritz,' Paul sniffed, commenting on their dark surroundings, when his nose bumped into some hanging metal, making it chime.

'Peter!' he hissed. 'This whole cell is chained!'

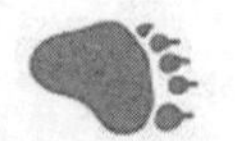

Chapter 15

CHAINS COVERED EVERY PART OF THE CELL

Chains covered every part of the cell. The walls, the floor and even the ceiling were covered, and inside, hanging in the middle, was another cage made from the same material, forming yet another chamber. Padlocks hung open on the small entrance into the inner chamber. It was a prison within a prison.

Outside, guards were shouting urgently and strapping on their swords. Peter sensed eight of them.

'They've found us!' Paul whispered, ready to go out and meet them, growing to his full adult size.

'Wait!' Peter whispered. 'Let's get them in here. They can only come through one at time. Between the two of us…' he left the rest unsaid and took up his position on the side of the door.

'They could be coming to lock the door on us. Peter, we can't get out of here – not through those chains!' Paul exclaimed, his eyes wide with fright.

He was right. The mesh was too fine.

The guards sounded terrifyingly close to Peter. Their steps echoed and boomed in the corridor.

'Let's get into the corridor,' he suggested. 'Stay small and wait. We can rush at them at the last minute.'

Paul didn't answer. He was too pumped up with adrenaline and ready for a fight.

They crept out, sticking to the shadows. The guards shambled into the corridor a little uncertainly. Peter could smell their fear, and knew they were egging each other on.

'Bring a torch!' one grunted. 'We'll show him a thing or two!'

As they approached, Peter and Paul crouched lower and lower, until their stomachs were level with the floor, ready to pounce. Peter felt his heartbeat speed up and something more primeval rising – a fury, a burning desire to lash out, to smash anything between him and freedom. He was convinced the guards wouldn't even react before the two of them would get through. He crouched lower, ready for a powerful rush.

The guards stopped outside the strange-smelling cell, the one with the silent occupant. One of them brought out the keys.

The scent of their fear and aggression was overpowering. 'Get ready,' the guard said roughly. 'If it moves…'

Peter. Are you there?

It was a call. Peter flattened himself against the wall. No! No! Of all the times to get one! He was scared of being heard and giving away their position, although he wanted to answer, he pushed the thought away. Staying silent, he forced himself into pretending he was made of stone. Paul did likewise. They felt the tingle fade but they stayed wary, just in case it returned.

The guards gathered around the other door, their weapons drawn, highly agitated and scared.

'His Majesty wants to see you. Give us any trouble and we start hacking. Do you understand, filth?' The guard inside the cell spoke loudly and with false bravado. The Changelings heard locks being opened and chains moved aside, followed by the sound of shackles being put on. By now, all the guards had entered the small cell.

Peter concentrated but couldn't see anything. He heard a small grunt followed by the sound of a guard hitting someone and making him grunt harder. They dragged the prisoner out and surrounded him in the corridor.

Peter expected him to be bigger.

They hauled the man to his feet, and two of them, armed with spikes, prodded him forward. It seemed like ages before they managed to leave the corridor and started to climb the small stairway in the main chamber. From the entrance came the unmistakable silky-smooth voice of Lord Killjoy.

'His majesty is waiting for you.'

There was something evil and cruel in the sound of that voice. Peter reined himself in. He didn't like it, and the badger within, was only just being controlled. A deep fury rose at the treatment of the shackled man. Badgers didn't do that to their own kind!

Peter heard the shackled prisoner shuffle forward, closely followed by all eight of the guards. 'Now's our chance!' he whispered.

In the dark stillness, Peter's whiskers picked up the movements in the air created by Paul's nodding. He twitched them to stop them tickling.

They started down the corridor, and again Peter found the same odd smell haunting the vacated cell. It was so odd that he felt compelled to have a quick peek in the chamber.

'What're you *doing*?' Paul asked frantically, trying to pull him back out. 'Have you lost your mind? They'll be back soon!'

'Yes, I know, but there is something very strange here.'

'I can't smell anything, other than unwashed bodies. *Ugh!*' He snorted in disgust. 'Otters need to be clean. Make it fast, for Pete's sake!'

The cell turned out to be exactly like the one they had just left. There were fine chains all over, forming an inner cage. The guards had unlocked the padlocks on the interlaced entrance. An empty plate lay in the centre of the room and there was a bucket to the side, which stank.

Apart from that, there was nothing.

'There's nothing here. Let's *go*.' Paul nudged Peter from behind.

Peter just couldn't quite place the smell. It bothered him, but he reluctantly agreed.

A solitary guard was busy clearing up in the other chamber and the washroom was open. That was all the opportunity they needed and they were off. Peter dived for the opening he knew was there – and almost bounced straight into the wall. The drain had been filled with stones and the buckets smelt awful.

Paul panicked. 'Oh my god! Peter, what're we gonna do?'

'Back up. The other washrooms – they can't all be filled in.' Peter couldn't think of anything else to say. *Why fill the holes if they think we're dead?*

They raced out, but had to wait for a man and a woman to vacate the next chamber before checking the drains. They could hear the couple's voices trail off.

'Those filthy Changelings! Romulus should have fixed them,' the woman was saying.

'Careful. That's "his majesty" to you and me,' replied the man.

The voices faded away and Peter peeked in before diving through the drain hole, which was open this time. He didn't stop until they got to the underground lake and jumped straight in. He was followed by a more elegant splash.

'I thought we'd never get out of that horrible place!' Paul said.

'Nor me.'

'We could've died when Jasmine called us in the corridor. Everyone in the world could hear that,' Paul grumbled and then looked at him as if listening, adding as an afterthought. 'You should.'

'Should what?'

'Call them.'

'How did you – ?' Peter started.

'I don't know. I just did.' Paul was far too occupied to answer him seriously.

'Otters! You're so easily distracted by H_2O,' Peter teased as he prepared himself by thinking invisible thoughts. He closed his eyes and cloaked his mental image with air, concentrating on the image of Jasmine. He picked up the magical stone from where Paul had dropped it – and hit a grey blank wall. He tried again and again.

Nothing!

He was just putting it down, dropping his mental image, when the picture of the guards dragging the prisoner along the corridor slipped into his mind.

Immediately, his mind flew through the ground and the walls above, finally coming to a stop above a thin man, who was on the ground and bleeding badly from the face. He was in the Shankar hall, and the glowing stone pulsed with a blood-red light. Peter couldn't remember it beating like that.

Lord Killjoy, in the throes of his demonic persona, hovered menacingly over the man. Sitting behind him was a bored, dark-

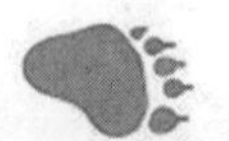

haired Romulus, the golden mask nowhere in sight, his sculpted features revealed and tainted only by the scar on the left side of his face. The raven-haired woman stood next to him, her eyes feasting on the tortured man, her hair almost alive and her cloak moving of its own accord.

The prisoner's head snapped up, turning this way and that. He sensed Peter and in a horrible voice pleaded, 'Ebo, help me…'

'It's no good calling for Ebo. They are gone – hidden by your co-conspirators,' Lord Killjoy informed him, viciously taunting the broken man.

'Ebo, help me!' the prisoner begged again.

'You have no one. They have all left.'

The man didn't respond.

'Oh, I almost forgot, we did have some visitors – friends of yours, I think. Unfortunately their visit was cut short by the Dragon's Breath. Pity.' Lord Killjoy seemed genuinely disappointed.

As his words hit home, the prisoner screamed and lunged at the king's counsellor, reaching out for the man's throat with his skeletal fingers.

A glowing red flame leapt from Killjoy's hands and struck the man, hurling him backwards.

King Romulus yawned in the background and crossed one leg over the other.

'Pull his brains out through his nostrils and ask him again. If he still refuses to speak, let him go.'

'But sire – he will die.'

'One hears this time and time again – it's *soo* tedious.' Romulus sighed dramatically. 'Death is so clichéd. Give One another line to work with.'

The raven-haired woman draped an arm around Romulus's shoulders. 'We *should* kill him,' she suggested, her voice slippery and insidious. 'Slowly.'

'Pari, you really should broaden your activities, my dear,' he responded, twisting a long velvety strand of her hair around his finger, 'otherwise One gets *sooo* jaded.'

Peter couldn't think clearly. Rage welled up inside him, and

he felt like striking them. He didn't want to leave; he wanted desperately to help this tortured creature, and lash out at his enemies.

What are you doing? Peter thought, trying to remind himself about not letting his mind wander. He was hovering in a dangerous place and the only thing saving him was the fact that three of the people in the hall were not aware of him – only the prisoner!

Peter felt Paul's hand descending on the stone, wanting to join the call.

Instantly, Killjoy flinched and looked down at his balled fists as the red glow flared. 'Someone is listening outside.'

That snapped Peter out of the spell and he was transported back to the cavern. He couldn't open his eyes fast enough, the sudden fright gave his whole body a jolt.

'That wasn't Jasmine!' Paul said accusingly.

'No. I – I accidentally stumbled into the Shankar hall…' Peter said, his voice trailing off uncertainly.

'That wasn't good!' Paul shook his head. One glimpse had been enough for him. 'If they were who I think they were… Are you *nuts?* What were you doing, staying so long?' Paul was ranting, now, his usual playfulness gone. 'They could've *seen* you! They would come looking for us after that! *Then* what would we do?'

Paul was right; he hadn't thought things through. 'I'm sorry. I should've come straight back.'

The otter's anger evaporated and he let out an exasperated sigh. 'OK. I probably would've done the same. So what happened? What'd you hear?'

'We're dead, apparently. And they think we're related to the prisoner,' Peter said, thinking back. 'And he's a friend of Ebo's.'

'How d'you know?'

'Because he thought that's who *I* was,' Peter confessed.

'We've got to warn Ebo. What was that in Killjoy's hand? I saw it flare as I tried to join you,' Paul said excitedly.

Peter remembered the flame of red light. 'He was holding Lal Shankars. Those stones are evil.'

'You could use the one down there,' Paul suggested, looking at the lake, then adding: 'Just don't fall into it this time.'

'I won't. I'm more careful now,' Peter said, noting the sceptical glance Paul flicked in his direction. 'Besides, I can't hold my breath as long as you.'

With that, he dived in, changing into a badger in mid-air. Ahead of him was something darker, and sleeker in the water.

Show-off! he thought, as he watched Paul effortlessly outstrip him.

In the middle of the lake, they both took a deep breath. Peter had to remain focussed knowing well where he could end up if he didn't, especially with the sort of power that was below them.

Conjuring up his invisible image, Peter plunged straight down, trying to give himself the best chance of contact. As he came closer, he reached out with his paw. Because he was approaching directly over the top of the buried stone, Peter was able to glimpse straight into the rest of it. The fracture lines were bright, now, and seemed almost to form a curled-up shape of some kind, but there was a big piece missing from the top.

Contact.

The images of Jasmine and his mother mingled as he tried to concentrate on a single person. He felt tempted to call his mother, but at the last instant, his need to get out of Castle Craven was more immediate. The image of Jasmine cleared and so did his conflict.

His mind's eye rushed over the heads of hundreds of people at fantastic speed, only slowing when he approached a large fireplace where various people were gathered. Jasmine stood with her back to him, her hands extended over large clay pots with boiling liquid in them.

Jasmine.

Peter? She sounded shocked.

I don't have much time, but we're back in the underground cave, Peter said, concentrating on thinking straightforward sentences. Although he felt detached, he could still feel his powerful badger body holding onto his breath. His fur felt strange as it swayed from side to side in the water.

Thank the Maker. I will get the Shaman. Stay there.

I can't wait that long, Peter thought.

Michelle, who had been standing to the side, looked up

suddenly, and in Peter's mind she became real. 'Peter,' she said, raising one contemptuous eyebrow, 'you look like a prat.'

Her remark made Peter laugh, and all the air exploded out of him. People turned in his direction, just as the contact broke and he was dragged to the surface by a vigilant otter. They broke surface laughing and gulping for air.

'She's right! You should check out the Hawaiian dance your fur does in the water!' Paul sniggered.

It was not long after they swam ashore that they felt the icy tingle of the call. Paul dropped the stone into Peter's outstretched palm.

Jasmine, Ebo, Charm, Michelle and the Shaman were there. The Shaman sat cross-legged, gripping a large green Shankar stone, his face was calm but showed deep lines of concentration.

Good to see you.

Ebo's response was measured, but his lips curled up at the corners, for once giving away his feelings of relief.

I thought I told you to stay out of the Castle, Jasmine chastised them, her concern turning to anger.

Easy. Ebo laid a restrain arm on her. *It was a brave thing you did for us, and I am glad to see you are both unharmed.*

'We were hungry, and when we couldn't find anything here, we went up to get some food,' Peter explained. He told them everything, up to King Romulus appearing at dusk.

So he is back, Ebo said, nodding thoughtfully. *You will have to be more careful now. He has awesome powers through the Lal. I suspect that he does not completely know how to control a lot of them. Michelle here is fully healed and –*

'Ebo,' Peter interrupted, 'a member of your Clan is imprisoned here.'

You are wrong. There are no Clan members in their prison, Ebo replied emphatically, his full attention on Peter.

'No. He knew you. And he called out for you.'

There are no Clan members in that castle anymore. Who is this man anyway? How did you meet him? Ebo sounded very concerned.

'Well, I tried to call Jasmine earlier,' Peter began, 'only I came up with a blank. I tried several times, and then as I was about to

break contact when I accidentally thought of this prisoner we'd seen, and there I was, in the hall with Romulus and Killjoy.'

You were with ***whom****? They will know!* Jasmine was horrified.

Charm gasped, and even the Shaman flinched.

Romulus – did he see you? Ebo eyes were so intense and severe, his eyebrows knotted so hard that straight lines stood out between them.

'No. But the prisoner did,' Peter said.

What prisoner? Ebo said, exasperated.

'The prisoner they were questioning,' Peter answered. His frustration was beginning to get the better of him.

Why were they questioning him? Ebo asked.

'I don't know!' Peter practically yelled at the leader, 'but he looked straight up at me and said "Ebo". And then the woman said -'

There was a woman in the room? Ebo asked, not even bothering to hide his astonishment this time.

Raven-haired? Jasmine whispered.

'Yes, that's her.'

Pariah Paine. Ebo spoke softly.

'She said that they should kill him as he didn't know anything.' Peter was relieved to get the story out at last.

Stay where you are. There was a haunted look about Ebo. With that he touched the Shaman and broke contact.

'But –' Peter started to say.

Paul gave him a quirky wide otter smile. 'Nothing more I can do. I'm going for a swim. Coming?'

He didn't bother waiting for a reply as he did a double flip and disappeared in the water.

'No. You go ahead,' Peter said preoccupied. Something bothered him about Ebo's manner. Something wasn't quite right.

Paul came back after a while. They waited and grew bored, and eventually they curled up in their furs, and slept.

A faint whisper woke him.

Peter.

He came awake fast, reaching for the rock in Paul's open paw.

It was Ebo, looking drained, with Jasmine, Michelle and Charm.

There is no one from the Clan inside the castle, Ebo stated. He sounded tired.

That's not what you said earlier, Michelle accused loudly.

I know what I said, and I was wrong to say it, Ebo replied through tight lips.

Peter, Michelle began, *he thought–*

No! Ebo's command was that of a leader and a parent. *We have to get Peter and Paul out of there.*

'What?' Paul shouted it out.

Peter looked from Jasmine to Michelle to Ebo. Ebo took a deep breath.

For a moment, I thought that maybe one of your parents was still alive. But even if he had been, he is no longer.

'What? How – how do you know that?' Peter stumbled over his words. He wasn't about to be told twice that someone he loved had died.

The Shaman and I have searched the whole castle. If a person we knew had been alive, with the power of the Shankar, it would have taken us to him, Ebo explained. *The person must be a Rumanni.*

'But why – ?' Peter started to object.

But nothing! We have searched all night. We would have found him, if he had been alive. Ebo's face dropped, the eyes became soulful. *That woman is called Pariah Paine. She likes to torture. She has killed many* – he changed his mind on what he was about to say – *things. If she wanted to execute him, then there is no one there who would have stopped her. Not even the king.*'

Peter had barely controlled his nature the first time he was told such a thing and he would definitely not do it twice without a fight. 'But maybe you haven't searched hard enough,' he demanded, hanging on desperately to this thread of renewed hope.

Yes, we have! Ebo sounded furious.

The badger growled.

Now. Griphand will bring Michelle to where she can come and get you. There are too many patrols to get very close, but you have to get to the surface.

'But that means you will be seen by the Sight if Michelle isn't

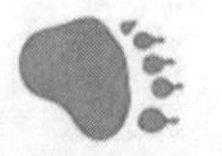

with you,' Paul butted in.

Ebo nodded thoughtfully. *Yes, that is right, but it is a chance we have to take. We are in the mountains. They will not be able to penetrate this far, especially near water. Griphand will need the protection from the Sight more than we will. He insisted on being up all night, and he needs to be alert for this journey. Can you hold out for another day?* Ebo asked in a weary voice.

Peter was silent.

'Of course we can,' Paul answered, glancing furtively at Peter.

I'll catch you later, Michelle said with one of her predatory smiles.

With that, they were gone.

'Peter, I'm thinking – you're thinking – what I think you're thinking…?'

Peter merely smiled.

'You *are* thinking what I think you're thinking!' Paul exclaimed.

Chapter 16

'WE'VE GOT A DAY TO KILL'

'We've got a day to kill, ' Peter said. 'Besides, they'll never know,'

'No, we haven't! And they will!' Paul grumbled, his worst fears confirmed. 'We have to stay right here. Ebo can't be wrong…'

Yet the doubt was clear in Paul's voice.

'And if he is?'

That did it.

'But – they would've found him.' It was a feeble reply and even Paul didn't believe his own words.

'We have to try for ourselves,' Peter suggested, and then a thought struck him. 'How about from right here? Like the last time?'

Paul immediately brightened at the suggestion, and retrieved the Shankar. 'No heroics. If you end up in a strange place, it's right back here,' he said, pointing to the ground.

A feeling in the pit of his stomach nagged at Peter, and for a moment he didn't say anything.

'No heroics. Not one,' Paul demanded again.

'OK, OK. Not one. Got it.'

Closing his eyes, Peter prepared his mind and recalled the image of the man's eyes, his overgrown beard, the pain in his voice. He nodded to let Paul know that he was ready. The dead weight of the stone felt cold as it dropped into his hand, his stomach tightened in readiness for the mental flight –

Blank. Nothing.

He concentrated again, trying to recall the features of the man more clearly: the long, matted hair, the torn clothes, even his treatment by the guards. He tried to recall every detail to help him focus just on the man.

Nothing!

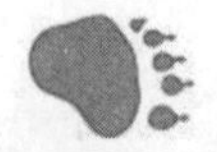

Disappointed, he tried again, concentrating even harder, holding his eyes tightly shut. He had been so convinced that he would find him again. He dropped his concentration and thought of Paul and what he would say if he suggested going up to have a quick look.

In his mind's eye Peter seemed to be hovering above his real body and looking down on Paul. The otter sensed his presence and rolled his eyes heavenwards.

'I thought I said come straight back into your body!'

Peter wasn't listening. It was the weirdest sensation, floating above yourself. He couldn't feel the temperature, just a pleasant coolness and a constant but gentle pull from his body.

Really cool. Surreal.

He could see the odd mixture of badger paws for feet up to the knees, some human leg followed by more badger in the midriff. He looked strange – but good! You wouldn't mess with that on a dark night. He opened his eyes with a sigh.

'You know, for a moment I really believed I'd find him again.'

He was unable to hide his disappointment. He would do anything to get their parents back.

'I believed you would, too,' Paul said as he laid a consoling hand on his shoulders. 'Listen: he *must* be dead. Ebo must be right.'

'Something doesn't make sense, though.'

'How do you mean?'

'About him being a Rumanni. Why would he call out for Ebo? These people hate the Clan,' Peter observed. He had to be sure. He had to be certain, no matter what. 'I'm going back up,' he said, coming to a decision.

'I know. Besides, there might be some more food up there,' Paul replied, smiling.

Peter smiled back. He hadn't wanted to go alone, but he didn't want to ask.

'Race you up?' said the otter.

The badger wasn't about to ignore a challenge. He expertly flicked the stone to Paul, who caught it in his mouth and was already heading towards the tunnels.

★

When they got to the small cave, just below the sewer, Peter suggested making another attempt to contact the man. Paul was all for it.

Blank.

It was just a grey fog – nothing at all. No sensation whatsoever. Peter concentrated on the image of the man. His desperation to find him had grown on the way up, convinced that Ebo had been right – the Rumanni had a different attitude to life, and they were more than capable of killing a prisoner.

He didn't know who this prisoner was, but even if there was a slim chance that he was one of their parents, Peter had to find out. He was missing from home, his mother was probably frantic, his father had probably been killed by Romulus and now he was being asked to give up the only chance of doing something good.

He wanted to add more than a scar to Romulus's face.

'Just one of us should go,' he said to Paul. 'I'll just take a quick look and come right back, OK?'

'I'll be here. Call me the minute anything happens,' Paul insisted.

Peter prepared his mind, took the Shankar in his mouth and set off. He had to wait for two chattering women to drain their buckets before dashing through the washroom and down the spiral staircase. His fear of being caught added an extra sharpness to his senses.

Getting across the main chamber was easy. Peter squeezed through the bars and stole into the prisoners' corridor. He found the stone choking him when he became too small – if only the stone could grow and shrink with him!

The first few cells were occupied and the odours were horrible – Rumanni. He decided it must be something they ate. The moans, grunts and coughs of the other prisoners grew louder, but Peter was interested only in the penultimate chamber.

Apprehensive and nervous, his breathing shallow, he realized he was afraid of finding someone in there. On the other hand – or paw as it was now – he was also afraid of *not* finding someone there. He had to know.

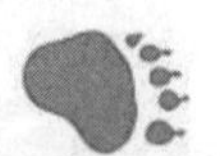

The door was closed. Silently he grew into an adult-sized badger and peered through the bars at the window.

Empty.

Inside the cell, it was dark. As he leaned on the door, it swung open a little. Not locked! He quickly pulled the door ajar, stepped inside and quietly closed it behind him.

The fine chain netting hung away from the walls, the interlaced opening in the cage in front of him was open. The strange salty smell of the previous occupant still lingered. He transformed into a human and stepped through the chain entrance.

The bucket and plate were gone, but the chains on the far wall were still there. All the padlocks were open and the cell was deserted.

He dropped the Shankar from his mouth, cupped his hands on the rock and concentrated. He wanted to let Paul know that he was on the way back; that he'd been wrong.

It felt like he had struck a blank wall.

He concentrated.

Still nothing.

Peter suddenly felt a terrible urgency to get back.

Could they have caught Paul?

He tried to calm down, and set off back to where he had left Paul. He paused at the bars to the main chamber before sneaking past. Through the open doorway he saw that the hole in the washroom was unblocked. It was the fastest way back and Peter took it.

He couldn't understand why Paul would've gone somewhere else. The thought panicked him, and he was soon back in the main drains. He rounded the corner – and there was Paul, waiting for him.

Peter let out a sigh of relief.

'Did you find him?' Paul asked excitedly, coming up from a crouching attack position. There were bits of meat and bread in front of him. 'I thought you'd be hungry when you got back,' he said, smiling that wide otter grin of his.

So that was it! He had gone somewhere else and Peter had been concentrating on the exact place he had left him!

'There was no one there. The cell was empty,' Peter said, tucking in. He could see the disappointment in the slight slump of Paul's furry black shoulders. 'All the padlocks – everything was open. Including the hole in the washroom – that's why I came back that way.'

'What do we do now?'

'Now we wait for Michelle.'

Back on the sandy shores of the underground lake, Peter went into the shallow water to cool off, but Paul dived straight in again. Splashing and shouting, he went further and further into the middle, enjoying himself. He disappeared for a long periods, re-emerging in a different place. Peter watched, his stomach growling. He knew what his stomach wanted – worms, mainly – but he tried to ignore the images.

Yuck!

Neither Paul nor Peter bothered changing from their animal forms most of the time now, and they were acquiring a finer control over their changes when they did make them. Peter felt as if he was only now truly discovering his powers.

Watching Paul frolic in the lake, it was clear that he was certainly having fun and could not keep away from the water. He was a bit of a scatty otter, really. Several times he had come out only to go straight back in without saying a word. He seemed fascinated by the water, almost as if he were seeing it for the first time.

Suddenly, Paul popped up and shouted to Peter from the middle of the lake.

'Peter! Come and have a look! I started to clear the area around the Shankar. Come on!' Paul was so excited that he could barely contain his enthusiasm as he tried to drag Peter into the water.

'OK, I'm coming! What is it?' Peter was shouting at the top of his badger voice, but Paul was already on the way back.

In the middle of the lake, Peter took a deep breath and dived. The light from below was much brighter than last time. Peter followed Paul down, concentrating on the sleek flippers. He caught glimpses of what Paul had been up to all that time.

Sand was piled high in places and the stone had fallen over onto its side. It was enormous. Paul swam off to one side, revealing the whole Shankar.

It lay on its side. The lines Peter had originally thought were fractures were in fact the edges of a gigantic dragon etched inside the rock, its wings folded on its back. Except for the fact that part of the head was missing, it looked real.

The lines burned bright, and molten lava flowed through the etching, complete and perfect down to the last fine detail. The claws, the scales; the fluctuation in colour; the open mouth, the set of the teeth… It looked dangerous – even as a mere etching.

Several times Peter went up for air, going down each time to inspect it in greater detail. Eventually, needing rest, he collapsed back on the sand, breathing hard from his exertions. It was almost a complete dragon. What did it mean?

Peter.

The whisper brought him out of his thoughts quickly. He retrieved the green Shankar from the sand. Jasmine was there with Ebo, the Shaman and Michelle.

Where is Paul? Jasmine asked, alarmed.

'Having a swim,' Peter replied and everyone visibly relaxed. The last thing Peter needed was for Paul to blurt out he'd been to the castle again.

Michelle and Griphand will be setting off soon, so as to arrive just before dusk, Ebo explained. *I am glad to see that you have stayed at the lake,* he added, smiling for once.

'It was the only safe thing to do,' Peter replied. He didn't see any reason to say anything else. After all, the cell had turned out to be empty.

How quickly can you get to the surface safely? Ebo asked.

'No time at all. Where do you want us?'

The dining hall roof. From what you said last time, the Rumanni have no reason to guard that building heavily, and they would not have moved into it by now. They will still be expecting to recapture our children again. The jaw muscles on his face stood out starkly.

Peter could see the ghostly outline of Paul coming out of the

water towards them. He needed to end the conversation quickly, well aware that Paul would probably want to join the call, and then might say something unnecessarily. 'OK, I'll tell Paul. Michelle, see you soon, but keep yourself as small as possible until the last minute,' Peter advised.

Don't worry. Two little weasels shouldn't be a problem.

'Fine. We'll be on the roof waiting,' Peter said, rushing to close the call. With that he lifted his hand and opened his eyes.

'Ebo?' Paul enquired.

Peter nodded, relieved, and filled him in on the plan.

'What were you doing all that time?' Peter asked, curious as to why Paul had stayed in the water so long.

'I gathered all the big shards together. The dragon's almost complete. There's a large piece missing with part of the jaw and an eye, but the rest is all there. And Peter?' There was something odd in Paul's voice. 'I swear that dragon's not in the same position.'

'It's a *rock*,' Peter sighed. 'You've been underwater too long.'

They reached the dining hall roof as the day was drawing to a close. A brilliant red sun was going down behind the mountains as Peter crouched in the shadows. He glanced back to the two nearest towers, one leading to the red Shankar hall.

'There she is!' Paul said, pointing to something tiny in the sky.

The feeling at the back of Peter's mind was nagging him again.

Something about the towers…

He tried hard to remember, but all he could see was the flash of red when Michelle was first hit by something from one of them.

An image of two weasels cowering in the shadows came strongly into Peter's mind, making him look up. The hawk seemed tiny at that distance.

She seemed to hover for a moment. He could feel the sheer determination behind the vision, and then she was ready to get them. She went into a vertical drop that made Peter's stomach lurch.

'Did you feel *that*?' Paul said anxiously, trying to disappear into the wall. 'I hope she remembers we're her friends!'

The dive was spectacular: almost a vertical drop – more of an

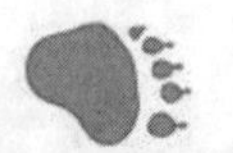

attack then a rescue – levelling off at the last moment. And she wasn't just showing off. Michelle grew fast in size as she closed the distance, ready to snatch them.

Peter and Paul moved out of their hiding place onto the main empty part of the roof. Paul had his eyes tightly closed, and Peter wanted to do the same, but a part of him needed to see everything.

Somewhere below, an alarm sounded and was soon joined by others. All of Peter's instincts screamed for him to run and hide from the terrifying predator descending with such incredible speed. When Peter couldn't control his nature any longer he closed his eyes just as a huge set of talons plucked him from the roof. Suddenly there was nowhere for his paws to go.

Their stomachs jumped into their throats as Michelle went into a steep climb, still flying silently. Her speed alone lifted them swiftly into the air before her powerful wings began to beat.

There was more screaming and shouting from below, but it quickly faded. It was replaced by the sound of rushing air and the pounding of powerful wings. Peter couldn't help but wonder about his situation, and he tentatively opened one eye.

Immediately, he wished he hadn't. An animal generally only got that kind of view when he was about to be somebody's meal.

He couldn't help himself and swore. His mother wouldn't have been happy – but then, she wasn't hanging from a hawk's talons hundreds of feet in the air.

The ground receded rapidly as they headed away from the castle, and arrows came up at them in slow motion, dropping before they reached their targets.

Peter didn't want to contemplate falling from this height, but he had never been clutched in a set of talons before, with nothing but air below him. His mind was spinning at the thought: the awful drop and then the sudden impact.

He became aware of Paul, who had been squealing for some time. Paul still had his eyes tightly closed and he continued to wail.

By this time, the two side towers were getting smaller, and a welcoming river in front of them began to come into view.

'Toughen up, boys,' something squawked above them, followed by a choking sound that Peter assumed was Michelle's laughter.

Below them, in the distance, a giant of a man stood at the tiller of a boat, waving at them. Peter spied mounted guards racing out of the castle after them, and sensed the other dark things moving in the woods below.

The sun was disappearing over the horizon, along with its protection, and the shadows began to stretch and race towards the trees. Dark shapes with flickering eyes flitted from tree to tree.

If he fell now, it would be worse than anything.

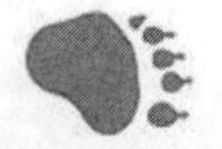

Chapter 17

TRAVELLING BY AIR WAS OVERRATED

Travelling by air was overrated. Michelle descended slower than she wanted because she was trying to be sensitive to her cargo's feelings. From the noises they were making, they didn't appreciate the gesture. Peter even suspected that this might be fun for Michelle by the squawks and trills she made on her way down.

He could see horsemen racing hard towards the boat, which was quite near but close to some woods in which the shadows moved. Occasionally he caught the glinting flash of ivory teeth. A shudder ran through him.

Dusk was when this land transformed.

Michelle banked and went into a shallow glide to land. Something warty and with stunted wings suddenly jumped out from the branches and tried to bite them, but the sunlight hit it first. It screamed in agony as its body caught fire and fell. The last rays of the sun still danced on the creature's flaming body before it dragged itself back into the shadows.

Michelle dropped them on the deck of the boat before transforming and coming to a running stop herself. Peter thumped onto the wood and rolled, grateful to touch anything firm. He instinctively transformed to his part-animal, part-human form. Paul was still lying on the floor, holding on tight and kissing it.

Charm and Jasmine rushed forward and passed them a rope that ran all the way along the boat. Gratefully, they grabbed it, twisting it round their wrists just as the boat lurched forward. Arrows began peppering the boat from the shore.

'Hold tight, everyone!' Griphand shouted.

'Glad to have you back!' Jasmine said, relieved.

The sun finally disappeared and darkness fell.

Behind them they could hear screaming. Swords clashed with unseen things; the arrows stopped abruptly and Peter could hear panic-stricken orders: 'Fall back!'

The boat picked up speed while the magic runners unfurled and filled the sails. They sped away upriver, all other noises quickly drowned out by the rushing of air. Darkness had descended completely by the time the mountains started to grow in the distance.

'The Mighty Mountains!' shouted Griphand, pointing, his enormous bulk jiggling with the gesture.

The mountains rose majestically, high enough for clouds to form around their snow-covered peaks. The temperature was dropping and they were now travelling perceptibly uphill, cutting their way into the valley. By the time they levelled off, the strain showed on Griphand; he was sweating, his great knuckles stood out white in the torchlight.

'I must get more exercise,' he muttered to himself.

His trousers sinking lower and his great bulk held up only by his own will, Griphand turned the boat from the main river and brought it to a stop in a small basin where other smaller craft were moored.

Torches danced in the darkness, trailing down like snakes from the mouth of a large cave. People were coming out to greet them, and a dozen armed Clansmen, led by Ebo, arrived to escort them back.

Two of the men went to aid Griphand, who was still standing, transfixed, to his tiller. He accepted their help gratefully, and each took an arm and wrapped it round their shoulders, hoisting him up. Determined not to accept defeat, but failing miserably, they yelled for assistance.

Lifting Griphand was not a task for the weak-willed!

They marched quickly to the cave's heavily guarded entrance and crossed a makeshift plank bridge which stretched over a trench of water. Inside, the enormous cave throbbed with life. Hundreds of Clanspeople were gathered there, all of different origins, but

united in joy. The sound of rushing water, the smells of cooking mingled with body odours, the hustle and bustle all made it seem as if the Clan had been there forever. Stalagmites and stalactites stood guard everywhere, their white limestone shimmering in the flickering firelight. Drawings on the wall gave the place an ancient feel.

Peter found his senses reaching out to all corners of the cave, reacting in a different way than when he was in danger. His senses seemed to glide in and out of the place, alternating between what he could smell and what he could hear: one moment sharply focussed and the next roaming the length and breadth of the cave. His head buzzed with the effort to keep up with all the bits of conversations, the snapshots of images, the different fragrances in the air.

Not unlike my Book, he thought.

Even the Shaman surprised them by coming to greet them. 'Foolish, blood and damnation!' he said, shaking his dreadlocks. 'Like the fathers and the mother, the sons and the daughter...'

As they sat down, Ebo came over with Ginger. She gave them a wide grin and went to hug her mother. 'My deepest thanks to you three, and not just from me but from everyone here,' Ebo said, glancing around.

Peter turned and noticed the warm looks everyone was giving them. Their gratitude was obvious.

Michelle nudged him and whispered: 'Super-hero.'

'I'm just an animal,' Peter growled, turning and drifting away just as a man came up.

'Ebo,' he said. 'It's time. The council has gathered.'

While the Clansmen attended their council, the three Changelings wandered through the Sanctuary Cave. Heading back to Jasmine's dwelling, they stumbled into a dark section that Michelle hadn't explored earlier. They heard chanting that was similar to what Peter and Paul had heard in the mines. Worried, Peter crept forward to investigate; darkness was never a problem for him.

The Shaman sat cross-legged and was chanting into a shallow pot of liquid that hung over a small fire. Peter couldn't help but reach out with his senses – the chant drew him in, and yet the

vibrations altered everything. He felt faint, and his vision was slammed by images the Shaman conjured.

Romulus Blackheart strode towards the doors to the Lal Shankar hall. The guards barely pushed them open in time before the king's cloak brushed past the bowed heads.

'Is the bloody spell ready or are you as incompetent as your servant?' The king crossed the hall in a few strides, and stood towering over a ghoulish figure.

Lord Killjoy blanched. 'I shall be meticulous, sire.'

'Harm the little ones and our pet project will be completed by you and your priesthood,' Romulus said, looking lovingly towards the Lal Shankar.

'I have prepared the charm as Dread had taught me – melding their old ways with ours, making the charm strong enough to reach them in the mountains.'

'And more selectively destructive?'

'Of course, sire.'

'Splendid. Dread – what an idiot. Believed anything you told him. Even We do not believe what you tell Us.'

'Sire, I wouldn't dream of –'

'We are bored. Find Our helpers, Killjoy. Preferably yesterday.'

Abruptly, the vision ended, and darkness descended on Peter, who was perspiring heavily. Michelle and Paul supported him as they dragged him away from the Shaman's domain as fast as they could.

In the morning, Peter kept his eyes closed. He was aware that Paul and Michelle, wrapped up in their animal forms next to him, were also awake. The most gorgeous cinnamon and herbal smells floated through the place, and Peter didn't need his eyes to track the aroma back to the fireplace.

'I know you are awake,' Jasmine said, without turning.

'The Dragon's Breath is not a problem at this distance,' Ebo was arguing as Peter dragged himself up and sat down heavily on an empty log.

'Malshees, Ebo! From the Hawk, you heard it: the bloody

Shankar's nearly half-complete. That is sufficient, even with their Boom-Basa incompetence; they can reach us with their filthy Dragon's Breath!' The Shaman's one eye bulged with passion.

'Conjurings *you* taught them –'

'Excuse me, sir,' Peter interrupted, 'but what exactly is the Dragon's Breath?'

'Damnation! Do you not know anything, boy?' The Shaman's contempt was obvious. He seemed more hostile than usual. 'All that time in your dreams: five cycles teaching you about our world and you come here with no memories. At least your parents remembered everything!'

'They didn't come back,' Peter said quietly.

'Damn it, the Dragon's Breath can kill everything before it,' the Shaman continued. 'Even people with good intentions cannot use it – it corrupts them. We can only guess at what it has done to those Rumanni who have used it.'

'So, what is it?' Michelle asked, cutting through the argument.

'The Rumanni have been mixing the Shankar's power for years, corrupting it with the powers from the Clan,' Ebo answered slowly. 'They combine to form a new destructive element that Romulus and Killjoy seem able to use.'

'That's what we heard, just before the rushing air tried to get us,' Paul chimed in.

'Why don't you destroy it?' Michelle suggested, direct as ever.

'That is what we were discussing,' Ebo said cautiously. 'The Shaman has the spells of exorcism. They can be used to drain the Shankar's power.'

'So what's the problem?' Paul said. 'You do the exorcism, and *voilà*.'

'That is *exactly* the problem,' Ebo replied. 'The exorcism is performed by being next to the stone. You say that the Shankar is housed in one of the towers?'

They nodded.

'The left tower as you look at them from the front,' Peter replied.

'We have to try to get the Shaman inside,' Ebo explained.

'I could go,' Storm offered.

The thought of the repellent, stinking castle and the last image

of the receding prison towers came back to Peter. Suddenly, he knew what it was he had missed.

'How about one of us?' he said, looking at Paul and Michelle. 'How about me?'

'No!' Ebo exclaimed adamantly, getting to his feet. 'You have risked enough on our behalf.'

Peter could hear a protective note in his voice, but he felt that the chieftain was being obstinate. He *had* to go back – especially now that he'd figured out what had been nagging at him.

'It makes sense,' he said doggedly. 'Neither Storm nor the Shaman can get in there as easily as I can.'

'You're not going without me,' Paul piped up.

'You're not getting away from me, either,' Michelle added.

'I said NO!'

Ebo got up, angry and upset, his face flushed. He stormed off, leaving an uncomfortable silence behind him. Jasmine went after him and no one moved.

The Shaman eyed Peter speculatively.

'You are like him,' he grimaced, 'but this time it will be as Ebo commands.'

'What do you mean: "this time"?'

'Malshees! Your father persuaded Ebo to try something similar, Blood and damn, it went wrong and we lost him.' The Shaman wandered off in a fit of expletives.

I'm going, one way or another, Peter thought, resolving to sneak out.

'Why's Ebo so angry?' Paul asked.

'Who knows? He is the Chief.' Storm shrugged his shoulders, then tried to find a way to lighten the glumness that had settled over them all. 'Would you like me to show you more of the Sanctuary? Oh, and by the way: watch this.'

He pointed his fingers towards a simmering pot on the fire.

As they watched, droplets of the boiling liquid lifted from the pot. Starting small, they grew and floated up one side of the handle and then into the air, forming little pockets of clouds above the rod holding the pot over the fire. It started to rain back down into the liquid, little flashes of lightning striking between the clouds.

Peter moved to get a closer look. Suddenly, the miniature thunderstorm collapsed. He glanced back to find Storm's attention caught by his mother, who was approaching them with a very disapproving face.

They explored the Sanctuary and its grounds for most of the morning, wandering about the valley, which was surrounded by the dangerous evergreens filled with unnatural creatures and watched over by the Mighty Mountains. The snow-covered peaks were visible only when the clouds parted.

The mooring basin had several different-sized boats in its docks, including the one that Peter had seen when the tribe escaped. Here, the river sparkled and was clear even in the shadows; it had none of the foulness of the Sindu.

Most of the forest was so thick that it seemed to be in semi-darkness, even during the day. Not surprisingly, the area around the cave had been cleared of trees all the way to the river.

In the early evening when the Changelings returned, they found everyone sitting around the cave with dejected faces. Ebo and Jasmine in particular seemed totally miserable. Only the Shaman was his usual crabby self.

'Who broke the egg?' Michelle asked, for once without a hint of sarcasm in her voice.

Ebo stared back unhappily. 'We have been discussing this all day. The longer we wait, the greater are the chances that Romulus will attack us and take back our children. The Shaman says that we must stop the possibility of the Dragon's Breath being used. You are right, Peter. We cannot do this without you.'

Peter clenched his fist and punched the air. '*Yeesss!*'

'I meant *one* of you,' Ebo said, a little taken back.

'Ebo, it's OK. I'm ready.' Peter's mind was already racing.

'But it is not you, Peter. It is Michelle that we need.'

'*What?*' Peter was flabbergasted. 'That's absurd!'

'Watch it, weasel,' Michelle bristled menacingly.

'She doesn't even like tunnels!'

'Storm will go, and Michelle will drop him in,' Ebo explained.

'But –' Peter started to protest.

'No. This is no light thing that I am asking. I let someone down once.' Ebo spoke as if greatly ashamed. 'You will stay here. We must have Michelle's help or we stand no chance of getting Storm into the castle.'

It doesn't make sense to send Storm! Peter thought furiously. Yet he knew there was no point in arguing with Ebo. Swallowing his frustration for the moment, he apologized for his outburst. To his surprise, Ebo suddenly softened.

'It is only for your own good,' he said, gently, trying to mask his own emotions, but Peter could smell the man's inner turmoil. 'The plan is this,' he continued, focussing on the business at hand. 'The Rumanni will be organizing their army by now; that much we have already seen. Under the cover of darkness, we can travel to a place where Michelle can fly Storm in at dawn –' he gave Charm a quick glance – 'and drop him on the Periculum without being noticed. They should not be guarding that area too closely. Michelle can come straight back and hide us from their sight.'

He paused, but no one said anything.

'I would not even be asking Michelle to do this if I absolutely did not have to.' Ebo's miserable face told its own story. 'However, I have asked the Shaman to create something for you.'

Shaman Dread got up and slowly walked over to them. 'Boom-Dread – "something". This isn't "something". This, blood, will stay with you whatever form you take,' he said, holding out his hand and obviously adoring his own handiwork.

Four black-painted, intricately engraved torques dangled from his palm, an amulet embedded in the centre of each.

'These stones,' he said, 'are *Herya Shankar*. Normally the torques would be golden, but we, damn it – *so* good! – painted them to stop the glitter, the glow, the power from showing. You simply put your hands to the bloody stone to receive a call.'

He placed one around the necks of each of the Changelings, then gave the last one to Storm. He then produced a larger one for Storm to carry.

'This will be the eye. When you get to the hall, Storm Bringer,

call me,' the Shaman finished, and Storm nodded. 'Once the ritual is complete, get back to the roof. Michelle will come and get you.'

The Shaman looked intently at the Changelings, especially at Peter. Peter hid his thoughts and emotions, and got up to leave with Paul in tow. He felt frustrated and angry.

'I'm going,' Peter stated, not wanting to lie to Paul.

'I thought you were thinking that,' Paul whispered.

Michelle had come up quietly behind them, and they both tried to hide their thoughts.

'So did I. Ready for another flying lesson, boys?' Michelle said cheerfully.

Paul groaned.

'What's the plan?' Michelle asked, looking at Peter.

Momentarily he could see himself through her eyes: spiky animal hair going off in various directions, with a let's-pick-a-fight sparkle in his jet-black eyes. He sighed. 'We'll have to pretend that we're still asleep when you leave tomorrow. Paul, can you grab some sacks so we can put them in our beds?'

Next morning, the noise of people coming down to the docks woke them. Peter and Paul had slept in the boat so as not to miss their departure. It was dark; the torches cast deep shadows as Peter went to the side to take a look around.

Michelle, surrounded by a protective circle of the Clan warriors, came down and boarded the smaller vessel.

'Paul!' Peter whispered. 'We're on the wrong boat!'

'Swimming time. Come on – best shrink to our smallest forms. And Peter? *I'll* do the swimming. No splashing. Just take a deep breath, and let me do the rest,' Paul said, taking a peek as well to make sure he knew which boat they needed to get aboard.

The cold water came as a shock, and only then did Peter truly appreciate Paul's abilities in the water.

As instructed, he took a deep breath and went under the dark surface. His senses blazed: everything was blindingly bright. Various shades of green light echoed off the boats and the bottom of the basin. A frighteningly fast black shape appeared from nowhere,

grabbed him and sped away underwater to the other boat. They came up on the far side, only to find Michelle casually dangling her hand in the water. She grabbed Peter, whipped him under her seat and covered him with her blanket.

Peter desperately wanted to shake the water off his fur. Instead, he squeezed it out with his paws, just as Paul joined him.

The whole of the deck was clear to his senses. Griphand was now fully recovered and seemed even larger in the torchlight; Ebo sat still as a rock; and Jasmine was helping Charm, who seemed drawn and was perspiring heavily. Further out, Peter sensed things moving among the trees, but even with his super senses, he could not make them out. They feared the light.

The boat lurched forward and Paul managed to grab him before he stumbled out from under the cover of the blanket. Griphand stood at the tiller with another man, who was as big as he was; they looked like a pair of titans standing guard. The boat was full, and silently they sped into the chilly semi-darkness.

When the boat eventually started to slow, Michelle casually put her hand underneath the blanket, grabbed Paul and dropped him in the water. Her hand reappeared, grabbed Peter and dropped him into the dark water, too.

He immediately took a deep breath, right before the otter grabbed him and dragged him away towards the shore, where they could see creatures milling about on the shore.

The boat went round the bend and left them treading water in the dark.

'*Now* what do we do?' Paul squeaked.

'I hadn't thought of this,' Peter admitted. 'I was thinking more that we could wait on the bank.'

The otter looked first at him, then at the snarling, snapping creatures on the shore. 'Not today.'

Peter became aware of the torque, the cold metal solid underneath the water. His paw grabbed it, his mind already latched onto the image of Michelle – and there she was, in hawk form now, ready to take off. Storm looked really scared.

Michelle.

She squawked, and Peter knew she had heard him.

We're in the water near where you dropped us.

Peter spotted Michelle as she came round the bend. She swooped down and dropped Storm in the water next to them.

'What the – ?' Storm began. Then he spied the badger and otter. 'Oh no.'

'We need that stone,' Peter growled.

'No! Ebo will be furious.'

'Storm, we don't have much time. It should be *me* making this attempt. And don't call Ebo until we're gone.'

Paul popped up behind Peter with a small pouch between his teeth. *Michelle, we've got the Shankar. Do you want us on shore?*

Peter didn't even have time to notice the silently gliding hawk that came down from behind him, seeming to walk on the water before she plucked the bobbing badger and otter from the surface. They were suddenly airborne and headed steeply upwards. Paul squealed and Peter had to close his eyes. The sound-images he was getting of the wood below showed hundreds of animals of all shapes and sizes. They climbed and Michelle hovered a moment at the great height, waiting for dawn.

The clouds on the horizon started to bubble, the stars dimmed and winked out; it seemed that time was running faster and a breeze had whipped up. The clouds gathered into an odd shape, a bit like the etching in the stone at the bottom of the lake, and suddenly the sun burst through – earlier than usual.

How had Charm done that? Peter promised himself to ask when he got back. The warm sunlight hit their fur and a shiver ran down him.

As he looked down, he froze. All sorts of monsters and creatures screamed and howled in agony. Some burst into flames, others caught fire, but all tried to dash for the shadows.

The noise was inhuman.

Both fascinated and horrified, Peter watched. He had completely forgotten where he was when Michelle went into a dive and he screamed. Paul whimpered and prayed that she knew how to stop.

Chapter 18

DURING THE DIVE

During the dive, despite the terrible sinking feeling in his stomach, Peter tried to recover his composure. Most of the guards were semi-recumbent, the light dazzled the few that were groggily coming awake, the sudden dawn making them shield their eyes against the unexpected brilliance.

Before anyone noticed or paid any attention, Michelle the hawk had swooped swiftly past and dropped onto the deserted plateau. She released her cargo, turned on a wing and swooped past them. She wished them luck and then was gone into the blinding light. The badger and otter automatically went into a tuck and tumble and ran for the cover of the tunnels.

'Paul! I know where he is!'

'Who?' Paul asked, distracted, still trying to bring his stomach under control.

'The prisoner, of course. He's in the other tower.' The more Peter thought about it, the more convinced he became.

'You can't be serious. We *can't!* We have to do the Shankar thing.' Paul was adamant, his otter features fixed.

'We can just look in on the way back,' Peter suggested persuasively. 'Ebo would never have let us try it, but I have to know.'

The otter nodded reluctantly. 'So do I,' he admitted at last.

'The detour isn't that long. Besides, did you see how many patrols and guards were on the surface?' Peter was convinced that all the bodies he had seen, huddled around the fires, were all extra guards on duty.

Paul had squeaked all the time during the flight and had kept his eyes closed. From what little he'd seen, the guards around the towers had been doubled, which meant they had to be extra careful.

Peter. Paul.

It was the moment Peter had dreaded: when Ebo found out. They looked at each other before reaching for the darkened torques round their necks, conscious of the fine light metal for the first time. It was just the right size! Peter didn't ponder the thought as the contact was made.

The image of a serious-looking Ebo and the Shaman appeared. The dreadlocked man now wore a darkened torque around his own neck. Storm stood to one side, looking bedraggled, his wet curly hair sticking to his forehead. He gave them a weak smile, then his eyes darted to the chieftain.

Ebo looked like thunder. His fierce eyes bore into Peter, but the Shaman had a detached, bemused expression on his face.

Remember, as soon as you are inside the hall, just call me. Stay alert; there are many more guards on duty and some of them have started their patrols outside already. That means they will be getting ready inside the castle as well, Ebo said, his tone controlled, his message short. Showing anger at this point was obviously a waste of time compared to the urgency of their mission. *May the Maker go with you,* he finished, his features softening at the last instant before contact was broken.

Storm must have done some explaining, Peter thought, and looked hopefully towards Paul. He decided he couldn't break his word to Ebo; he had said they would go straight there. He would have to find out about the prisoner afterwards, even if it meant more danger.

'We have to go to hall first,' he told Paul. 'We don't want it to be occupied. It's early and there should be fewer Rumanni about. We can search for the prisoner afterwards.'

Hurriedly they set off on their mission. Peter easily picked up their previous trail from his earlier scent-markings. The kitchen showed signs of life; a few coughs and curses gave away the presence of people getting things ready. Peter led them deeper to the entrance in the prison washroom. It was the safest way. He peeked carefully through the hole, already aware of a solitary snore from inside the chamber.

'Paul, it doesn't take both of us to sneak in there and make the call. You wait here. I'll call if anything goes –'

Peter was about to say 'wrong', but Paul cut him off. 'If you need me, which you will,' he said, finishing the sentence.

'Yes. That's it.'

Peter did a furtive search of the main chamber and dashed through – he didn't want to think of failure. He sped up the stairs to the main guard chamber and jumped straight through the grate without breaking stride. Using all of his senses, he negotiated the pitch-black spiral stairway downwards.

The place was deserted. He was reassured by the emptiness; it meant that he could pay more attention to the task at hand. As he came to the end of the stairs, a slight red glow crept from under the twin wooden hall doors, providing the only light. Despite his senses already telling him that it was empty, Peter put his ear to the door and listened carefully.

Not a whisper!

Transforming his paws into hands, he turned the big circular wrought-iron handle and pushed open the door. He vaguely wondered why it wasn't locked, but then he remembered Ebo's words about the Rumanni being superstitious about magical powers. They were scared to come down here – too scared of Lord Killjoy.

Quietly, Peter crept inside and gently pushed the door closed behind him. The bright-red light was blinding compared to the darkness. He stretched his senses to all parts of the hall; adrenaline made his heart thump louder. His mouth was dry.

The hall was deserted. He did another quick search, not quite daring to believe his luck, before cautiously approaching the broken rock in the middle of the hall. Its golden armature glistened, the internal fractures burnt bright; molten lava pulsed through it. Its jagged top was razor-sharp.

Peter quickly put his hand on his torque, and the Shankar within it exploded into life, his mind focussed on a solitary image.

Instantly Ebo was there, along with the Shaman. Separately he called up the image of Paul and a more ghostly vision of the otter appeared, his whiskers twitching and his otter eyes alert.

Ebo looked at him with concern. *You are not together?*

Before Peter could answer, the Shaman interrupted and was already giving instructions.

Blood! Peter, you have to be my eyes! the Shaman commanded. *It means the hall has to be real to me so you have to concentrate. Open your eyes while holding onto this link between us in your mind.*

Peter thought he understood. He concentrated, butterflies in his stomach. He felt detached as he tried to feel the link – a ghost chain that could reach anywhere.

Just breathe – regular but deep, and when you open your eyes concentrate only on the Shankar. Hold up the piece we gave to Storm and look through it.

Peter opened his eyes, his mind a blank, his thoughts suspended. The blood-red colour of the stone turned black through the green magic stone.

The Shaman started an incantation. *Lau-go Thumara Thuschman They-Koo! RaqSheshs! Lau-go! Thuschman! RaqSheshs! They-Koo Tomara Thuschman. Ja-oo Yahn-say! Ja-oo Yahn-say RaqShesh. Jahn-say a-ya Wa-hi ya-oo – Kali-Rath.*

Peter could not tell how long the Shaman chanted. He lost track of the time, but the rhythm kept going on and on.

Slowly, and almost imperceptibly, a scream started to resonate from the huge stone. As Peter watched, the bright fracture lines flared, the lava pulsed faster through them and the noise got louder. It flared brighter still and then it began to dim, just like when they had extracted the stones in the mines. The bottom point of the stone started to turn grey. The grey colour seeped upwards, turned black and fell through the veins to the bottom.

The horrible scream rose in pitch, deafening Peter. He couldn't make up his mind if it was in his head or in the hall. The cry became insistent, urgent and nasty; the stone sputtered fire and sparked. It shook and tried to dislodge itself from its armature.

Gradually, a change took place in the fractures, and from the broken top, gelatinous red liquid oozed out of it. It flowed from the top and poured over the sides – thick and sticky – congealing into lumps as it cooled. The black ash, slowly at first, raced through the veins and the angry virulent colour started to drain from the stone.

The cry rose to a crescendo and threatened to burst Peter's eardrums, yet still the dark veins raced upwards, turning first grey and then black.

The shriek rose higher and the shaking became more violent and panicky.

Something distracted Peter, and out of the corner of his eye he saw Lord Killjoy come screeching into the hall, moving with inhuman speed.

'What have you *done*?!'

Before Peter could react, Killjoy raised his staff, and with a speed Peter couldn't have imagined, launched it at his head. It smashed into the side of his face with tremendous force. Stars exploded in Peter's skull as he was thrown sideways from the force of the blow. His face landed in a pool of the oozing red liquid.

The stone's blood took on a purpose and congealed into a thick, viscous fluid that tried to choke Peter by going down his throat, the rest oozing over his hair. Involuntarily, he swallowed some of it; its spicy saltiness was bitter and it burnt his mouth and tongue. The fire quickly spread to his body, and Peter convulsed with pain, jerking in spasms.

Before his vision failed, he looked at the Shankar. Now it was mostly clear, shot through with black veins. Killjoy was screaming – out of control. The evil man bowed reverently before the unholy relic, his head lowered, and he sobbed in anguish, one knee bent on the dais.

Despite the numbness that was now spreading through his body, Peter smiled. He lost consciousness; the smell of the sulphurous Shankar blood filled his senses and clogged his nostrils. He came around feeling something sticky on the side of his face, and an unbelievable pain exploding in his head. His eyelids were stuck together and refused to open. He moved his hand slowly to feel his skull, still not daring to open his eyes, vaguely aware of someone in the background ranting about *it* being lost, *it* was all gone.

Eventually, Peter forced his eyes open, but even the dim light was piercing. He quickly closed them again and was violently sick; pain racked his body and dulled his senses. Before he could do anything else, he was suddenly grabbed by his fur and hauled upright.

'*What have you done?!* You are going to tell me!' Lord Killjoy screamed at him, his ugly face contorted in agony.

By this time, Peter had recovered enough of his senses to realize he was in trouble and danger lurked close. The fear helped him rebound when a blistering slap across the face sent him reeling to the ground. The fresh pain cleared his head sufficiently for him to open his eyes properly and see Lord Killjoy advancing on him. The man grabbed his hair, pulled him up and an inhumanly hard hand slapped him again, sending him sprawling across the floor.

Peter's whole face exploded with pain and he couldn't stop the tears that poured out. Lord Killjoy moved with frightening speed, as if possessed.

'You are going to tell me what you have done! Then you are going to –'

He struck Peter again, and Peter did not catch the rest of the sentence as he crashed to the ground.

Lord Killjoy grabbed him around the throat, and drew his face close as he screamed for the guards. 'You are going to tell me!'

Anger, the sense of imminent danger and his returning senses shocked Peter into realizing that his life was now in peril. The thought of the guards and Killjoy all on him made him panic. He would be trapped, just like his father, and he knew that if that occurred, then something much worse was going to happen.

Suddenly, Killjoy's malevolent face registered shock. His inhuman strength drained and was quickly replaced by terror. The clear evil eye opened wide in surprise as he realized that he had just grabbed an angry, snarling, man-sized badger.

'I'm going to tell you *nothing*!' Peter growled, his claws slashing out across Lord Killjoy's face, meeting soft and yielding flesh. The badger enjoyed extracting a different kind of scream from the evil man while adding three deep, bleeding wounds to the Killjoy's face.

Peter's senses had already informed him that two guards were about to enter the hall, and that several more were tramping down the stairs. He moved with animal reflexes, grabbed Killjoy and flung him bodily at the door.

The guards stormed through the open doorway, their expressions changing to terror on seeing a screaming Lord Killjoy hurtling towards them. They immediately forgot the messy scene in the hall and tried to scramble out of the way. Killjoy collided with them with great force and knocked them to the ground. The other guards who were arriving behind the first group had just enough time to avoid the toppling bodies.

Peter headed through the opening and launched himself at the soldiers – growling, snapping and swiping them aside.

He raced up the stairs. Shouts rose in front and behind as he put on a burst of speed, desperation adding strength to his frantic need to escape. He was angry at himself.

The Shankar had not been destroyed.

He had failed.

A guard, wondering at all the noise, peered through the door when a rather small, snarling, blood-covered badger flew through it. The surprise knocked him backwards and off the stairs. Peter could already see Paul peeking around the washroom door.

'What happened?' Paul squeaked, racing after Peter as the badger shot past.

'Later!' Peter shouted back. 'Come on!'

Paul didn't need to be told twice.

'Where are we going?' he squeaked in frustration.

'To the other tower!' Peter answered.

'But they'll be everywhere!' Paul said with a loud groan.

'Not yet, they won't. I gave Killjoy something to remember me by,' Peter said, his head pounding with pain. 'They'll be looking around here for us for a little while.'

Breathing hard, Peter stopped when he got to the other prison washroom.

'Peter, you're –'

Blood poured profusely from the gash in his forehead, although it did not hurt much. The rest had congealed all over him.

'I know. Leave it,' Peter answered, and yelled, 'Ouch!' as Paul licked his wound.

'Sorry. Don't know what came over me,' Paul said. 'Look,

you're not in any state to go anywhere. I'll go and find out if he's one of us. Besides,' he added with a wink, 'I'm the better thief.'

'Yes, you are.' Peter did not want to argue. 'I'll call you,' he added, 'just like in the cave – that way I'll know if you're in trouble.' Although he was desperate to go to the prisoner himself, now that he'd stopped running he found that his head was pounding inside his skull.

'Good idea. But – Peter, what if he is?' Paul asked quietly.

'We get him out. We get him out now! Killjoy is looking to punish someone, and we all saw what that's like.'

'Get him out – gotcha,' Paul said with a nod, his thin otter lips going even thinner for a second.

Peter closed his eyes and placed his hand on the torque, the power coming alive at his fingers' touch. *I'm here*, he said, floating invisibly above his body, *if anything happens*.

'I know.'

Paul set off to ferret around with the badger's invisible spirit in tow. Peter felt odd floating alongside the otter, being able to pass through anything. He felt like a ghost dragged along by the living.

There was a noise from the stairs and a guard got up to investigate. Another snored in the main chamber with a blanket over him. A set of keys dangled from his belt and his fat belly oozed copiously over the side of the bunk.

Paul saw his chance and took it, rushing to the cell that they had previously explored. Quietly he tested the door.

It was locked.

Peter saw Paul change back into human form and then peek through the spy grate in the door. Paul squinted to get a clear view. He whispered tentatively in the Clan's native Bhasha, 'Sir, are you awake?'

Someone stirred within the cell, but in his present form, Peter couldn't use his abilities to see into the cell. Instead, he heard a grunt. His heartbeat sped up, seemed to be in his throat.

'What do you want?' It was a rough voice, and the manner was extremely aggressive.

'Sir, I was wondering...'

Paul had reverted to his native tongue.

From inside the cell, Peter heard a horrified voice croak, 'Oh my god!'

It was in plain English!

Peter's heart leapt.

'Sir, please keep quiet! We're here to get you out. Just stay there – stay there.'

Paul raced back to the main chamber.

Peter started to edge forward to a vantage point from where he could view the chamber. He wanted to be in a position to help his friend should he need it.

Paul sneaked past the bars and underneath the bunk of the fat sleeping guard. There he used his razor-sharp claws to saw through the thin rope the guard had used to secure the keys to his belt. The keys slipped off but Paul caught them before they hit the floor. The fat guard above him turned over suddenly onto his side, his weight banging the top of the bunk on Paul's head.

The otter froze, not daring to breathe until he heard the guard start snoring again.

Peter watched Paul slither back into the dark corridor and race to the cell. Paul had transformed into his now familiar part-human, part-otter state and was frantically trying one key after another, until one of them turned.

He opened the door quietly and slipped inside, stealthily closing the door behind him. Inside, Peter could see that the chains that hung on the walls and formed another barrier which had been padlocked closed. He was having difficulty in seeing anything else clearly, other than Paul.

Again Paul went through the routine of finding the right key, eventually opening all eight locks to gain entry into the chained cell. The chain fell away, revealing the opening. That left only the hanging inner cage inside. Peter watched intently as the Changeling stepped inside.

Instantly Paul winked out, snapping the connection between them so sharply that Peter was thrown back against the wall. He was convinced everyone would hear his heart beating.

He was stunned for a moment, then came out of it, startled, his senses raw as if he had just been burnt.

He was ready to rush in despite his still-pounding head, but noises in the corridor drew his attention. People were rushing down. Worried, Peter tried quickly to re-establish contact with Paul, tried desperately to let him know what was going on in the chamber.

The pounding in his head had been made worse by hitting the wall, and the wound had opened up again. Blood trickled into his eyes and made it hard to see clearly.

Paul might need him, but for now he had to close his eyes against the pain.

A single guard had come back down the stairs and the other one continued to snore, rolls of fat dangling precariously on the side of the bed, ready to drop to the floor, his belly overhanging the edge like a mellon.

After what seemed like ages, Paul and the prisoner emerged into view. Both of them stuck to the darker areas, but the prisoner was in a terrible state and seemed unable to help himself. Paul tried to unlock the barred chamber door, and to Peter's sensitive hearing, every chink was like the toll of a great bell. Anxiously he watched, fully expecting someone to hear Paul's effort to open the door, and attack them. To his surprise, no one did. The sound seemed loud only to him.

Finally, there was a *clunk!* from the chamber door, and instantly the guard on duty shouted something obscene to the sleeping one. Groggily, the fat one stirred, still not aware of the escape.

By now, Paul and the prisoner were through the barred door and into the chamber itself. The fat guard tumbled to the floor, sleepily grabbing for a nearby club. He got up, tried unsuccessfully to get his bearings and wondered what all the noise was about.

The fat guard spotted the prisoner and started shouting, just as Paul transformed completely into an otter and launched himself to attack. The club dropped from the fat man's hand and he fell back in surprise.

'Come on – this way!' Peter shouted to the prisoner, who also seemed transfixed by the transformation.

Paul screamed. 'Go to the door!'

The prisoner stumbled up the stairs and started tugging at the door.

'*This* way!' Peter shouted again, more vehemently.

Peter didn't understand, but watched as Paul too headed for the stairs as well. The pain in his head was making it difficult to think, and he decided to follow Paul's lead.

The skinny prisoner was jerking wildly at the door, finally collapsing when he failed to budge it, breathing hard.

The guard had grabbed another club, and was advancing on the prisoner. Something furry and clawed grabbed him from behind, and threw him backwards. The fat guard screamed as he hit the floor.

'To the dining hall!' Paul squeaked from in front.

Peter rushed past the exhausted prisoner to help Paul pull the door open.

The man, badly emaciated, was in no condition to help anyone, and Peter noticed that his odour was awful – unhealthy. He had barely managed to get up when Paul grabbed him and dragged him through.

Peter raced up the stairs, and in the kitchen he encountered a man and a maid whom he scared half to death with his snarling. They ran screaming from the sight of a growling man-sized badger. Peter looked back towards Paul, who was having to help the struggling man.

'The roof!' Paul shouted, only to find Peter already heading there.

They found the underground passages deserted and the hall was empty. Peter waited for them to catch up before taking the lead again. The man still had his hand shackled and was close to fainting; his eyes rolled alarmingly in his head. They flickered open momentarily as Paul changed direction to drag him up the stairs, but he was barely conscious. Then, he fainted altogether and they both collapsed in a heap. Paul cursed as he increased his size in order to carry him.

The otter hauled the man onto his neck, but the prisoner slipped off and bumped his face on the floor. Peter understood what Paul was trying to do, and he grabbed the man before he could receive yet another bruise.

'My fur's coarser,' he explained to the surprised otter.

Paul immediately released the prisoner. They didn't have much time. There was noise in the lower passages and an increasing number of people were gathering there.

The badger hauled the prisoner bodily onto its shoulders, expecting him to be heavy, but to his surprise, the man weighed hardly anything – he was mostly skin and bones.

Peter relied on Paul, who followed, to scare off anything behind them. Once on the roof, he lowered the man into a shadowed area and reached for his torque, his fingers going automatically to the now-familiar piece of jewellery.

He focussed, his anxiety adding an extra urgency to his plight.

Michelle!

It was a cry as well as a request.

She looked up. 'Peter?'

We need you right now! We're on the dining hall roof!

Michelle took off abruptly and Peter followed her with his vision until the sight of the land dropping away made him feel ill.

Paul scrambled through the roof door. He spied Peter and the still-unconscious prisoner in the corner, then looked back unhappily towards the door. 'They're coming,' he said.

The guards had moved into the hall and were searching the landing.

'They think we're still downstairs,' Peter replied, his senses flickering. He was about to ask about what had happened in the cell when he heard a squawk. They both searched the sky, but could not see anything. Then, from out of the sun, Michelle dropped like a stone, descended with blinding speed, and landed beside them.

'What happened to *you?*'

'Not now. Come on,' Peter said pointing to the man. 'He's not as heavy as he looks, but we have to get him away. Can you do it?' he asked anxiously, seeing the shock on Michelle's face.

'*Can I do it?* That's not even a question,' Michelle said, transforming into a hawk larger than even Peter thought possible. He stepped back, his primeval instincts panicked at having such a fearsome predator so close. An involuntary snap at him made Peter step back further. 'Sorry,' the hawk squawked. 'Couldn't help myself.'

Michelle hopped over to the man, examined him as if deciding whether he was for eating or something else, then grabbed his shackles in one of her talons. She eyed the badger and otter, who were ready and waiting in their smallest forms. The otter had his eyes tightly closed.

Just then, the roof exit burst open, guards poured out and immediately spotted the giant hawk. They spread round them like vultures. Michelle screeched loudly, startling the soldiers, then snatched the badger and otter before they could react, and took off.

Paul's eyes snapped open as arrows started whizzing past. The encumbered hawk weaved about frantically, lurching to the sides randomly in a vain attempt to duck the arrows, but they were coming thick and fast. Despite her speed, the arrows were faster.

Suddenly, Paul cried out.

An arrow had pierced his side, and blood was pouring out of the wound. It looked like a javelin compared to his small size, sticking out at an unnatural angle. Peter and Michelle both screamed as Paul's mental agony communicated itself to them. Being so physically close together, the images and feelings coming from Paul were raw and powerful; each of his friends felt the pain in his side, the weight of the arrow trying to drag him down. He tried frantically to stop the bleeding with his paw.

The hawk lurched to one side, her grip on them weakening. Paul, already doubled over in pain, had no chance due to his sleek fur. He slipped from Michelle's grasp and plummeted to the roof below.

Peter clung on desperately to the sharp claws, the sympathetic pain in his mind making him believe his side was blazing like fire. He watched helplessly as Paul hauled himself up and scrambled towards the edge of the roof.

'Michelle, take me down! I can help him!'

'No! He's going to make it!'

'TAKE ME DOWN!' Peter screamed, and struggled against the impossibly tight hold.

'No! We'll all get killed!'

Paul made it to the drains, leaving behind a bloody trail. He turned, stood up and waved with one paw.

'Michelle!' he squeaked. 'Get away to the plateau!'

He had forgotten the guards.

An arrow smashed into Paul's head and pain exploded in Peter's mind, while the hawk screeched and dropped like a stone. The pain pouring out of Paul was severe, and he was struggling for his life.

The otter tumbled down the drains, his life ebbing away fast, the tearing agony in his side cripplingly intense each time he hit the wall. The painful blaze in his head raged out of control. It made him dizzy and disorientated. Everything was spinning. Everything hurt.

The otter was fighting and losing, trying to stay alive as he saw the exit approaching rapidly. Paul struggled, desperate to grab hold of anything to stop his descent, but the walls were too slippery.

He reached the exit and shot through it into the air, the sudden daylight blinding. Vaguely, Paul gazed down at the rocks and river below and wondered, 'How long…?'

Then the pain stopped abruptly, and the agony in Peter's mind vanished.

'Paul!' he screamed, again and again. *'Paul!'*

Chapter 19

'DROP ME!'

'Drop me!' Peter shouted, trying desperately to wriggle free from Michelle's clutches.

'No!'

'We have to get his body!'

'We'll all get killed!' Michelle simply held on tighter.

'Put me down!' He struggled in vain against Michelle's impossible grip, distracting her and making her fly erratically, his mind on the last image of Paul as his lifeless body tumbled into the drains. 'Just drop me!'

'No! You're not helping me here!' Michelle screeched as she flapped harder, twisting and turning out of the way of the arrows that were dangerously close. A few found their mark and made the hawk screech louder. Peter felt every one as Michelle swerved and dived over the wall into the mining area.

He wanted to be on the ground, wanted more than anything to get to Paul. He continued to struggle against the hawk's iron-like grip but Michelle only squeezed harder and held on tight, despite having to deal with the mismatched weights in her talons.

Peter tried to grow larger, but couldn't – the talons only cut into his skin. He tried to change and the grip stopped him. Michelle, with the flailing badger and the limp man in her talons, made it to the plateau.

By now the arrows had stopped. Only the sound of orders being shouted could be heard, and even those faded quickly. All Peter could hear was the flapping of wings as they descended into the green mists below. The glowing grains of the stones glistening around the mine settled on their bodies, cooling them and bringing a same surreal calmness to their descent.

Michelle could hardly see for the tears stinging her eyes – an empty feeling of loss was consuming her. Peter could feel her conflict, her doubts that she should have tried to drop Peter on the rooftop, that she could have held on tighter to Paul, but the hawk inside had dealt with the situation. It was not a coward, but it wasn't stupid, either.

He couldn't feel Paul's presence in his mind. During their time together, he had always felt the aura of both his friends, but now only the hawk was there. The enormity of his loss just beginning to dawn on him.

Michelle had been right.

They landed on the deserted plateau – only to find Romulus alighting from the lifting platforms. His face was rage incarnate, the veins in his forehead stood out and throbbed. Guards scattered before him.

He had spotted them but continued striding purposely towards a large cage on the other side of the plateau. He threw off the covers to reveal a blood-stained pen. The creature within it lurched forward at the sight of another animal, bashing into the bars and raging against its confinement.

Romulus didn't flinch; instead he threw open the door. The creature immediately charged out on thousands of legs, its big head snapping at the exposed man standing at the entrance to its torture chamber.

Romulus grabbed it around the throat before it reached him and drew it close to his face.

'This is *not* a good day to play!'

He stared back at it, clenching his jaw while the creature struggled to get free. The beast's eyes glazed over as Romulus stared at it, then the king jerked its head towards Peter and Michelle and pointed. 'THEM!'

'Michelle!' Peter screamed, changing back into human form so that he could grab hold of the prisoner as he entered the tunnels. 'Follow me!'

Peter glanced over his shoulder. The beast had turned towards them and it disappeared from sight but the badger could still see it.

It was coming. It was coming with frightening speed. And, it was invisible.

He was running blind in the darkness, dragging the body of the man, and all the twists and turns he made to avoid his stalker seemed to lead to a narrower and narrower place until finally there was nowhere else to go but back. He could feel himself changing as he turned around – tough, coarse hair sprouting all over him, the hands becoming thick and padded, the nails elongating into points, and his jaw becoming wider and more powerful – and then his vision altered. He was breathing hard, he was sweating, and fear made his hair bristle. There was nothing he could do but turn and face it.

Hovering over the bleeding man, hunched on all fours, he waited.

He could see it gliding forward on thousands of legs. The jaws snapping, the staring blind eyes, the wild movements of its large head – it lurched forward and came closer. The predator was hungry, its body covered in boils, its back scraped raw and haemorrhaging. He could see the long, hairy tentacles whipping around. It was searching, hunting, but not for food – for *life*. The man beneath him hadn't moved and he was going to die. He could not save him.

The creature dived at them, opening its jaws and revealing its vicious fangs. He could see them in the dark.

There was no way out…

If he was going to be torn apart, it wouldn't be without a fight. He met his nightmare. The beast lunged, only this time it was met by the most powerful jaws in the animal kingdom preparing to close around the creature's throat. *If I'm going to die,* the badger thought grimly, *it's going to die with me.*

The jaws closed round the creature's throat and blood poured from the badger's teeth punctures. It issued a choked screech, and whipped its worm-like body around, grabbing hold of the badger with its many sharp, tiny legs, latching onto Peter with the strength and desperation of a parasite in its last death-throes. It was squeezing the breath from the badger – he could feel the thousands of tiny, sharp toes biting into his skin despite his thick fur.

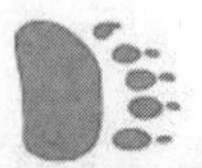

He doubled his effort to break the creature's neck, but it was powerful enough to hold its own, even though its neck was ripped open.

A beak came out from behind the warring animals and tore off the creature's head. Peter turned to find Michelle trying to wipe her beak on the tunnel walls. For a moment, he could do nothing else but stare at her.

'What?' she asked, smoothing her feathers back into place. 'Just how much trouble and gore did you want?'

Peter was too tired to argue. They were both still thinking about Paul and did not even bother looking at the decapitated creature, which was now disintegrating before their eyes, leaving only dust behind.

'I'm going back up to get his body,' Peter said quietly.

'No, you're not,' Michelle stated, her wings brushing at her face, trying to wipe the tears away before Peter could see them. 'I've lost one friend. I'm not about to lose another. He's gone. I *know*. You can't feel him any more, either, can you?'

Peter shook his head. Deep down he knew that was exactly what he felt, but he tried to reject it, to push it away with anger. He grasped the amulet round his neck in desperation, willing himself to find Paul, to find his friend.

A horrible sensation made him feel sick.

There was just darkness.

Paul had been the best friend he had ever had.

The enormity of Paul's sacrifice forced Peter to his knees. He hid his face in his paws, smelling the animal fur, steadying his emotions, trying to come to terms with it. He wanted to weep, but no tears came. Eventually he shook his head from side to side, growled and got up, his jaw set.

'Let's get out of here,' he said.

Michelle, who had been watching him, dropped her beak uncertainly.

'You two are my best friends,' she said, and for once awkwardness choked her voice. 'I meant to say –'

'I know what you meant to say.'

He could feel her wrestling with the need to be strong and the desperate need to get away. Finally, her head come up and the steely look was back.

'So who's he?' She nodded at the unconscious figure on the ground.

'I don't know,' Peter shrugged, 'but he speaks English.'

'*Our* English?'

'I watched Paul through the Shankar as he went to get him,' Peter said, and then hesitated before continuing. 'He – he disappeared and then he reappeared, dragging him along.'

Peter.

Both of them heard it, and they automatically reached for their torques. Ebo, Jasmine, Griphand and the Shaman appeared.

Peter looked at the members of the Clan. 'I failed,' he said miserably. 'I'm so sorry. You're all in danger. You must get away from here.'

Boom-Basa, boy! The Shankar's dead! The Shaman's word stopped him short.

'So is Paul.'

Griphand flinched. *How?*

Peter couldn't bring himself to answer.

'He was shot as we were escaping,' Michelle replied.

He could still be alive, Griphand said hopefully. *You have to –*

'No. He isn't.' Peter voice was strangely unemotional.

The big man uttered a foul curse and broke off from the call.

An awkward silence followed before Ebo spoke in a subdued tone. *They have doubled all the guards. We have to get you out of there. The Shankar is drained, so their priests are effectively useless. However, Romulus and Killjoy are not – their powers are their own. That was a great thing you did, Peter, and we will all miss Paul, but we now have to concentrate on getting you two away from Castle Craven.*

'We can't get back just now,' Michelle said. 'There are too many Rumanni to come back right away.'

Peter, you are bleeding, Ebo pointed out, his anxiety cutting deep lines between his brows.

It was only then Peter felt the trickle of blood dropping

down his fur. 'Killjoy threw me at the Shankar and I struck my head on it.'

He should have been more careful; the burning sensation in his stomach was still churning and he threw up.

Everyone bolted upright in alarm.

'It's nothing,' Peter said, recovering.

Ebo was distracted by something on the boat. He turned quickly. *We will call you later. Stay there. Stay together.*

With that they were gone.

'Why didn't you tell him about the prisoner?' Michelle asked.

'He told us to go to the hall and then get out. It was me who persuaded Paul to do those crazy things...'

All he felt was sick – with grief, with guilt – and the pain in his stomach wasn't helping.

He wanted Paul back. He wanted him back alive.

Noise broke through their thoughts. The sound of guards entering the tunnels was unmistakable. Even at so great a distance, Peter could sense them. He decided to investigate, and what he saw froze him with terror.

Lord Killjoy was on the plateau – *and he was chanting!*

Peter raced back to where Michelle was waiting for him. 'We have to go now,' he said. 'It's Killjoy.'

Michelle looked at the unconscious man on the floor.

Neither of them were ready to abandon him. He could be the reason all of them had come – their lost years, their lost lives. Now that they had a glimmer of hope, they would fight for him fiercely.

'Peter, can you find a way out that's big enough for all of us?'

'No, but I can find a way *down*,' Peter said, thinking that the deeper they were, the less chance there was of anything reaching them.

As he gathered up the prisoner to put him on his shoulders, Peter couldn't help but notice the many scars on the man's back. They had all healed, the skin stretched thin over them. He had obviously been tortured.

Out on the plateau, the chanting was getting louder. The sound faded rapidly as they moved deeper underground.

It was awkward in the tunnels with the man on his back, and Peter rested frequently. Eventually the ground became brittle, and Peter knew they were approaching the massive underground lake. Finally they broke through a wall, a little higher than Peter wanted, but sufficiently close to get down relatively easily.

The man hadn't stirred. With his long beard and smelly clothes – mostly torn rags – and long black and silver hair, he was not a pretty sight, but then again, he *had* been a prisoner.

Michelle, however, jumped into the opening and took off. Her squawking filled the cavern with echoes. She returned after she had explored the underground structure.

'This is good,' she said breathlessly. 'There's a dragon looking at me from the bottom of the lake.'

'Actually, he's lying down with his wings folded on top.'

'No, it's hunched up, as if it's about to take off, but its head's stuck to one side,' she stated with conviction.

Peter knew how Paul had left the dragon, and it hadn't been like that…

Peter! Michelle!

They reacted instantly. Jasmine and Charm were there.

I wanted to let you know… Jasmine's voice trailed off. Her eyes grew wide. *Who is that?!*

'He's the prisoner we told you about.' Peter said, trying to calm her fears.

Peter, we searched. There is no one we know in that castle. He is one of them, Jasmine spoke quickly in alarm. *Get away from him! I'm not going to lose you or Michelle!*

Ebo and the Shaman searched all night! Charm added her protest to convince them. Both of them looked ready to jump through the Call to get them away from the unconscious man.

Get back into the tunnels! Go! Go now! Jasmine pleaded.

'But we can handle one man between the two of us,' Peter said, baffled by Jasmine's extreme reaction.

Some of their priests have taken on powers from the Shankar. Peter,

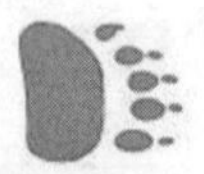

please – get away from him. The priests can channel through each other. Just like the Shaman asked you to be his eyes, this man could act as the eyes for Romulus. Peter –' Jasmine was desperate.

Peter looked at the dishevelled man curled up on the sand. He glanced towards Michelle for help. He didn't want to abandon the man, but a small voice in his head whispered that Jasmine was right. He hadn't been able to save Paul, and he wouldn't put Michelle in any more danger.

'Let's go,' Peter decided, breaking the contact.

They backed away from the prisoner.

'Come on. Jasmine's right. If he is one of their priests…' Peter left the sentence unfinished. 'Anyway, he's not going anywhere for the time being.'

'I'll put this on him,' Michelle said taking off her torque, 'That way we can keep tabs.'

'Good idea.'

Peter wished he had thought of it first.

Michelle lifted the man's head with steely determination and gentleness, and slipped the torque around his neck. It fit.

'Let's go and help Ebo. They need us,' Peter said dejectedly. He could see that Michelle had her doubts.

Peter glanced back once, before entering the glowing passages. The man still had not moved.

Peter led them back to the plateau, thinking hard about the events that had led up to the rescue. Even when he had been struck, his head blazing with pain and ready to burst, he had still been able to transform. So why hadn't the prisoner changed if he was one of them? The man *must* be a Rumanni – and he had got Paul killed for that.

He felt crushed.

Michelle found it hard to keep up with him. At first, she had hopped along in her hawk form, but kept getting hurt as she scrambled through the hard tunnels. Eventually she changed back into a human, but even so, she was breathing hard when she finally came through.

Thankfully, this time the plateau was deserted.

'They must think that creature of theirs finished us off,' Michele said. 'Like *that* would ever happen –'

'I'm sorry,' Peter said suddenly. He had been stupid and had led them into rescuing a strange man, clutching at straws.

'For what? Trying to find one of our parents?' Michelle's reply was as blunt – and as truthful – as ever.

'*I* should've gone and talked to him.'

'No. You did everything perfectly. We need to get out of here, fast.'

'I should have seen it when he didn't transform.'

A silence fell between them.

'Michelle, I'm –' Peter was about to apologize again when she cut him off.

'Don't beat yourself up. Let me do it instead,' she said, throwing a mock punch at his shoulders before adding: 'Time to catch me a badger.'

On cue, she transformed her hand into a talon and flexed it. 'As much as I would prefer that you were bigger for fighting's sake, I think it's better if you stay small. And don't wriggle this time.'

'I wasn't "wriggling". I was struggling.'

'Oh. So *that's* what it was.'

The hawk shot up into the sun like an arrow from the plateau with a small furry animal in her talons. Peter tried hard to control his queasy feelings, and looked back from the great height. He could just make out the guards and patrol groups below. They moved out and marched towards the river, where a large, defiant boat waited.

Michelle dived and dropped Peter on the deck. Jasmine and Charm rushed forward to greet them. Ebo gave him a nod. He was on the top deck with Storm, the Shaman and Griphand, who seemed to have lost all of his bounce.

The ship was crowded with people, and more of the Clan warriors were on the banks of the river. In the distance, Romulus advanced with his troops, their armour and weapons glinting in the sun.

They were coming to get revenge.

Chapter 20

AN ARMY WAS COMING TO GET THEM

An army was coming to get them. By mid-afternoon, Romulus and his forces were close enough to the river to be clearly visible and within striking distance of the Clan. Their temporary defences – barricades of wood behind dug-out trenches that boasted a line of spikes in front – were crude compared to the shining armour of the well-disciplined castle troops.

The Clan's warriors were armed with bows, arrows and swords, and some weapons Peter hadn't seen before, but they would be no match for the force assembled against them.

He didn't care or wonder why they weren't running away from the superior numbers coming towards them. He didn't care if Ebo had a plan. He was going to stay and help them anyway. He was going to stay and get even – for Paul.

A vision of his lost friend came back to him: his quirky behaviour; his awesome power in the water, always splashing around; his wild squealing whenever they flew.

The last image of Paul haunted Peter. He had been in so much pain... but Peter didn't want to think about it. Death hadn't been something Peter had ever experienced. He had lost his friend and he missed him. But he promised himself to see to it that Paul had not died in vain.

Michelle was thinking similar thoughts and had the same resolve on her face. He could feel it.

The troops halted and three figures on horseback advanced towards them. They cantered at a lazy pace, led by Romulus, who was dressed, as always, in shiny black armour with a red hexagonal

symbol emblazoned on his chest. He seemed in no hurry; casually, he took in the scenery, his manner relaxed, his expression serene, the scar on his face glistening white against his sun-tanned skin. The raven-haired woman by his side smiled and laughed as if out for a Sunday jaunt. By contrast, Killjoy's hood was up, his face hidden in shadow.

Ebo walked forward. Griphand followed, hauling up his trousers with one hand, and came to stand protectively next to his friend.

'Bravo, Ebo! One is amused by all your silliness,' Romulus said with a flourish and a small bow. 'Beg for forgiveness and your king will forgive you.'

'You are not my king.' Ebo words echoed clearly and were easily heard by the people of the Clan.

'You break your king's heart with such cruel words. One watched you grow up into this man, when you should have been by Our side as an overlord.'

'What about the man you have become? Not a shred of the boy I knew.'

'Ebo, One hates such intense conversations. By the way, we were trying to break this gently to you, but your Changelings are dead. Alas! So is Pariah's pet, who went after them. So much death and destruction, such a waste – the pet, not the Changelings,' he sighed heavily. 'She is very upset with you. It took endless hours in the torture chamber for her to get over her grief.'

Pariah's stare bore into Ebo.

Romulus leaned forward menacingly, the golden sunlight of the late afternoon glinting on his every move.

'We've been excessively diverted by this creative streak – truly, Ebo. We'll be generous and overlook your treacherous act. One has an idea: return the children and you may return to your farms.'

'We will not deliver our children into captivity *ever* again.'

Ebo's words brought a cheer from the Clan.

The king merely looked amused and waited for it to die down.

'Ebo, you know how much One hates arguments, so why do you vex Us?

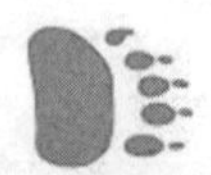

'We are leaving now. You should do the same.'

At this point, Peter couldn't figure out why Ebo was spending so much time talking with a man he despised.

'Why is he bothering to speak to him at all?' Peter asked Charm quietly.

'The longer he talks, the better. Have you not noticed that the sun has been going down all this time?' Charm pointed behind them. 'Just as the day came early, so will the night fall. Romulus has no time.'

'There's also a lot of woods around them,' Michelle said appreciatively.

Peter walked across to the barricade and climbed up. He could hear Romulus ranting.

'You will bury your head between *Our* royal toes and beg for forgiveness. You will –' Romulus stopped mid-sentence as he spied Peter.

Peter stared back, his heart filled with loathing for the man who had killed his father, and had been the cause of the death of his friend. Hate boiled in his badger's blood and he could sense fear in the king. He was close enough to smell him, close enough to leap across the barrier and get to him, even from this distance. For a long moment they simply stared at each other, hatred raging on both sides.

'So,' Romulus shook his head. 'Changeling, you think you can change our world? We have killed your kind before!' Romulus spat out the words.

'You should beg my forgiveness for killing my father.'

'One tries so hard, but it's just not in Our nature.'

'Your father was useless to us anyway,' Pariah Paine hissed in the background. 'His spirit died like an ugly thing in a trap.'

At the mention of his father, Peter's fury erupted. 'I'm going to get you!' he shouted from the wall. 'Remember your dream, Blackheart? You want me? Come and get me!'

Romulus's face went ashen at Peter's words.

Michelle climbed up to join him, anger blazing in her face.

Romulus tried to regain his composure. 'Oh, please!' he attempted a contemptuous laugh. 'You two can do nothing more

than your parents.'

Slowly he half-turned as if to leave, but suddenly he screamed: '*Get them!*'

At Romulus's side, Pariah Paine flung out her hands towards the Clan's barricades. Vines erupted from the ground and shot straight at the people on the walls, rapidly becoming thick and sprouting deadly spikes.

Even with his quick reflexes, Peter wasn't fast enough; a vine slammed into him, knocking him off the top of the barricade, the thorns only just missing him. He had just enough time to notice Killjoy beginning to murmur.

The hooded man's head was bowed in concentration. An evil breeze sprang up, turned quickly into a wind and passed through them. Peter felt his life being sucked out, and watched the men and women around him double over in agony. The desperation was sudden, the panic frightening. Their very lives were being drained.

Michelle shot off vertically, with the vines in pursuit.

The badger twisted this way and that, trying to evade the murderous spiked vines which were still growing at a terrifying rate. He headed instinctively for the river and dived in, coming up for air just in time to see the vines, which now stretched hundreds of feet in the air, still pursuing the fleeing hawk.

Ebo dashed through a gap in the ugly green walls while his men hacked desperately at the vines but to no avail. They couldn't make any impression against the unnatural growth.

All of a sudden, the vines stopped. They had halted short of the river, but even those that chased Michelle fell back to earth, just as Pariah Paine tumbled from her horse.

Peter climbed out of the water and ran back to the top of the barricade. The animal inside, angry and snarling, threw himself recklessly at the vine wall and tried to get through to the other side.

A thicket of intertwined thorny vines protected the king and his consort, and through their tightly interlaced stems Peter caught glimpses of Pariah being helped back gently onto her horse by Killjoy. She had aged: her face was now covered in wrinkles, her hands were all withered and bony. Her armour seemed to have

been made for another person altogether. This old hag was not the brash young woman that had come riding out with the king.

Romulus stood staring, a twisted hatred written on his face.

'We will return to extract your essence, as We did your father's!' he screamed, wheeling around and racing for his troops, shouting, 'Attack!'

Having helped Pariah onto her horse, Killjoy was laughing manically as he got onto his. His alabaster hands extended in front of him, and his hood was drawn back, revealing a hideous face that had been further disfigured by the three deep long gashes Peter had inflicted. He screeched incoherently, and his normally pallid skin glowed with stolen health. He seemed to be bigger.

Peter didn't hesitate. He launched himself at the hysterical man, who didn't even seem aware of his presence. Only at the last moment did Killjoy realize that something snarling and dangerous had got through the protective vines.

Peter felt a satisfying thud as he collided with the man and toppled him from his horse, but Killjoy was too fast. He lashed out, sending even a man-sized badger sprawling to the ground. Killjoy continued to convulse with laughter as if possessed, but his concentration had been broken, and the evil wind that had surrounded him died.

'Peter, get back! Mistall: to me!' Ebo shouted from the barricades.

A squawk alerted Peter to the approaching hawk and he changed his size, ready to be picked up. Michelle plucked him from the ground, banked and swooped over the treacherous vines to drop him safely on the other side of the barricades.

Peter ran to help Jasmine. 'What was *that*?' he asked.

'Killjoy. He destroyed our hope and fed on our life,' Jasmine replied. 'The bleakness descends quickly, then your will to live goes. That was a foolish thing to do, Peter. Your father was the same: always thinking of others – and always ready to risk his own neck.'

'They are coming! Get to the boat!' Ebo shouted over the mayhem.

Everyone headed for the boat and scrambled abroad – all

except a lone figure who climbed up the wall.

'Peter!' Jasmine ordered. 'Get to the boat quickly! Mistall will link herself to the river and bring down the fog!'

One of the Clansmen threw a rope into the river and dragged the wet end up to the old woman, who proceeded to rap it around her bony wrist.

Mistall raised her other hand in the air.

The castle, bathed in the golden glow of the dying day, began to disappear. The land cooled; a mist rose and surrounded it. Its thickness increased and tiny wispy vapours merged together to form a dense, moving cloud. It gathered speed and came towards them like thick soup, flowed over the castle troops and overtook them. The land lost its warmth and froze over. Soon the enemy advance had halted.

The river bubbled where the rope dipped in the water. Soon the magical mist had reached its banks.

From out of the mist, Romulus's voice boomed, 'Nice – very nice! Is this a time for talking, now? Then let's talk!'

The noises from the soldiers had stopped altogether and an expectant deathly silence hung around the fog.

The silence lasted only a moment, but it seemed longer, before someone shouted to form a defensive formation. Someone else shouted to retreat.

Groggily, small dark things moved out from the woods. Peter sensed that they weren't troops, but he couldn't see their shapes clearly through the magical mist. Further in, other creatures started to stir.

Ebo rushed on board last, and with a lurch, the boat moved off through the thick white soup that blanketed the entire area.

'It's all the way up to the castle, but that's only going to slow them down,' Michelle said, relaying what she had seen.

'Romulus's own monsters are going to attack them now,' Peter replied, his mood subdued. He wanted to be pleased that Romulus was getting what he deserved, but he still felt an overwhelming sorrow for his friend, the otter. He wanted to take the smile off the king's face himself – for his father, and for Paul.

The Shaman stormed over to Peter as the boat moved off.

'Blood, boy! Jasmine says you rescued a priest from their prison?'

'Yes, sir. I'm sorry,' Peter apologized. 'We realize now it was a dangerous thing to do.'

'Boom-Laga, perhaps we can take a look at this rescued person,' the Shaman suggested. For once, he seemed to be in a good mood. 'Obviously, he meant something to you.'

The Shaman's hand rose to his Shankar.

'That should be easy,' Michelle said. 'We left him one of those.' She pointed to the torque.

'Blood!' The Shaman's tone changed to alarm, his hand withdrew from the magical stone.

'Wait here,' the Shaman ordered, rushing away. He seemed shaken and afraid.

The boat had escaped the mists and they could see that the sun was disappearing behind the horizon. It blazed crimson red for an instant and winked out, plunging them all into sudden darkness. The Clan warriors, however, had already lit torches around the boat in anticipation.

'That is what happens when Charm weaves her magic. Night comes quickly – as Romulus is about to find out,' Jasmine said, quietly, glancing backwards towards the mists.

With his super-sensitive ears, Peter thought he heard the clash of swords and screams as the boat picked up speed.

Ebo came to join them with the Shaman in tow. 'You have left an enchanted Shankar with a *priest?*'

'We didn't know –' Peter began.

'I realize that,' Ebo cut him off, 'but the Shankars we gave you were specially enchanted so that we could find you more easily and channel through them. If the priest has it, then he can channel straight through it to *us*. How easily can this priest get back to the castle?' Ebo's expression was full of concern.

'We left him by the underground lake,' Peter said, his voice trailing off as he remembered that the priest would be able to see the other stone in the lake. The same thought had just occurred to Michelle.

'If he is that far down, it will be days before he can find a way out – if at all,' Ebo said thoughtfully, 'but we cannot risk spying on him. He would immediately latch on to us.'

They all nodded.

'But he was in prison. And afterwards he just collapsed into – into a sort of coma,' Peter added.

'They periodically discipline their priests that way,' the Shaman said with distaste. 'Mal-shees! It focusses their simple minds.'

'But the red Shankar is destroyed, so –' Peter was trying to work out whether the priests' power was truly gone.

'So nothing,' Ebo interrupted him again. 'As you saw, Pariah and Killjoy's power is still there because of their long association with the Shankar.'

'This Shankar in the lake,' the Shaman said, also thinking of the possibilities. 'It could be very powerful.'

'Yeah – if you get past the dragon,' Michelle said.

'What dragon?' the Shaman thundered.

'What do you mean?' Ebo shouted for Griphand to join them. He turned to them slowly. 'Say that again.'

That was it – Peter had to tell the whole thing: how Paul had uncovered the stone in the lake; how the fracture lines had pulsed with lava; how fractures formed a dragon with a few missing pieces; how the dragon moved when no one was watching it; and how its head seemed to be stuck in one place.

'It is one of the Guardians. An *Original*. Did you look through its eye?' the Shaman asked in awe, for once forgetting to swear. 'Its *one* eye?'

'No. Paul –' Peter voice caught on his friend's name – 'he gathered up most of the pieces, and when they were close enough to the Shankar, they would sort of get sucked into it, all by itself. There are only two jagged edges at the top missing, where its eye ought to be.'

The Shaman took a deep breath and closed his one eye. 'We cannot go back but they must not get hold of it.'

'Are the pieces so big?' Ebo asked, indicating an invisible size with his hands.

'You've got them?' Michelle asked.

'Yes, although we did not know what they were: a circular Herya Shankar with molten light pulsing through – occasionally it moves. It is the All-seeing Eye. We can find anyone with it,' Ebo said miserably. 'Using it, we had searched for weeks for your parents, night and day. We found nothing. No trace.'

Peter shook his head. Inside his heart, his last hope died.

'We have kept the All-seeing Eye a secret for hundreds of years, passed down the generations,' Ebo explained. 'We have kept all of the treasures from the Maker hidden from the Rumanni. They are used only for the good of the Land, as the Maker intended. It had not occurred to us that a Guardian was trapped.'

Ebo turned to the Changeling, his face serious.

'Peter?'

'What do you want me to do?'

The chieftain smiled and shook his head ruefully. 'You really are just like him.'

The Shaman was already deep in concentration.

'He is asking for the pieces to be sent here, ' Ebo explained. 'The dragon must be complete. Only you can do it because you have been there before.'

'I thought so.' Peter looked at Michelle. 'One for Paul.'

'And the priest?' Michelle asked.

'We have no choice. You will have to handle him if he has not started back up to the castle already,' Ebo said. 'The Eye and the other piece must be taken to the Shankar to complete the dragon.'

'The dragon has to be made whole,' the Shaman said with unshakable faith. 'I will go with you.'

'To be honest, I don't think I can carry you, Peter *and* the stones safely. You're just too big,' Michelle admitted grudgingly. 'I'll have to do two trips.'

'No,' said Ebo. 'One is all we can risk. By tomorrow morning we will lay siege to Castle Craven. The Rumanni must leave our land.' The chieftain had decided. 'We will act as the distraction for you two to get in.'

The Shaman came forward, and produced another black torque.

'I think you will need this,' he muttered. 'Try not to give it away this time! Damnation! We have only so many!'

'I won't,' Michelle said sweetly, giving him one of her most disarming smiles.

'And, you,' he turned to Peter, 'will be my eyes. You look and I will see.'

On the shores, the howling from the forest creatures increased, as if they could sense the imminent battle.

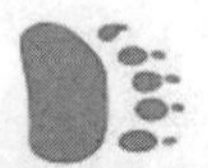

Chapter 21

THE CLAN'S BOATS CLUSTERED TOGETHER

The Clan's boats clustered together: a small island of defiance against the darkness, where shadowy murderous things moved. None of the creatures dared to approach the water or the light. The noises and howls of the night broke through the Clansmen's fatigue and crept into their dreams. The boats, roped together, stood still in the middle of the river, not drifting with the current and not swaying with the breeze. The large men at the tillers stood as if made of stone.

Peter slept fitfully, his mind in turmoil, his feelings focussed on Paul; there was guilt and a nagging conviction that he had caused his friend's death. He dreamt of the otter coming out of nowhere to save him in the lake. He relived the moment when he had first seen him, heard him say cheerfully, 'I'm a bit of an animal myself.'

The dreams changed to those of home; Uncle Ramsey had taken the house and was lording it over his mother. He strutted about, giving orders. Uncle Lorenzo was there, breaking things and telling everyone to clear up, and Peter's horrible Aunt Petra was being simply vile: chopping down all the plants and wafting through the place like a noxious fume. Peter woke often, each time sensing the danger skulking in the darkness and each time deciding to go straight back to sleep.

Morning came, laying its soft, warm, glorious hands on everything, and with it came a gentle breeze drifting across Peter's fur. Warm, fragrant drinks and spicy-smelling rock cakes were being handed out in the chill semi-darkness.

In the distance, Castle Craven looked as magnificent as ever.

No mist remained from the previous day, and there were no obvious troops on patrol. Peter's emotions lingered on his absent friend. In his mind he was still searching for the feeling that the otter was there.

'The tribes will surround Castle Craven today,' Storm said. 'We have recovered most of our strength and our gifts. It is almost as if, after a certain number of us had recovered, the healing process speeded up. Combined, we could…' He gestured towards the sky mysteriously.

A sombre Ebo came over. 'Good morning,' he said. 'The Rumanni are about to find that walls are not only to keep people out.' He said it with a smile, and seemed completely relaxed, despite the dark rings under his eyes that showed he had not slept.

Peter felt the absence of Paul. He wanted to do more than just help the tribe; what he really wanted was to take a swipe at one man: Romulus Blackheart. Peter ground his teeth in misery, contemplating something unsavoury.

'Pariah Paine almost caught me yesterday,' Michelle said. 'She was close – and then all her power just fell away. Why? I'd never give up if I was that close.'

'Because,' Jasmine said joining them, 'when you use such power, the strength has to come straight from the spirit of the wielder, and that will always fail, eventually. Especially if you use it full force like she did yesterday.'

'So that's what happens when *you're* using it,' Peter said, pieces coming together finally in his head, 'but *we* don't get tired when we transform.' He didn't know if he was asking a question or telling her something.

'I am not a Changeling. I can only tell you about us. The Maker rarely gives gifts that you do not have to pay for in some way.' Jasmine spoke reverently. 'We cannot do what you so obviously do naturally.'

The glance made Peter look at Changelings – half-human, half-animal – in a new light. They looked good, he decided, even if they were such a strange mix.

An exhausted Shaman wandered over, his dreadlocks hiding his

face. 'Boom! I have thought about it, the dragon in the lake is definitely one of the Original Guardians.'

'What's that mean?' Peter asked in between mouthfuls.

The Shaman shook his head in disbelief. 'Blood and damnation! You really don't know? Boom-Basa! I wasted all that time with you! The Maker's Guardians protected the Land and its people. As the hand of time flew, they fell, like fire from the heavens, because the cycle had come full circle. The creators and destroyers – their balance lost – they fought a terrible war.'

'The Lal was a destroyer?' As usual, Michelle's logic was faster than Peter's.

'Not was – *is*. It can only be drained by us – not destroyed, and over time, boom-basa, we go through it again,' Shaman said, drifting off into his own private thoughts.

'It's not *destroyed*?' Peter asked, frustrated. 'But what did we do all that for?'

'The rest of it will have to be found before the Rumanni realize,' Ebo spoke softly, 'and this time, it will have to be destroyed completely, otherwise it will regenerate in time, and return even more powerful than before.'

'But it was all black and ash,' Peter said, his stomach churning at his failure.

'A Guardian is eternal. It is no easy matter to destroy one.' Ebo's words carried weight. 'It is not the Guardian that we need to kill; it is the container that has to be obliterated.'

'But you're asking us to make one *whole*?' Michelle stared at them as if they'd lost their minds.

'The Herya Guardian – the dragon – is an Earth Guardian; you see bits of it everywhere. It moves through all living things. If it is trapped, you can use it, and abuse its powers,' the Shaman explained, confirming their worst fears.

'So if Romulus got hold of it, while it was down there –' Peter started to say.

'And now they know, because the Rumanni priest will see it,' Michelle added.

'Then we would suffer darkness under his rule. With that

power, anything we can do will not matter,' Ebo finished flatly.

'What happens when it's freed?' Peter asked. 'I mean, we'll be standing right there. What do we have to do?'

'Get away – fast.'

Peter and Michelle looked at each other and swallowed.

At the end of the first day on the river, there had been no movement from the castle, but many more boats had come to join them in the meantime. The old, the young – the entire Clan was coming together. Jasmine explained that even the youngest among them had natural gifts and, because of their weakened state, they needed the strength of everyone.

Different leaders from the various tribes discussed things with Ebo. Wise men from other villages, wearing amulets on necklaces painted black, came to confer with the Shaman.

Even as the Changelings watched, a veritable town grew up on the water in a day.

In a short time, the separate villages had become an army, ready to lay siege to the power that kept them in slavery through blackmail and might. There was surprisingly little noise – just the background hum of people going about their business.

Evening approached. In the distance torches were being lit on the castle walls at almost the same time as the torches were lit and posts manned on the river. The atmosphere seemed as normal as ever, but everyone moved with a purpose. The children were being kept in the centre, protected at all times.

Peter could see and smell the aggression. The resolve from these people, even the children, was obvious. They were getting ready for a war. He spent the time talking quietly with Michelle.

Storm and Ginger came over to them just as night fell on the group like a thick black blanket. The conversations stayed naturally subdued as they huddled round the fire, where various unidentifiable things were being roasted. Peter found it strange, given his super-smell, that even he could not quite identify all the ingredients.

The cooking fires had been lit in a small, sunken area surrounded by stones. A long metal rod was suspended over it. People

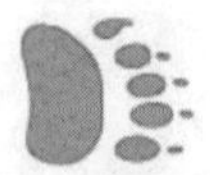

came with various pots to be hung on the rod, and the food was cooked and passed around. Peter was again surprised by the flavours and delicate tastes of all the different things that were being made. One particular woman, hunched over with age, was diligently examining each pot as it came off and others went on.

'That is our greatest cook,' Storm said.

Michelle raised an eyebrow. 'What's she called, then?'

'Foor.' Storm said the name with reverence.

'*Foor?*' Peter repeated. 'What kind of name is "Foor"?'

The lady in question walked over to them.

'Ah, you must be Peter,' she said with a toothless smile. 'I have something special for you.' She handed him a plate piled high with mashed white and green bits.

Peter wasn't sure exactly what he was supposed to do with it, but as everyone was looking on expectantly, he took a tentative spoonful, and then another.

'This is fantastic! This is great!' he said while the old woman waited patiently.

'My name is Foor Elements – with those I can make anything. My sister, the Mistall – the matriarch – is even more powerful. I could feed you the earth and you would not even know it,' Foor said, giving him her most charming toothless grin. 'Eat up, Changeling.'

'What – um, what exactly is in this?' Peter asked, having sensed the warning in her words.

'Oh, just some of your favourite foods: worm ends, raw eggs, fish innards – that sort of thing.'

Peter didn't wait to hear her finish the full description of her recipe before he turned green and ran to the river to bring up the contents of his stomach. He had thought the food delicious!

The next day, they were all ready to move as soon as the sun lifted past the horizon. There wasn't much conversation, and Peter noticed that, this time, the children were kept at the rear.

Ebo went forward and climbed onto the deck of the nearest ship.

'When the Changelings first came among us, we did not know how or why they had come. We know now!' he shouted, and joined

his hands together and bowed to them. 'The others have been hurt and our children are back among us where they belong. We will always remember Paul, who has recently fallen. He helped free our children, courageously giving up his own life.'

Michelle laid a hand on Peter's shoulder as he listened silently to Ebo's words.

'We will never again give up our children, and never again will we allow them to take the life of a Changeling. Be strong and have faith. Look and you will see.'

A thunderous roar went up from the people on the water.

With that, Ebo bowed and walked from the deck to the sound of cheering.

'I miss him, too.'

Michelle spoke softly by Peter's side.

'I know.' Peter tried not to sound upset.

From the northern mountains came more of the Clan's people, effectively cutting off that route of escape to the Rumanni. From where Griphand had first put them ashore, from the River Sindu, even more people came to join them.

'This will be our only chance, so we must get it right,' Jasmine explained to the Changelings.

'What can you fight them with?' Peter asked. 'Small walls and pretty smells aren't going to contain *that*.' He pointed to the lofty towers and the great walls of Castle Craven.

'Our powers are returning. We do not want them dead, but they must be made to leave. Walls can be made from other things than stone,' Jasmine said. Her enigmatic words hung in the air.

As Peter looked back towards the river, two channels appeared on the banks and ran alongside the advancing crowd.

Jasmine saw his look. 'Just wide enough to be a danger to the creatures of the night. We are not leaving until this is done,' she said, striding forward.

'Do you get the feeling they're upset?' Michelle asked quietly.

'Almost as angry as we are,' Peter agreed. 'Are you ready?' he asked, remembering something else.

'Are you?'

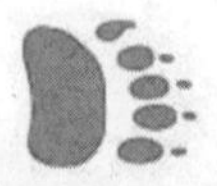

★

By mid-afternoon, they were all camped at a safe distance from the castle. Some Rumanni had come to talk, but they were sent back. Ebo was visible at the front, directing different groups and talking. He seemed to be everywhere – like a king getting ready for battle.

The water channels ran alongside the advancing crowd. Those Clanspeople arriving from different directions had cut channels ahead of them, too. Water filled each trench almost as quickly as it was cut.

A tribal band had come to give battle to the stone and might of the Rumanni.

'Ebo!'

It was Romulus's voice – not shouted, but easily heard.

'They still have their powers,' Jasmine observed.

'Ebo, let us talk about this. Fights are always bad for business,' Romulus ranted.

No one listened but continued to work at what they were doing.

Ebo joined them briefly.

'Michelle, will you take him over as evening falls?'

The hawk nodded.

'Once you have completed the Guardian, get back fast and do not go into any part of the castle. We intend to release their own demons in there.'

'How?'

'We will build the channels and close them off around each gathering. If you have not noticed, the channels run back to the rivers,' Ebo explained.

'You're not protecting us – you're surrounding *them*,' Peter said, his mind leaping ahead.

'Exactly.' Ebo smiled at him in a fatherly way.

'That's not going to get them past that drawbridge,' Michelle observed flatly.

'We will have to open it then,' Ebo replied.

The people of the Clan began to sit on the ground in symmetrical patterns. Peter remembered seeing similar patterns in the

Sanctuary Cave; each one led directly into the next. Everyone seemed to know where they belonged.

At dusk, the whole area was bathed in golden glow, for torches had sprung up on the plains as well as on the castle walls. The water channels started forward again, each curving until it met the one that had been running parallel to it, protecting the people in between. The channels of water came together just short of the castle's own moat.

Jasmine took a last look at Peter and Michelle. Her jaw was set as she said, 'Be very careful, you two.' Impulsively she hugged them before hurrying away and hiding her tears.

Darkness fell fast and the whispers and sounds from the woods moved closer.

The Shaman approached them with several men carrying something covered in a cloth. Peter guessed that it contained the missing pieces, but his ultra-vision wasn't able to penetrate the strange wrapping. The bundle had been tied with rope, and another bit formed a handle at the ends.

'Ebo thought it would be easier for you to carry if you had them tied to your legs, Michelle, and then your –' The Shaman was at a loss for the exact word to use – 'your *hands* are free for Peter. He said to wait until darkness falls. The crater's light will guide you and there is less chance of being seen.'

'See?' Michelle told him. 'You *can* speak like a human being when you want to. Not a single swear word!'

Once Peter had tied the ropes to Michelle's legs, she turned to him with her customary predator smile.

'Hunting time. How's your stomach for flying these days?'

Peter remembered his last flight and wanted to believe it was getting stronger. However, he had his doubts.

Michelle grabbed him as soon as he had changed, and then there was no more time to think about how bad it was going to be.

They rose fast, Peter trying desperately to control his feelings. He remembered Paul's constant whimpering when he had been at his side; it made him chuckle and saddened him at the same time.

The scene below them was captivating. The patterns Peter remembered from the Sanctuary Cave had been replicated by the Clan on the ground. They intertwined each other like serpents, or dragons battling each other, forming part of a much larger and intricate pattern. Men, women and children all took their places in what had become a chain of life.

As they rose even higher, Peter saw Storm go to the back of the boat and reach down with his hand towards the water. Lightning sparked and he sent it towards Castle Craven. It jumped from person to person – a spark that got brighter and brighter and raced towards the Rumanni.

Their ascent slowed, and for a moment Michelle hung in the air until she headed for the green lights of Plateau Periculum.

The plateau was empty, but Peter could still hear the noises, shouts and panic coming from its surface. The panic grew, and he strained harder to listen, then wished he hadn't as a great thunder-clap shook the ground and sheared through his eardrums.

Michelle almost lost him as he struggled to close his ears against the noise. She wobbled in her glide, but recovered.

They landed quickly, and for once Michelle did not look completely composed.

They dragged the stones into the tunnels before anyone could spot them. 'We can't carry these like this,' Peter said, struggling with the awkwardly shaped parcel. 'Michelle, help me tie them to my back.'

Michelle held the wrapping between Peter's furry shoulder blades as he used human hands to tie the ropes around his neck and shoulders. That done, claws emerged once more.

'Let's go.'

They sped quickly downwards, Michelle struggling to keep up. Peter sensed her frustration and claustrophobia.

'I'll get you back later,' she warned.

Peter ignored her. He led them swiftly to the brittle walls and then down to where they could come out by the sandy shore. They were both apprehensive, and stopped just before coming out of the tunnels.

Michelle crept up the tunnels and took off. Peter, his hand going to his Shankar, called her. Suddenly, in his mind, he was flying above a green crystal lake.

He's not here, Michelle trilled, after making several passes.

Peter went forward, still not letting down his guard. They were alone as Michelle landed. They undid the binding and took off the strange wrapping, revealing the stones. Peter tried to rub an oily sensation from his fingers. He felt a tingle in his hand as it reacted to the inside of the material.

One stone was triangular and completely clear. The other was bigger and more rectangular; it had the curves of an eye etched in it. Liquid light flowed through it. Peter held the stone in both hands, looking straight through it to his furry feet.

'Before we do this –' Peter began.

'I think we should,' Michelle interrupted him from behind, knowing exactly what Peter had in mind.

Peter took a deep breath. He hoisted the stone to head level, his entire being concentrated on their parents. He had no idea what the others looked like, so he concentrated even harder on the remembered pictures of his father. He lifted the stone to his face and looked through it.

Michelle starred anxiously at him from the other side.

'It's not working, is it?' Michelle asked.

'No. I can see you straight through it,' Peter said.

Michelle cursed. She bent down to pick up his stone and Peter immediately shouted. 'Look out.'

The priest had come up the beach towards them. Dropping the stone, Peter transformed completely, Michelle did likewise and took off, growing rapidly while Peter turned round with a snarl.

The priest came on, skin and bones, completely calm. They circled him. He stopped in front of Peter, a mere arm's length away from a growling animal. If he made any movement, Peter would attack him. He could tell from the man's scent, however, that he wasn't bothered in the slightest.

The man's voice broke, then, and tears ran down his face.

'Hello, Peter,' he croaked. 'Hello, son.'

Chapter 22

PETER FROZE

Peter froze. He didn't know what to say, or feel. He stood almost as if he were suspended in time. Slowly, his body transformed into its half-badger state. Meanwhile, Michelle landed and simply waited – alert but equally uncertain.

The man tried again.

'Hello, son.'

The words came as if from a great distance. Peter was unable to respond or even recognize them.

'Son?'

Peter couldn't bear to hear the man talk to him so personally. He'd had no interaction from his father for half his life, and he did not know how to react to it. And, to hear it from this – this – *creature* who didn't even look like a man… It was all too much for Peter could stand.

And yet the animal inside was nudging him. It wanted him to get closer, to feel the nuzzle from another badger – but Peter pushed it down. Instead he walked up to the man and pressed a threatening paw against his chest.

'What were you doing?' he shouted uncontrollably. '*Why did you go away to save another world and leave me all alone?!'*

Somehow, it came out all wrong. The tone, the anger, the aggression. He wanted to believe and he couldn't. He wanted to say it was fine, but it wasn't. He wanted to say 'Dad' but he didn't know the word. He hadn't tried to say it for such a long time that he had forgotten the sound, forgotten the feel of it, and forgotten the touch.

Yet he remembered a smell: something odd, something strange, something comforting, something that protected him in the dark.

Something he had smelled a very long time ago, something he had smelled again back in the prison cell.

The three of them stood there, Peter unsure of what he should do next.

His father gave him a tiny smile and turned to the hawk. 'You must be Michelle.'

She nodded, not daring to come any closer.

Peter took his paw away from the man's chest.

'Please – where are the others?' Peter asked, unsure of himself even though he had dreamt about this moment for years.

'I don't know,' Allan Badger replied hesitantly. 'We were separated.'

'Then they could still be alive?' Michelle asked.

'Yes, they could. I have not seen anyone for two and half years. They have been doing things to us…' His voice shook with horror.

Michelle simply nodded. 'Let's fix the gem and get out of here.'

Peter picked up the stone and walked into the glowing lake. He swam backwards with the stones on his belly, then, when he was halfway out, he cast a brief glimpse at the man on the shore before taking a deep breath and diving.

As he put the pieces into place, Peter saw a flash as the Shankar accepted it. He noticed that the one-eyed dragon was sitting up this time, as if waiting for him.

As he let the final stone slot into its place, the dragon abruptly pulled free. It swirled around inside the stone, then stopped and looked at Peter. Something enormously powerful whispered into his mind – a whisper that he didn't understand.

Then the dragon put its glowing talon outside the stone, flexed it in the sand, withdrew it and gave a deep growl. It began to swirl around, faster and faster.

It broke out underneath him, and the light in the cave suddenly increased. The dragon whirled round the lake in ever-larger circles – free, flexing its muscles and wings. The centre of the lake began to spiral, and a whirlpool appeared, dragging up the sand.

Peter broke the surface and gasped for breath. His felt as if his lungs were on fire, he had stayed down so long. He could see his father and Michelle watching anxiously from the shore.

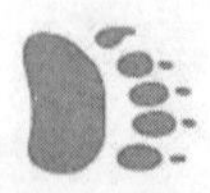

The whirlpool increased in power and strength as the dragon below became a frightening blur. He was being sucked in! He would never be able to make it out now!

Michelle was airborne within seconds and came at him with speed. She dived a few times, trying to catch Peter, but the waves lashed out at her. Their size and strength increased rapidly, and Peter knew that he had only moments before the power of the whirlpool pulled him under. He struggled harder.

Allan Badger waved frantically as he swam towards him. Peter tried to break through the ever-increasing waves, but the edge of the whirlpool grew higher and the shore became completely obscured.

He swam uphill in desperation, all the more certain that he wasn't going to make it to the top. Michelle dived again, heedless of her own danger, but her wings caught the water and she tumbled into it. Allan appeared above the crest of a wave, swimming frantically, but he, too, was struggling.

The light below was brilliant and its intensity blinded them. Peter's torque felt heavier – he was being sucked downwards. If only Paul were here! Peter swallowed water while trying to remove the torque; his vision blurred, and his lungs burst with pain.

A quick flash from the necklace showed that Michelle was struggling, too, and being pulled down towards the centre as well. The vision made Peter even more frantic, and he redoubled his efforts to remove the necklace.

Suddenly, there was flash of blinding green light. It felt as if it were going through him, his body seemed to be on fire and Peter could see all three of them – himself, Michelle and his father – struggling together. The whirlpool stopped spinning and the mountain of water came crashing down. That was the last thing he remembered before darkness engulfed him and he saw no more.

Peter felt a rhythmic pounding in his head. Slowly he recovered, his head resting in the middle of a sticky page. It was the early hours of the morning and the stone on the bridge felt cold and damp.

From where he crouched, he could see Blenheim Palace to his left, the most beautiful building in England. In the distance, straight ahead, he could see the lights of Bladon village. After all he had been through, and as much as he had wanted to get away from here at times, he was so glad to be back that he could've wept.

Another dream, he thought wearily, hanging his head. His mouth didn't taste good. His whole face was wet.

Oh god, Mum's going to kill me, he thought, as he realized that he was soaked through. Still on all fours, vaguely he looked down at the outline of the open book on the bridge, barely making anything out. It took him a moment to realize that it was still open. He slammed it shut, picked it up and turned to leave for his small inconsequential village northwest of some of the greatest spires on earth.

It was then that he became aware of something dangling around his neck.

His hand reached for the torque.

'My Shankar!'

Only then did he wake up fully. He looked around – and noticed a dark shape slumped on the ground.

He dared not move, nor touch him. His mouth was dry.

It was a man, all skin and bones, still curled up and wet. A dark necklace with a stone dangled limply around his neck, contrasting with his pale skin in the lamplight.

Peter knelt and placed a gentle hand on the man's shoulder.

'Dad?' he said softly.

The contact jerked the man awake. His eyes flickered. He looked stunned for a moment, then his eyes came to rest on Peter – dark eyes completely focussed. His lips moved and tears formed in his eyes as he reached forward. Peter didn't resist and returned the embrace.

When they parted, Allan Badger was more controlled, but still he didn't say anything. He didn't need to. Peter returned the smile and got up unsteadily, his thoughts turning to his mother. He glanced towards home – towards Bladon, a place he had once thought he might not ever see again – and then towards his father, who nodded.

They were only just stepping into his house, his mother yet again having left the door unlocked, when Jenny Badger appeared

in the hallway. She seemed confused for a moment, and stood staring at him for what seemed an age before she spoke.

'*Peter!*'

She rushed to him. She was shouting as she hugged him: about how worried she had been, where had he gone. Questions tumbled from her in a stream. She hugged him again and then tears and relief washed over her.

'Have you any idea? *Have you?*' she gasped, her face taut with worry and relief.

'I had to bring somebody home.'

His mother's gaze moved away from his face and she became aware of the man standing behind him. All pretence of control left her. She stumbled forward and grabbed at the man who caught her before she fell. Jenny Badger was shouting and crying for joy at the same time.

Somewhere in the midst of it all, Peter's parents began to talk. Then there was no stopping them. The morning came and went, afternoon started and finished, they ate, and the evening fell. They had moved down to the kitchen, and were still talking.

Peter went up to get the Book to show his mother. In his room, on his desk, was the leather-bound Book, lying face down. He turned it over, and then stood there staring at it, stunned. There, to the left of the curly figure of a three, was a red crystal.

The Book had been open. Where had the crystal come from?

He unclasped it and tentatively lifted the cover. No light came from it. He opened it fully. There, on the first page, was the pool, almost real, with a huge dragon at the bottom looking directly at him. The edges of the dragon faded into the water.

It winked at him.

At the bottom, straddling the pages, was an egg-shaped stone covered in symbols. He hurriedly closed the Book.

Another thought struck him as his hand went to the torque. He looked down at the blackened stone and thought of Michelle, then he thought of Paul. Had they been real, too? Was she still out there? Had he only wanted to find his dad?

He lifted his hand slowly, and closed it tightly around the stone dangling from his neck. Drawing a deep breath, he concentrated on Michelle.

Immediately, he flew through the walls of his room into the darkness outside. Everything became a blur. He flew faster and faster, until finally he burst through more walls – and there she was.

Instantly, she looked up, her hands going to her torque.

'Peter!' Her smile was bright and beautiful. 'What took you so long?'

Peter couldn't believe it. Even in his world, they could talk!

'How's your dad?' Michelle asked, a deeper sadness coming into her voice, her emotions under control.

'He's fine. He's –' Peter couldn't continue. He remembered that Michelle's mum was still missing. Both of Paul's parents had not been found, either, and Paul himself was dead.

'Michelle,' he said, 'if we found my dad, then we can find your mum, too, and Paul's parents.'

Her face fell. 'Nice dream, Peter. But they're gone. And Paul's dead.'

'But I didn't know what your mum looked like, or Paul's parents, so I could only search for my dad. And I almost didn't even know him,' Peter admitted, thinking hard. 'And, it was funny, but Ebo was the closest thing to my dad and it was only knowing by Ebo, that I could -'

Michelle interrupted him quietly. 'You won't believe this.'

She felt on the ghostly desk behind her and as soon as she latched onto it, it became real. It was a picture frame. She turned it around so that he could see it. There was a man, wavy blond hair parted in the middle, wearing a checked shirt with a sweater draped round his neck, but it was the woman he had his arms around that really caught Peter's attention.

It was Charm!

Peter stared at the picture, open-mouthed

Michelle spoke almost to herself. 'All the time we were there, I kept thinking that she looked so much like my mother – that it could have been *her*.'

Peter fumbled on his desk until his hand closed on the frame. 'What do you make of this?' he asked, turning the picture of his mother and father towards them.

For once, even Michelle was lost for words.

'Michelle?'

'I'm getting it. I bet you Paul's father looked just like Griphand. But Ebo said they searched…'

'They couldn't find my dad, either, but *we* did.' Peter sounded more and more convinced. 'Listen, I promise you that we'll find your mum, and Paul's parents.'

'I believe you.'

'I have to go soon – Grandad's coming tonight.'

'So's mine.'

Peter's spine tingled, and a shiver crept down it.

'I know this might sound weird,' he said, 'but he doesn't wear a white hat by any chance, does he?'

'Only comes at midnight…?' Michelle added, slowly.

'Carries a cane –'

'– with a dragon on it –'

'– clips his eyebrows –'

'– and never says a word.'

Just then, the clocks started to strike midnight in both their houses. The torque beneath Peter's fingers tingled, its vibrations getting stronger. He looked down to see it glowing amber through the magical black paint. The Book, which never moved when someone was in the room, fell off the bed with a *thud!* Light leaked out onto the carpet.

Suddenly, the faint image of a *well* appeared, and a ghost dashed out from between the pages. It chased itself round the room, flitting from pillar to post, as if searching for something.

It was black and sleek.

The vision faded.

Peter looked at Michelle. A hawk stared back.

'I have to go back,' Peter said.

'Not without me, you're not!'

Book 2

THE WELL

Chapter 1

PAUL STOOD BEFORE THE DARK ANGEL

Paul stood before the dark angel.

The darkness moved around them, killing any light, engulfing the small clearing in the shadow of the statue made of black stone. It was a statue of a demon, an angel cast out from the heavens. Standing twenty feet tall, eyes closed as if resting, its presence was sentient, six arms spread out like wings, each holding a different weapon and ready to defend its master.

Its evil seeped through the rock, destroying everything. This was not a place of worship. It was a place of pain.

The woman lay at its feet like a sacrificial offering. Her skin, the colour of marble, clung to the bones and made her look more like a skeleton than a human being. Withered with age, her life-force almost gone, she still had her hands out in front of her, in one last defiant gesture. She had defended herself against the impossible but lost.

Paul gazed upon the ancient face, his eyes brimming over with tears. His heart broke and he sank slowly to his knees, reaching forward to touch the woman's face, his tears fell on the dark angel.

The demon's eyes snapped opened, revealing molten lava that blazed in the darkness.

The woman screamed as the light hit her…

The second volume in the series

Book 2

THE WELL

is coming in 2006